The Love Curse

Arrow heart

The Love Curse

Arrow heart

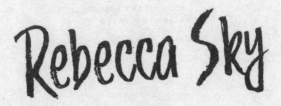

Rebecca Sky

HODDER

HODDER CHILDREN'S BOOKS

First published in Great Britain in 2018 by Hodder and Stoughton

1 3 5 7 9 10 8 6 4 2

A CIP catalogue record for this book
is available from the British Library.

ISBN 978 1 444 94005 3

Typeset in ITC Berkeley Oldstyle by Hewer Text UK Ltd, Edinburgh
Printed and bound in Great Britain by Clays Ltd, St Ives plc

The paper and board used in this book
are made from wood from responsible sources.

Hodder Children's Books
An imprint of
Hachette Children's Group
Part of Hodder and Stoughton
Carmelite House
50 Victoria Embankment
London EC4Y 0DZ

An Hachette UK Company
www.hachette.co.uk

www.hachettechildrens.co.uk

For the   girls who
feel like   they don't
fit in, with their Converse
sneakers, big dreams,
and brave
hearts
!

<---and for Dave . . . always<<

Anacreon, Fragment 413

Once again Eros (Love) has struck me like a smith with a great hammer and dipped me in the wintry torrent.

One

Boys were disappearing. Sometimes weeks passed before they turned up, dazed and confused, wandering in the park, down the street, on the rooftops of tall buildings. When asked about it, they had no clue how they got there, where they had been, and what happened while they were gone. Sometimes, if they thought hard enough, they'd have vague memories of a girl. But I know what happened. I know the girl.

I turn up the volume on the media screen in the taxi's back seat as a reporter sticks his mic in the face of the latest victim – an eighteen-year-old boy found sitting under the bleachers in Times Square a few hours ago. He'd been missing for two weeks.

'I . . . I don't know,' he says. 'I was biking to the store and then I woke up here.'

The reporter pats his shoulder then turns back to the camera. 'Three boys are still unaccounted for in the latest string of disappearances. Police are asking anyone with information of their whereabouts to call in to the hotline.'

A phone number appears in a thick, flashing font, followed by headshots of each of the missing boys, with their names, dates, and what they were last seen wearing. I turn off the screen and stare out the rain-streaked window, preferring a soggy New York to their faces. Besides, there's nothing I can do about it and right now I have more pressing matters to deal with, like coming up with an excuse for being late.

The taxi drives through a large puddle as it turns into the parking lot. I sink deeper into the seat, delaying the moment I'll be spotted by the tall blonde pacing the corner. I know that walk – shoulders back, arms crossed, quick determined steps.

She punches something into her phone and immediately my pocket buzzes. I pull out my cell to find our text thread filled with angry emojis. Marissa Bale, the pacing blonde, is the closest thing to a friend I have. Where I come from, we don't pick our friends – we're assigned accountability partners instead.

'Miss?' The driver clears his throat. 'Miss, we're here.'

I sigh, and sit up, flashing a strained smile to the man watching me curiously through his rear-view mirror.

Marissa spots me and stomps to my door, yanking it open before I'm fully upright. 'What time do you call this?'

'It was raining,' I say, rushing to hand over the fare and leave the cab. 'Finding a ride was—' My foot shoots out as it hits the wet pavement, sending me tumbling, rear first, to the ground.

'Classy, Rach, real classy.' Her deep blue eyes study my feeble attempt at righting myself.

I glare up at her. 'A little help?'

Instead she glances at her watch and adjusts a gold-blinged purse to sit higher on her shoulder.

'Seriously? I'll remember this next time you ask for something.'

Chunks of my black waves flop wildly about. I brush an escaped curl from my face, shoving it back in my ponytail. As I do, my skirt rises to expose the cut-off jean shorts smuggled underneath.

Marissa's eyes lock on the shorts; her lips curl into a sneer. *If it isn't* Vogue, *it isn't Marissa.* 'Really, Rach?'

She shakes her head and turns away, giving me the opportunity to take her in. At half a foot taller than me, though a lot of that is the navy heels, her height only adds to the fact that she looks like a model in our school uniform. The white dress shirt clings to her willowy form. It's covered by a meticulously pressed blue blazer with gold buttons, and the matching skirt stops just above her legs – whereas on me, it hangs down my calves.

I sigh and use the door for balance while I wipe myself off and straighten my skirt. The driver taps impatiently on the steering wheel, the taxi jerking forward. Before I can gather my things, Marissa whirls around, her eyes bulging.

'He's rushing you? And you paid him?'

'It's fine,' I say, loading my arms at record speed.

Still, she starts in a determined march to the door, making me drop my bag to grab her arm. All I can picture is the cab driver's face, flashing on the screen beside the three other boys.

'Just let this go,' I say, giving her a gentle tug back.

'Let it go?' Marissa's eyes widen even further. 'He got you here late, which makes *me* late.' She yanks her arm away. 'Besides, nobody gets away with treating you like that.'

'Oh really?' I purse my lips, half smiling, trying to lighten her mood.

'Really.' Marissa taps the passenger window, turning back to add, 'Nobody but me.'

I shake my head as her back arches like a cat readying for attack.

The cab driver glances past her, his eyes locking on me.

'Let me just get my things,' I say, rushing to the back seat and scooping up the bag. As soon as I shut the door he revs off, splashing water on to Marissa's shoes.

'Eww. Jerk.' Marissa grabs an envelope from my pile, balls it, and throws it after the taxi. It lands in a puddle a few feet away.

'That was my application for the social work program.'

Her arms cross, and she takes in my frustrated look. 'So?'

'So, it took me hours to fill out.'

'Time wasted.' She sighs at my glare, bending to wipe her shoes, and scowling at the dirty water left on her fingers.

'Wasted? There are so many kids in need of help. You of all people should know what it's like to be without a guardian.'

'Should I?' She glares and holds my arm for balance, her touch lingering extra-long, no doubt to dry her hand. The glare trails to my bird's-nest ponytail. 'You look pathetic.'

'How kind.' I bat her hand away, roll my eyes and adjust my armful of stuff, not sure if I should start walking to school or wait for Marissa, who looks to be rearing up for another lecture.

'We're late, remember,' she says, taking quick steps ahead into the park.

I shrug and jog to catch up.

'Why do you even pay the cabby?' she asks. 'Turn one into your personal driver. It saves a ton.'

'I don't think it's right.'

'Oh please. It's wrong to *not* use your gift. Even in good weather, it's impossible to get a cab in New York. At least you could do something about that.'

'Anyway.' I'm not in the mood for my lecture on tardiness to become a lecture on my lack of respect for our *ability*. 'How was your night?' I ask instead.

Marissa lifts her well-groomed eyebrows. 'My mom sent this bag from London. My reward for straight As last semester.'

'London?'

She pauses, thinking over her reply. 'Her and her new lover are on vacation there.'

Lover is a gentle way of putting it.

'Well?' she says slowly. 'Do you like it?'

I'm sure it's a nice bag, just a bit too flashy for my taste. But there's a certain spark in Marissa's eyes that I haven't seen for a while and I don't want to be the one to dowse it. 'It does make you stand out.'

Her smile becomes blinding. 'And it matches the buttons on our uniform. Mom thinks of everything.' Her face softens, and for a quick second she almost looks fragile. Then she hooks her arm through mine, nearly dislodging my armful of books, and uses my elbow as leverage to pull me through the park towards school, her gold bag whacking my side with each step.

Central Park is unusually empty for a weekday, a result of the morning rain. Still, a few people walk their dogs and a dark-haired boy sits by the Bethesda Fountain across the path. There's something about the way he holds his headphones to his ear with one hand, singing quietly to himself as he reads a magazine. He doesn't seem to care if someone notices, and I envy him for that feeling.

As we pass by, he looks up. I glance away, but out the corner of my eye it's easy to tell his gaze is following us. He's probably checking out Marissa. They all do. Still, his awareness makes my cheeks flush.

'When's your mom coming home?' I ask, distracting myself from the guy.

Marissa's pace quickens and her focus fixes on the ground. 'I don't know.' She clears her throat. 'No rush, though, I get the whole apartment to myself.' She raises her chin and squares her shoulders. 'Parent-free life is awesome.'

I force a smile. 'Say hi to her from me. Next time you talk.'

Marissa misses a step.

'Careful.' I twist to hold her, dropping my books in the process.

'I'm fine.' She yanks her arm free and kicks a binder out of her way, scattering lined paper everywhere.

I sigh and bend down to gather them.

'Great, we'll be even more late now.' Marissa crosses her arms.

'You could help.' It's not like I can leave the mess. Losing my college application to the puddle is one thing – schoolwork, however, must be protected at all costs. I grab most of them before looking up to see what Marissa's doing. She twirls a lock of hair, managing a playful grin while biting her bottom lip. I follow her gaze to the guy by the fountain. *Of course.*

He stands, smiles, takes a step our way.

'He's coming over,' she says, her voice higher than normal. Marissa smooths down her hair, then a sober look floods her face. 'You should probably stop him.'

'If you mean what I think you mean, the answer is no. Always no.'

'We can't very well let him see this.' Marissa taps her heel against the spine of a leather-bound book with a gold block font that reads: *Eros's Arrows: Indifference and Infatuation.* 'We have to do something.'

'I *am* doing something,' I say, picking up another loose sheet.

She lifts her chin, making her seem even more smug. 'I've got all the bonus credits possible for turnings and you're still at zero for the year. You really should do it. It's not that big a deal.'

'He's probably just coming to help.' I wave to the mess but she doesn't take the hint. 'He's not a threat, and as long as we keep our cool, there's no reason for him to become one.'

'You're the worst A.P. ever,' she says, the muscles on her jaw bulging – it happens every time she's mad. Marissa thinks being an accountability partner means me doing what she says. I do have to do everything with her, but I don't have to like it.

The guy approaches. He passes Marissa, giving her a polite smile, and continues towards me. She mouths, '*Do it.*' I shake my head a firm *no*, returning my attention to the papers. As I reach for one, the guy bends down and grabs it, our hands nearly touching.

'Here,' he says. 'Let me help with this.'

I smile up, noticing how bright blue his eyes are. He hands me the leather-bound book and smiles. I flip it over, hoping he didn't catch the title. Marissa's a few paces away, waving at me to get on with it.

I ignore her and jump after a rogue sheet, trapping it underfoot. It flaps wildly over the toe of my Converse. Marissa huffs and beelines for the guy.

'Hi, I'm Marissa.' She extends her hand to him.

'No! Don't—'

It's too late. She yanks him close, grazing his lips with her kiss. He jolts back – eyes blinking fast as he struggles against the power separating his consciousness and dragging him deep into a trance. Marissa screams from the pain of using her gift. One hand pressing her stomach, the other her head. But I focus on her victim. On the way his blue eyes now stare, his body twitches, and on the mixture of fear and release that pours over him the second his legs start to wobble under the pressure of it all.

Then I run to him. But before I reach the boy with the striking blue eyes, his legs give out. He falls hard to the brick walkway, convulsing at our feet. All I can think of is how there's now four.

Four missing boys.

Two

Marissa steps over his writhing body, straightens her skirt, and saunters on like nothing happened. The truth is, she doesn't care that she just stole someone's will. *And that makes me furious.* It's one thing to treat an A.P. badly, but this – taking away a stranger's choice – it's deplorable.

'You . . . you can't just leave him there.'

She spins, flicking her blonde hair over her shoulder with force. 'Don't be stupid, Rach, he'll find me. They always do. You really need to come to terms with it.'

I focus on the guy curled in a fetal position, rocking back and forth on the ground, his denim jacket bunching by his neck and his white T-shirt covered in soggy brick dust. I can't call for help – drawing attention to him could risk exposing us.

'Why, Marissa? Why did you turn him?'

She shrugs. 'Besides the obvious,' she waves to the sloppy stack of school papers in my arms, 'he's cute . . . and he has nice shoes.'

'*Nice shoes?*'

'A guy with nice shoes brings good luck.'

I'm fairly certain she just made that up. 'It wasn't too lucky for him, was it?'

'God, you're melodramatic. It had to be done and I'm glad I did it. I haven't turned a guy in days. I was starting to feel underappreciated.'

'You're out of control.'

Marissa ignores me. 'Nothing makes you feel as valued as a fresh turn. They're so desperate to please, all those heightened passions overcoming their other desires.' The side of her mouth curls into some freaky smile/snarl hybrid. 'There's nothing like a man doing whatever I ask to keep me happy. You really should try it sometime.'

'Do you hear yourself?'

She glares at the interruption. 'Maybe I should tell this one I want someone who can fly and watch him jump off a building.'

I shudder. She can't mean it, but I've heard of others doing similar things. It's reasons like this that make me hate my gift. If you could call it that. *Gift* feels like a sick term for what it is we really do.

Steal.

Forcing a man to love me is not something I want.

I kick rocks away from the guy shuddering into my Converse sneakers. There's nothing else I can do for him. He'll stay like this until he's fully turned.

Marissa lets out a long breath, waiting for me to say something. And I do. 'I just don't think it's right.'

Somehow this infuriates her enough to continue towards school. When she's a good few feet ahead, she pivots on her heels. 'First the cab and now this.' Her arms flail like one of those inflatable advertisements on a car lot. If it weren't for the particulars of this argument it would be hilarious. 'If this is your *I want true love* rant, Rach, I'm tired of hearing it. Those women in *true love* situations would die to get what we have. Well, what I have – a guy whose only purpose is fulfilling my every wish.'

I ball my fists and glance around, making sure no one heard her, or will hear what I'm about to say. Thankfully the park is still empty. 'If women really wanted that, they would get a dog. Nobody wants to be followed blindly by a boy. They want someone to see their worst qualities and still choose to love them.'

'God, you're such a downer.' Marissa nods back over her shoulder. 'If what we do is so bad then why would the gods gift us with the ability? Huh?'

It's a question I ask myself every day.

I hang my head, eyes closed to avoid seeing the guy. Why did the gods choose me to have this ability, to be a Hedoness? Why couldn't I have been born to another family and missed the freak gene? It pains me to open my eyes, but I do, and look one last time at Marissa's victim.

She's right about one thing, he's good-looking – even while mid-seizure with his headphones twisted around his head, and that's saying a lot. He's not much older than me. *And now he's Marissa's puppet.*

'Stop moping,' she says, glancing at her cell. 'We have first block in five minutes. We're supposed to pick a famous Hedoness to study for our final projects this morning. I want to get there before someone else chooses Marilyn Monroe.'

I point towards the guy on the ground. 'What about him?'

Marissa folds her arms across her chest, gripping tight to her gold purse strap. 'Haven't you been listening?' She lets out a dramatic breath. 'Seriously. Forget about him. He'll find me when he's fully absorbed my power. Until then, I have a class to get to.' With that, she flips a wave of blonde hair over her shoulder and struts off, wafting the familiar scent of rosemary and mint shampoo in her wake.

Even though my heart tells me to stay, I know there isn't anything I can do to help him. Who am I kidding? Marissa's right – I'm a Hedoness and no matter how much I want to, I can't change that.

I run to catch up, guilt washing further over me with every step away from the will-less boy. That quickly shifts to anger. It irritates me how Marissa seems to float over the ground and how her gold mane sways in unison with her hips. She doesn't even need powers to make men fall for her. It's out of laziness that she uses them.

Marissa's almost at the school by the time I make it to

14

her side. She acknowledges me with a curt nod and then starts right back into her speech from earlier.

'*Amor est vitae essentia*,' she says, pointing to the words carved into the wood doors. '*Love is the essence of life*. Until you come to terms with that, Rach,' she goes on, her tone dripping with contempt, 'you'll never experience any form of love. What we do might not suit your high morals, but it's our calling, our purpose.'

'Ladies,' a gruff voice barks from the doorway. 'You're late.'

I look up in time to see Marissa curtsy, bowing her head to the large black form. 'Yes, Mother Superior. Apologies.'

The woman in black turns her attention on me. She cocks her head, showcasing the wiry grey whiskers poking out from her chin. 'And why is that, Miss Patel?'

'Reverend Mother . . .' I pause and attempt a curtsy of my own. By the look on her face, it comes across like a drunk trying to plié. I glance at Marissa. I could sell her out, buy me some much-needed favour with the nun. Though I can't help noticing the uneasy way she grips the strap on her new gold purse.

'The taxi—' I begin, but Marissa cuts in.

'I stopped to turn a guy.'

I hold my breath, waiting for Mother Superior to yell about how careless Marissa was for using her power

15

without a teacher's supervision, especially now, with all the media attention on the missing boys.

'Good,' she says instead, clasping her hands and lifting the side of her mouth in what I can only assume is an attempt at smiling. 'What is your current turning span?'

'They usually last for a few days,' Marissa says. 'Then I either turn them again, or set them free, depending on what the class needs are.'

Mother Superior strokes her whiskers. 'That is passable, but you are an outstanding student and my expectations are high. You should be aiming for weeks, months – even years, soon.'

I'm pretty sure my jaw's hanging open. The nuns are constantly telling us to be careful and not get caught using our gift. But now she's practically encouraging it. It's not surprising the reporters are starting to ask questions.

Mother Superior puts her hand on Marissa's shoulder, but looks at me. 'It is important to learn to control your gift. One day you will turn a future mate and that requires no error – it must last for ever. It is your duty to be fruitful and multiply so we can ensure the survival of the gift you were given.' She drops her arm from Marissa, but her eyes remain locked on mine. I'm starting to see why Marissa didn't get in trouble. Mother Superior seems more concerned with my lack of embracing the gift than Marissa's overenthusiasm for it.

Her eyes wander down my body, taking in my dishevelled appearance. 'Heavens, what muddy tragedy has happened to your uniform?' Her voice cracks and her eyes bulge when they land on my shoes. 'Did you dip your toes in white paint?'

'They're Converse sneakers.'

'They're responsible for the demerit I'm adding to your student file.' She points to them, her nose turned up. 'I never want to see those on school property again.'

'Yes, Mother Superior.'

She nods and leans closer. 'Now, how are your studies going? Have you had a successful turning yet?' She glances at Marissa as she asks.

From the amount of times I've been sent to her office, you'd think she'd know.

I haven't done it yet, and I don't intend to.

Mother Superior clears her throat, waiting for my answer.

I hang my head and tug at my coat sleeve, wanting to tell her that I'm perfectly content to never test my ability. But instead I say, 'No, your Reverence.'

She tsks and steps closer, a giant wall of black blocking me from the doors. 'This troubles me, Rachel. Your mother was one of our best students – such a treasure. There's no reason why you shouldn't have developed your gift.'

There's that word again. *Gift*. If it's a gift, it's a stupid one.

The bell rings, and Marissa shifts from one foot to the other.

'You ladies better hurry or you'll be shut out of homeroom.' As soon as the words leave Mother Superior's mouth, Marissa takes off, dashing around the nun and through the doors. I force a smile and follow after.

'Miss Patel,' Mother Superior says. 'I want to see you in my office after school. Be prompt.'

I push down the wave of nerves and nod before continuing to the hall. Tuesday's turning out to be the worst of the week.

My shoes squeak on the polished stone floor as I pass the housing wing and turn down the corridor of classrooms. Marissa's way ahead of me and I realize I'm probably going to be late as I glance up at the domed ceilings painted with vivid scenes of angels and demons in a deadly war.

The halls, blue-striped wallpaper and wood trims, are peppered with art. Mostly historical pieces rescued from closing Greek museums, but there's some custom work too, like the ceiling. I take a quick moment to study my favourite – a baroque of Eros gripping that magical golden arrow in one hand and a charcoal-black arrow in his other. His hair is curly like mine, his skin way paler, and his eyes are a striking blue. But the bow slung over his shoulder is what draws me to this particular painting: it's carved with a celestial battle scene similar to the ceiling, but instead of angels and demons it's the gods of Olympus versus man.

I continue to the stairwell, taking the stairs two at a time, skidding on to the landing in front of a procession of Sisters guiding a classroom of first-year students to their homeroom. I feel for every single one of them. It's hard enough being a normal thirteen-year-old, but for Hedonesses, thirteen means discovering we have an ungodly ability, that we're monsters, and that everything we thought we knew about life and ourselves is one big lie. We're torn from our normal schools and sent to ones masquerading as religious institutions so as not to be detected. Schools like St Valentine's, which specialize in guiding us into our power.

First year is a whole lot of girls, with a whole lot of confusion and anger and tears – something that's evident in the group before me. They take in every inch of the hall, trying to make sense of this new place, this new stage of their lives, and they walk in parallel lines, forced to hold hands with their recently assigned A.P.s.

The nuns stop to send a warning look – they can't have my tardiness setting an example for the first years. I quicken my pace, less for fear of angering them and more because I can't stand seeing the cries for help hiding in the eyes of the girls. It reminds me just how stuck I am.

When I finally make it to homeroom, the large oak doors shut. I take a moment to straighten my uniform, though it doesn't really help, then ring the bell signalling to the class that a tardy student waits in the hall.

The door groans open, and Sister Anthony Christine peers out. Her hazel eyes fall on me and she offers a welcoming smile.

'I'm sorry I'm late, Sister. I was—'

'No need to give reason, Miss Bale's already informed me. Please come in and take a seat.' She motions me to a spot at the front of the class. I scan the room for Marissa to find her in our usual place at the back. She offers me a brief shrug before spreading her things on my section of the table.

As I take my new seat, the Sister hands me a paper. 'The other students have already picked their end-of-year projects. I'm afraid you're left with Joan of Arc or Queen Guinevere.' She looks on with anticipation.

I chew the inside of my cheek, flicking my pencil back and forth, thinking over the choices. Truthfully, I don't care which Hedoness I do my project on, but my teacher's dedicated her life to preserving Hedoness traditions, and after this morning with Mother Superior I want to be careful with my response. The last thing I need is more demerits – failing transcripts from St Valentine's would be even worse than regular ones, and I really don't want to take school all over again.

'Who will it be?' The Sister clasps her hands.

'Um, I'm not sure. Who do you suggest?'

She leans against her desk, crossing her hands in her lap, the shadow from her habit making her look like a sad doll. 'Hmmm . . .' She thinks out loud. 'Joan used her gift to turn men's will towards her cause and help end a war. She was not interested in love, *per se*. But Guinevere had men believe she was the most beautiful maiden in the world, when in truth she was a regular girl much like you.' The girls in the class fight back chuckles. But they don't bother me – I know I'm no Marissa. Still, I can't help running a hand over my wild black waves.

The weight of everyone's eyes on me, waiting for my answer, is too much. 'I guess I'll go with Joan of Arc,' I say, knowing I'd rather be a fighter than a beauty queen.

'Excellent choice.' Sister Anthony Christine jots some notes in her planner. When she finishes, she stands, smooths out her habit, and turns to address the class. 'Ladies, I'd like you to take the rest of this period to plan your essays and presentations. If you need any resources, please come to me for a hall pass before leaving for the library.'

I flip open my notebook and glance around – most of the class has already set to work. The girl next to me, Paisley, leans over. I know her a little outside of school. Our mothers were A.P.s when they went here, and they've kept in touch over the years. Plus we're the only students whose parents aren't from the US – my ma's from India and my dad's from England. Her parents are South African. Paisley's nice, and I think we would have been real friends if it wasn't school policy to only be friends with our A.P.s.

'Did you see *My Vampire Alien Life* last night?' she asks, her accent a more musical and wild version of my father's British one. She tugs on her necklace – a charm of a spaceship with vampire fangs.

'Not yet.' I smile at her.

'OMG, you have to. It's the new *it* show about hot vampires that come from outer space and go on dates with high school gi—'

'Paisley.' Sister Anthony Christine flashes a warning look. 'Just because your A.P. isn't in class today doesn't mean you can disturb Miss Patel.'

'Yes, Sister.' Paisley nods and leans against her hand.

It feels like hours go by before the bell finally rings. I glance at my notebook, where I've doodled the words 'Joan of Arc' and 'fighter' over and over in twisted writing. Sighing to myself, I pack my books and leave for the next class – Turning 101. As I walk past Sister Anthony Christine's desk she looks up at me, disapproval flashing in her eyes.

'Hey,' Marissa calls from the hall, giving me an excuse to rush past the Sister. 'I got Marilyn. Rita tried to claim her but I gave her the dirtiest stare.' Marissa hooks my elbow and chatters away as we walk towards second block. 'She caved so fast it was hilarious. You should've seen it.'

She stops to wait for my reply as a pair of A.P.s skip past us down the hall, heads together, giggling about their projects. I look up, trying to think of what Marissa said.

'Nice.' I force a smile, hoping it's the right answer.

'You're not even listening.' She watches the girls until they bound around a corner.

'I'm trying, it's just—'

'*What?*' She turns back, somehow managing to make one word a weapon.

My grip tightens on my books. 'After that guy this morning, then Mother Superior . . .' I sigh. 'My mind's someplace else today.'

She crosses her arms. 'It sucks being your A.P. sometimes.'

I'm too shocked to respond. Of the two of us, I thought I'd be the one saying that.

'I just wanted you to be happy for me,' she says. 'For my new purse from my mom, the hot guy I turned, for Marilyn. But all you care about is yourself.'

'I didn't mean—'

With a flick of her hair and a scowl, Marissa turns and stomps away, leaving me feeling like the worst A.P. ever.

I can't be a normal girl, and I suck at being a Hedoness.

Three

Maybe Marissa's right. Maybe I have been self-focused, and though I don't get why those things are important to her, they obviously are. She's stood by me for the last three years of struggling with school. The least I can do is be here for her now. It's what every good A.P. would do. Besides, somewhere along the way she's become more than just an A.P. – she really has become a good friend.

'Riss?' I call after her. 'Riss, wait up.'

As I enter the classroom behind her I cringe. Seated quietly on a bench at the front of class, where they've been told to wait since yesterday, are the three missing boys from the news report this morning. Though, unlike their serious headshot images, they have giant smiles now. Forced. False. But smiles nonetheless.

They wave and perk up when they see their girls. Paisley approaches her victim, a boy with the same shade of red hair as my father. He nearly stumbles getting off the bench to greet her.

'How was your night?' she asks. 'Is there anything I can do to make you more comfortable?' At least she cares about his wellbeing, in a way.

'Making you happy makes me comfortable,' he says with a giant smile.

I roll my eyes and turn my back so I don't have to see the rest of their exchange.

Marissa's already spread her things over my usual spot next to her. I ignore the message and plop down in the chair. She gives me one of her dramatic glares.

I force a smile. 'You got Marilyn, that's awesome. What are you going to do for your presentation?'

She crosses her arms and leans into the desk. 'Like you care.'

The bell rings before I can reply, and Sister Hannah Marie enters.

'Good morning, ladies. I trust you've come prepared to learn.' Her voice is all sing-song which means we're most likely having a pop quiz or a live demonstration. I hope to the gods it isn't either, but if it has to be one, I'm praying for the quiz. 'Why don't you push your tables back, grab some floor mats and make a circle at the front.'

I groan – floor mats mean demonstrations. After this morning, this is the last thing I want to do. I debate excusing myself to the restroom or the sickroom. But of all the Sisters, Hannah Marie loves her job the most. Her eagerness to teach often results in me with a detention. If

I don't want to be sent to Mother Superior's office early, I'll have to at least look interested in the lesson.

'How did your assignments from last class go?' Sister Hannah Marie asks, surveying the room and taking a mental attendance as we get to work setting up our mats.

Marissa's first to raise her hand. She kicks off her heels and stands on the edge of the squishy foam, waiting to be called.

'Miss Bale,' the Sister acknowledges with a nod.

Marissa's head jerks up and she flashes one of her pageant-winning grins. 'I turned a boy this morning. A cute one.'

The class bursts into a fit of giggles and Sister Hannah Marie claps her hands in joy at the news. I force a smile so as not to look too out of place.

She walks down the aisle to our corner of floor. 'How did it go?'

Marissa's posture straightens. 'It seemed to affect him more than anyone I've turned so far.' There's a pressure in her gaze, a longing for perfection, and it freaks me out.

'That's splendid news, Marissa,' the Sister says. 'You're well on your way towards top marks with all your accumulating turning credits. Where is he now?'

Marissa's smile slips. 'I haven't been notified of any visitors and it's been over an hour. Shouldn't he be here already?'

'For some it takes longer.'

26

It's hard to believe that I'm listening to them talk about taking the will of someone so casually. But then again, there are three boys sitting at the front of class waiting to be called on for experimentation. I roll my eyes at the absurdity of it and Sister Hannah Marie notices. She gives me a warning look before returning to the board to jot down some notes.

'It is important to learn to control your release. When you graduate you should be able to determine the amount of force required for the length of a turning you need. If you do not focus, you can under-turn your target. Too much, too soon can result in a very powerful but very short turning of a couple days. If you focus your release, you can turn someone for ever.' She diligently writes her points on the board, making sure to underline the key elements.

I can't help shuddering. I've seen someone who's been turned for ever – it isn't as glamorous as Sister Hannah Marie makes it sound.

The Sister stops writing and spins around, clapping for our attention. A cloud of chalk dust floats from her hands, sparkling in the colourful light from the stained-glass window as it drifts to the floor. 'It seems to me, Marissa, that you released too strongly and didn't control where you were targeting.' She returns to the board, rewriting CONTROL in big letters and circling it.

'Now, class, can anyone tell me what Marissa felt when she released her gift into the man?'

27

'That part sucked,' Marissa says, getting another round of laughter. She smiles, proud of herself, and takes a seat beside me on the mat.

Everyone in class has a hand raised, except me. It earns another look of disapproval from Marissa, and Sister Hannah Marie.

The Sister points to Paisley, kneeling on a mat a foot away, waving a little too keenly. 'Yes?'

Paisley jumps to her feet, the momentum popping a button on her cardigan. 'It's painful. Almost like when your arm is asleep, or like a bee sting, or like vampire venom.'

The class giggles and Sister Hannah Marie purses her lips. 'If vampires were a real thing, I'm sure it would be. Thank you for your contribution, Paisley.' She looks to the other side of the room. 'Now, can anyone tell me why it's painful to release their gift?'

I know the answer – I read it in our manual. It says that Eros wanted to keep the arrow of infatuation away from his mother, Aphrodite. Apparently, Aphrodite wasn't happy with his choice to marry Psyche, and Eros was worried she'd use the golden arrow to turn Psyche's love towards another man. So while she was asleep, he hid it inside Psyche. But he didn't know she was pregnant and the arrow pierced their unborn child, the power transferring to baby Hedone. Thanks to that we, the descendants of Hedone – *Hedonesses* – have the power of

Eros's golden arrow in us, but when we use it, we feel what that baby felt.

I don't bother raising my hand. It's one thing to read it, it's another to announce it as truth.

When no one answers, Sister Hannah Marie walks to the middle aisle. 'Pull out *Eros's Arrows* and turn to page 230.'

I slide the textbook out from under my pile of papers. The leather cover's still dirty from this morning. I run my finger over Marissa's heel indent before flipping to the page. It's a full-colour fresco of Eros shoving a gold arrow into Psyche's swollen belly and the words IN THE BEGINNING. This is how we came to be – the Hedonesses' origin is one giant mistake.

The Sister nods with excitement. 'It all comes back to the arrow. The act of creating love is painful. All the tension, embarrassment, all the emotions balled together and injected into someone, just like an arrow piercing a heart. That is what you chosen ones feel when you use your power. What you feel is the physical manifestation of what Hedone felt when she was stabbed while inside the womb: fear, pain, isolation, the absence of love, and then all love at once.' She pauses, letting us take it in. 'Can any of you tell me why Eros gave up his arrow, his greatest power?'

I drift off, thinking back to the painting of Eros in the hall, and almost don't notice Sister Hannah Marie calling my name until Marissa nudges me in the side.

'Yes, Sister?' I rub my ribs and glare at Marissa.

She raises an eyebrow and mouths, 'You're welcome.'

'I was asking if you knew why Eros hid the arrow?' the nun repeats.

I shrug. I've heard the story more times than I'd like. I just don't want to be a participant in this conversation.

The Sister frowns, stepping back to scan the classroom. 'He gave up the arrow in order to keep Psyche to himself.' She places her hand over her heart, trapping her rosary beneath her chalk-tinted fingers. 'You Hedonesses are a product of an act of love. Eros gave up his greatest power to keep his true love. This is no small gift from a god, and that makes it a huge responsibility bestowed upon you. Each time you turn a man, you give over a piece of your power, much like Eros.'

Marissa's hand shoots up.

'Yes, child?'

'Will we lose our ability to turn men if we give over too much of our powers each time?'

I laugh to myself. Of course she'd care about that.

'There's no need to worry,' the Sister says. 'The love your charge gives you will fill you up, make you stronger. Most young Hedonesses' power sparks for the first time when they feel love, or choose to pursue it. And some Hedonesses even learn to return the love of the men in some way. In those cases, we've seen their powers grow exponentially. In very rare cases, they can even turn men with their touch.' She smiles and looks right at me. 'Much like your mother, Rachel.'

I fidget in my seat, too afraid to look up for fear of locking eyes with anyone. I hate people talking about my mother's heightened ability almost as much as I hate being a child of forced love. I imagine Joan of Arc riding into the classroom, the word *fighter* painted in red on her back, a fierce look in her eyes as she rams her sword through the Sister.

Marissa shoots up her hand again. 'So if I love a guy I turn, I might be able to get powerful enough to turn by touch?'

'Love is a most powerful magic,' the Sister answers.

I'm so tired of all this. 'What we do isn't love,' I blurt, regretting it when I see the look on Sister Hannah Marie.

'It is love,' she says with an icy sharpness. 'Don't you see? It's the amount of love you offer that gets transferred into your charge. The more the intentions are true, the more power surges into him, the longer he stays turned, and the more it affects you.'

The class erupts in murmurs of understanding, and the fact that they buy everything they hear without question only makes me madder. If we're really offspring of a god, shouldn't that give us the right to some power of our own, something stronger than making puppets of men?

I glance at the boys seated up front and anger burns through me. 'Who decides the intentions? One person might believe in something that another person thinks is wrong.'

Marissa inhales sharply and the hopeful expression on Sister Hannah Marie's face fades to stone.

'I am tired of your doubt.' The Sister scribbles something on a piece of paper, a long something – it takes up the whole sheet. When she finishes, she seals it with wax from her altar candle, and lays it on the corner of her desk. 'Take this letter to Mother Superior and remain in her office until she permits you to leave.'

I set to work packing up my things, running through every excuse I can give my ma when she finds out. Because she will. She always does.

Marissa watches me with a mix of sympathy and confusion. This stuff is important to her – she seeks her identity in being a Daughter of Hedone. All I want is to be normal.

The Sister claps and the class turns from watching me. 'Marissa, come partner with Paisley. You can be first to demonstrate.'

Marissa hops to the front, assuming position at the corner of the mat. Paisley stands inches away, palms out, feet spread, shoulders braced. Marissa takes her hand and gives it a gentle kiss. Instantly Paisley's eyes roll back and her knees wobble, but it's not as strong as how the boy with the blue eyes in the park reacted. The Hedoness power doesn't work the same on us. It's why they make us practise on each other first.

Paisley giggles and rubs her hand. 'That was intense. I almost blacked out.'

'Very good, take a seat in case you do.' The Sister motions Paisley down. 'What did you feel, Marissa?'

'It hurts much less than kissing a boy,' she says, 'but it's a lot less fun.'

The class giggles again. Even the Sister chuckles. I fight the urge to shake my head.

'Paisley, can you call your gentleman friend up? We shall have Marissa demonstrate on him.'

Paisley hesitates. 'It won't hurt him, will it?'

Sister Hannah Marie smiles. 'I assure you he won't remember a thing. What we don't know doesn't hurt us.'

I roll my eyes. Paisley nods and waves her boy over. He stands on the mat in her place, waiting for Marissa's kiss, his eyes never leaving Paisley's.

'Who knows what happens when a turned boy is injected with the powers of a different Hedoness?' the Sister asks.

Paisley raises her hand and the Sister nods for her to answer.

'Does it erase the instructions of the last Hedoness?'

'It does not,' the Sister says firmly. 'Every command given to a turned man stays in place even after the

Hedoness's ability wears off. Unless, of course, the next Hedoness instructs him differently. But thank you for your question, Paisley. Now, could you please command him to do something? Then we will have Marissa demonstrate the change.'

I finish gathering my things, and approach Sister Hannah Marie for the letter before I have to witness any more of their experimentations. Her eyes offer a look of disappointment, much like the look Sister Anthony Christine gave me earlier. I try not to read into it as I take the letter from her outstretched hand and head for the door.

'And Rachel?'

I pause, not turning around.

'It's your own heart that's the judge,' she says.

Mother Superior's reading spectacles slide down her nose as her eyes dart across the note.

I gulp and shift in the doorway, waiting for my verdict, my Converse shuffling awkwardly on her tiled floor.

She glances up from the page, those dark eyes assessing me, then carries on reading.

A few throat clears and a 'hmmm' or two later, she lowers the note to her desk. 'Take a seat, Rachel.'

She points to an altar chair in the corner. I place my books beside it and shakily lower myself in, then sit rigidly with my hands folded in my lap, and my shoes tucked under so she doesn't see them and get mad all over again. Sister Hannah Marie's class on turning is maddening, but anything's better than Mother Superior's office. It's dim and dusty, a collection of Gothic crucifixes line the walls, and dozens of lit prayer candles – each painted to depict the death of a saint – clump in random groupings about the place. It's more like a funeral parlour than an office. My eyes are drawn to a grey rock with bright gold veins, under a glass dome on a corner of her desk. It's the only thing in the room that isn't staged and it's the only thing not covered in dust.

'That's a philosopher's stone,' she says. 'It's used to turn base metals into gold. Though this one has run out of magic.' She rubs a phantom smudge off the glass. 'It could work again, if I find a god willing to give me their magic-restoring blood.' She smiles to herself before looking up. 'It was a gift from the Committee.'

When I don't reply, Mother Superior sighs and adjusts her seat, resting the letter and her spectacles on her large mahogany desk. 'You don't like it here at St Valentine's, do you?'

My first instinct is to apologize. But I take a deep breath and lift my chin, noticing a particularly gruesome candle with a caricature of a decapitated man. 'Not really, no.'

'You have no desire to use the gift given to you?'

35

My stomach flips. It's this belief that makes me twitchy – the idea that I have one talent, one purpose in life. I'd like to believe I have several gifts and being a Hedoness isn't one of them.

'Which *gift* are you referring to?'

Mother Superior slams her hand on the desk. 'Don't play games with me, Rachel. You know what I'm asking. I will not tolerate disrespect.'

My breaths come short. 'Honestly? No, I don't think it's a gift to steal a man's will. I think it's selfish. Awful, even.' Heat floods my cheeks and I cringe, waiting for the shouting, the anger, but the nun stays calm. I lean forward, my hands gripping the side of the chair, its tattered wooden edge gripping back. 'Shouldn't love be a—'

'Rachel.' She hisses my name, causing me to jerk back. The tension of her *on again, off again* temper has my entire body in knots. 'It's time you stop thinking about what you don't have and start being thankful for what you do.'

'And what's that?' I ask, a little too sharp.

Mother Superior locks on to me, those dark eyes holding me captive. 'You are a strong, intelligent young woman who has been given a gift that could change the world for the better. *The greatest of all things is love.* If you used that brain to think of solutions instead of problems, imagine what you could do. Look at the good done by the Hedonesses that have gone before you. There are women, who started right here in St Valentine's, in key political positions in nearly every government. If necessary, the Committee can step in and take control – we have you Hedonesses to thank for that.'

'How good of them.'

'Rachel . . .' She says my name like a sigh. 'It's a disappointment that you refuse to embrace your gift. With your mother's extraordinary ability, I had high hopes for you. There was even talk of the Committee continuing training during your work years and placing you in a respectable position. But your lack of acceptance makes us doubt you're ready.'

The last thing I want is to sign up for the 'strongly encouraged' after-graduation work years. And I certainly don't want to spend them training with anyone who values utilising Hedoness power.

'At this point I'm going to be advising the Committee to hold you back for an additional year at St Valentine's, unless you show some major progress in your last semester.'

'What?! That's not fair.'

'The life of the gifted is rarely fair.'

'So if I turn someone, I can graduate and go on with my life? Is that all you care about?'

She crosses her hands over her desk and takes a calming breath. 'That and law and history. It is imperative you learn your power before your next stage of training.'

'Next stage? What if I don't want it?'

'Then you are the Committee's problem.'

'Isn't the Committee busy with important things? What would they want with a Hedoness who doesn't want to be a Hedoness?'

'The Committee oversees everything we do. But we can discuss them later. Right now, we're discussing you.' She puts her glasses back on, but doesn't go back to reading the note. Part of me thinks she just needs an added barrier between us, as little and insignificant that it is.

'Rachel?' A look of disapproval washes over the nun's face. 'This is a serious matter. The gods have given you a gift and you refuse to embrace it.'

I absorb the nun's penetrating glare and try to keep my breathing calm, collected. It's not working. It's like I'm on trial.

She takes my silence as doubt. 'How can you have such a gift and still question the gods' existence?'

'It's not that I don't believe in the gods. It's that I'm not sure I agree with them.' I regret the words the moment they slip off my tongue. Not because I don't mean them. I do. But because I don't want to sit through the lecture that's twitching on her lips. 'And anyway,' I say, hoping to change the subject, 'I just don't understand why the Committee needs Hedonesses to do their work when there are actual gods around.'

'The gods are not allowed to interfere with humans and as such are not allowed out of Olympus. The

38

commitee sealed the doors to Olympus and the otherworlds. You know this.'

'It seems strange that those who are supposed to keep the gods and demigods from interfering would encourage Hedonesses to—'

Mother Superior sighs. 'Over the years, the Committee learned that it was easier to control the gods with the help of Hedonesses. Now that the gods no longer interfere in our world, the Committee's efforts have turned to world politics, trying to spread peace by placing Hedonesses in influential and strategic positions. You should know this also, Rachel.'

'Maybe they'd be better off letting them out than having a bunch of forced-love children do their work.'

'I see what this is really about.' She pushes up her glasses and re-crosses her hands, leaning over the desk to be nearer to me. 'A child who is a product of forced-love is a form of beauty birthed from darkness. A gift. You are born of sinners, yes. We all are. Still, future sins are your choice, not your right. You can be a part of greatness, Rachel.'

The nun's quiet response stabs my heart.

She's confirmed what I've always known – I am a product of sin.

I am birthed from darkness.

I am a monster.

39

Four

When I get home, I practically run through the door and straight into the kitchen. I'm greeted with the familiar smells of cardamom, asafoetida, coriander – my parents have been baking again.

Ma stands by the counter. Her dark hair is neatly pinned off her face, showing off the beautiful gold and black beaded necklace that I've never seen her without, and she's wearing a long navy-blue saree. 'How was school, sweetheart?' she turns to ask, her warm brown eyes squinting at the side as she smiles.

'Please don't make me go back, Ma.' I toss my books on the table next to Ma's navy leather going-out gloves, and flop into the chair.

'I can't remember the last time you said something like that.' She laughs. 'Oh wait, yes I do. Yesterday.' She returns to filling the teapot.

'Ma, I'm serious. Why can't I just go to another school?'

'Rachel—'

'Hate isn't strong enough a word.'

'If St Valentine's is that bad I can send you to Gujarat. You could stay with Nani and go to one of the Hedoness schools there.'

'No thank you. I love New York. I don't want to live anywhere else. And I want to go to school here, just . . . not a Hedoness school. I never want to use my *gift*.' I hiss out the word 'gift'. I can't help it.

'Location I can work with, but Hedoness training is mandatory.'

I sigh.

Ma reaches across and puts her hand on my shoulder. 'My love, you know you won't need university when you graduate school. It may not be what you wish, but Hedonesses have higher callings. It's our job to use our gift to protect the human race. And it is our duty to grow our families.'

More Hedoness kids. I shudder at the thought. Obligations, expectations. I don't care what Ma, or the Committee, wants me to do after – I'm done. For as long as I can remember, I've wanted to become a social worker and help children without families, children who are abandoned, children who have no choice.

I fiddle with the salt shaker, spilling granules over Ma's gloves and her hand-dyed tablecloth. 'Hey. You're supposed to be supportive of me.' I shake off the gloves and flick the salt from the table as I wait for her response.

41

'I do support you. But I also worry for your future happiness. Your happiness is more important to me than my own.' She places a mug of tea and a plate of perfectly rolled khandvi on the table. My stomach rumbles and my mouth salivates to inhale the savory treat.

'I want to be a Nani one day,' she tells me.

'I thought you were worried for *my* happiness.' I squeeze a lime wedge over the khandvi, then pop one in my mouth.

'Speaking of which, have you looked through any of the biodata husband profiles Nani sent over for you? I know she'll ask next time we talk.'

I don't bother answering. She knows how I feel about Nan's matchmaking attempts. My Nani's an older, wrinklier version of Ma, with even more love for our Hedoness heritage, if that's possible. We visited her once, when I was thirteen. All I remember of Gujarat, India, is that it's colourful, and busy, and hot, and it would've been the most magical trip of my life if it wasn't also the most embarrassing. Instead of getting to see sights and experience the culture that makes up one half of me, Nani paraded me around the Hedoness convents, showcasing me to the students who would be my competition for what she referred to as 'Our generation's most powerful Hedoness.'

'It wouldn't hurt to look through them,' Ma says, taking a seat across the table, patting her gloves out of habit, before cupping her steaming mug. 'I know you're not comfortable turning anyone. The Patel men in Nani's forms are of the few that know what Hedonesses are. They're willing and wanting to be with one. To them it's an honour.'

I think about the envelope of profiles sitting unopened in my room, with a handwritten note from Nani on top that reads, 'You are nice-looking girl, not too skinny, not too fat, wheatish complexion. You have top choice of biodata.' Then it hits me. Ma's siding with Nani – she's serious. She wants grandkids.

'Oh no, no, no.' I wave my hands and lean back in my chair, my mind returning to that frightening phone call I had with Nani on my thirteenth birthday, the day I first found out what I was. She told me I was lucky to be born a Hedoness, and a Patel. She said Patels must stick together, that my bloodline has done remarkable things throughout history, even ended wars. But mostly she said it's important that I don't make the same mistake as Ma and marry a non-Patel.

If I was born to a family without the Hedoness gene, I wouldn't even be called Patel. I'd be like every other girl and take my dad's last name, not my ma's – Rachel Madhu Groundwater.

I glance up to find Ma studying her mug and fake a smile. 'I'm not so sure the whole marriage and family thing is in my future.' What I don't say is that the idea of forcing a man to spend his life with me and raise my kids isn't my dream. I'd love a family – just not the Hedoness way. 'Besides, I'm serious about wanting to be a social worker, so that'll take up a lot of my time.'

She looks over her mug, eyebrow raised. 'I know you want that,' she says. 'You've brought enough stray children home for me to feed over the years.'

'They didn't choose to be abandoned by their parents.'

'And the gods know why you keep giving Marissa chance after chance.'

'Well, she is my A.P.'

'You have a big heart, Rachel.' Ma smiles. 'But perhaps you're selling yourself and your gift short. I graduated top of class and I didn't turn out so bad. Besides, Eros looks out for his descendants. It's because of him, I met the love of my life.'

'The love of your life?' She can't possibly mean Dad.

'You, silly.' Ma reaches over and pats my hand. 'Just remember – *if you surrender to love, Eros will find you.*'

I am wondering if this is going to turn into one of Ma's 'embrace your gift' speeches, but her smile is so big and hopeful, it's hard not to take her seriously.

'Right,' I say, unsure. 'Speaking of Eros's version of love, where's Dad?' It is unusual for him to not be around Ma – in fact, it's weird.

'He's out in the garden. I asked him to do some weeding.' She takes a sip of her tea.

44

'Gardening? How's that going?'

Ma glances up. 'You know your father – the same as usual, I suppose.'

'Usual' is glued to Ma's side. But he's not here, so that's got to be a step in the right direction. 'I'm going to go say hi.' I stand, pushing out my chair, watching my mother struggle to keep her face expressionless. On my way to the backdoor, I straighten my shirt and fix my ponytail.

'Hey, Dad,' I say, pushing past the screen into the small side alley between brownstones that Ma's turned into a flower heaven.

He doesn't hear me, or if he does, he doesn't turn to respond. Instead he stands over Ma's exotic lily bed, his face in his hands, crying.

'Dad?' I call again, this time louder. He raises his head and wipes his freckly cheeks, the same dark brown of my freckles. A smile spreads over his face, and it lifts my mood.

I return it with one of my own. 'Your garden—'

'Does your ma want me? Did she send you to come get me?' His British accent has a sombre cadence to it today.

I should've known that smile wasn't for me.

'No. I just came to say hi. Why are you crying?'

He runs his mud-stained hands through his thick ginger curls. 'I miss your ma so much.' He starts back into a fit of sobs.

45

'She's inside, like ten steps away!'

His answer shouldn't be a surprise – it's the exact same every time.

'It seems so far.' He collapses to his knees and carries on plucking weeds.

I can't stand seeing him like this. I run back to the house, to my room, and flop on to the bed. I lie there wondering what Dad would've been like if he'd never met Ma, and whether the free-spirited boy from the park is just like my father now too.

My chat dings with a notification. I pull over my laptop to find a new message.

MARISSA: *Turn on City News and see what I did to Paisley's guy in class today. It's hilarious.*

I search for City's livestream. My heart drops when it loads, and the frightened face of the red-haired boy fills my screen. He presses a blood-soaked cloth to his neck, and Paisley's alien vampire necklace hangs over his shirt. I turn up the volume as the reporter asks a question.

'Are you certain that's what happened?' He holds the mic out.

'Yes,' the boy says, his voice shaking. 'It bit me. I . . . I was taken by vampires. Alien vampires.'

'Did they give you that necklace?' the reporter asks.

'Necklace?' The boy looks down, his eyes widening. 'Get it off me!' he screams, clawing at the chain.

A police officer steps in to help, and the camera swings back to the reporter. 'The latest victim in the abduction cases leaves us with more questions than answers. Are monsters real? Are they in New York? Are they taking our boys?'

Five

The next day, we're barely ten minutes into third period when Marissa is called to the office. She slowly packs her gold bag, glancing at me with a smug smile that reads, *I told you so*. I roll my eyes but, truthfully, I'm glad for her. Even though I hate the reason, I haven't seen her this happy in a long time. Marissa's smile is a mix of relief and excitement. Her new conquest – or 'Nice-shoes' as I've taken to calling him – showed up at the office. He's a day late, but here nonetheless.

The class watches her with an eagerness that makes me uncomfortable. You'd think Marissa just won the lottery or something.

I shake my head, wondering if she's taking her time to revel in the class's admiration – only seven girls from our grade have been able to turn someone so far, and this is Marissa's fifth time. Knowing Marissa, it could also be for the game of it, keeping her guy waiting and wanting, and driving him mad with desire.

The brass tardy bell rings, interrupting Marissa's gloat. Sister Hannah Marie rises from behind her desk and walks to the door to see who it is. She opens it a crack, then slips into the hall. It's odd behaviour for a Sister. They don't normally leave us unattended. The class chats among themselves, a mixture of excitement for Marissa and gossip over *My Vampire Alien Life*'s latest episode.

I think I'm the only one who hasn't seen the show.

After a few moments the Sister returns, breaking up the chatter. A serious look has spread across her normally bubbly face. I can't help but sense something isn't right.

'Rachel, pack your things and escort Marissa to the office.' The Sister doesn't make eye contact. Instead she rushes to the board and hastily wipes the bullet points from yesterday's class. Marissa and I share a worried look.

'Am I in trouble?'

It's a perfectly valid question, but Sister Hannah Marie hangs her head. 'Just go,' she mumbles.

Marissa shrugs and I gather my books, following her into the hall. It's only Wednesday and it's the second time this week that I've been sent to the office – this has got to be a new record for me.

'I hope he's as cute as I remember,' Marissa says. 'I have a good feeling about this guy. Who knows, I may even keep him.'

I roll my eyes and fall into step beside her.

'Ooh, what if he has a six-pack?' She squeals and quickens her pace and I have to speed-walk to keep up.

She has her mind on Nice-shoes. But all I can think about is how strange Sister Hannah Marie was acting.

The halls are unusually empty – we don't even pass patrol nuns ushering first-years between classes. That only adds to my nerves. I bite the inside of my cheek. The closer we get to the office, the more uncertain I feel. Everything in me screams to turn and run. Instead, I stop in the middle of the hall.

'Something doesn't feel right.'

Marissa rolls her eyes in her typical belittling fashion. Then she pushes past me, reaching for the office door. She steals a quick moment to straighten her outfit and smooth down her eyebrows, even though they're perfect.

'Eyebrows?' she asks, pointing to them.

'Good,' I say.

'The rest of me?'

Flawless. 'Also good.'

Satisfied with my answer, she grabs my hand and strides into the office, dragging me in tow. When she stops abruptly, I slam into her, sending us both stumbling into the room. I regain my balance and gasp, staggering back.

In front of us are three police officers, guns drawn, pointing straight at us.

One of the men wears thick red-framed glasses and a wool sweater the same shade of brown as his skin. I only know he's an officer by the badge hanging around his neck. He pushes his way to the front of the group. His shaky hand clings to a gun. I glance from him to Mother Superior, hoping for some form of understanding. She stands behind the officers and gives a weak smile. When they're not looking she mouths something, and I'm pretty sure it's, '*We'll get you out of this.*'

'You're under . . .'

His words fill the room, and everything slows as the officers grab me and push me to the ground next to Marissa. I fight back every image I've seen on TV of police brutality and tell myself it won't happen to me. But then they yank my books out of my arms, jerk my wrists back to handcuff them, and then lift and shove me against the wall.

Marissa is guided beside me. The difference in treatment is startling. They've so wrongly judged which of us is the threat. And Marissa doesn't even seem to notice how scared I am; instead she looks bored by the whole thing. It frustrates me that her cool, cocky demeanour doesn't even slip when we're handcuffed. I fight the need to cry and instead focus on taking slow, deep breaths.

'Don't worry,' Marissa whispers, her eyes darting to the officer holding me. 'We got this, you ready?'

I can't believe what she's suggesting. Still, another part of me is tempted to try using my ability, to see if I can save myself. My guess is the nuns will act like this is a normal Catholic school and turn on us if they need to.

Still, I can't, not even for this. Not only is it wrong, but I'm unpractised. Even if I did somehow manage to successfully turn one of the officers, and Marissa another, we couldn't fight off the third officer. *Could we?*

I shake my head *no*, and she rolls her eyes.

So I do the only thing I can. I lift my chin and try to be brave. 'What have we done?'

The officer holding me shoves me further into the wall, and the one in the red glasses begins reciting our rights. All I really understand is that we have the right to remain silent. It's hard to focus on what he's saying when he's staring at me like I'm about to shoot laser beams from my eyes. It's like he's scared of us.

He wouldn't know about our *ability*, would he?

I bite my lip and return the stare, hoping to read something on his face that could give me answers. His eyes bulge through the thick lenses, and he steps back.

'Take these . . . these . . . girls to the holding cell.'

I'm jerked around, landing face-to-face with a large sweaty man.

'I'm Officer Tucker Johnson, that's Officer Mark White, and that,' he points to the officer with the glasses, 'is Officer Ammon Matos. You two are coming with us.'

The officers thrust us towards the door and Ammon watches, cleaning his glasses on his sweater.

I twist in their grip to look at him. 'Will you tell us what we've done?'

I'm knocked back around.

'When I find out exactly what you two girls, if you even are girls, have done, I'll . . . well, I'm going to make sure you never reach the mother ship, that's what.'

That confuses me at first, until realization sinks in, slow and painful – they *are* scared. But it's even worse than I thought. They think we're the vampire aliens.

Six

I slide closer to Marissa as the squad car pulls in front of the precinct. Ammon exits, putting on surgical gloves as he comes to the back and opens our door. He waves us out, reaching down for Marissa first. Even with the gloves, he hesitates to touch her, acting like he's being forced to put his palm on a hot stove instead of a sixteen-year-old girl.

She plays into it, snapping her teeth, smiling proudly at the way he jolts his hand back.

I lean and whisper, 'Stop that, if they didn't already think we're vampires, they do now.'

'Oh please.' She rolls her eyes. 'If he's forcing me to be here, I might as well have a little fun.'

Ammon pulls on the neck of his sweater and wipes his brow. 'Careful when you handle them.' He steps aside for the other officers to get us out.

They look at him like he's losing it. Still, they grab us and jerk us from the car to our feet.

'Open your mouth.' Ammon holds out a long plastic tube, and it's not until I'm fully yanked around that I see there's a cotton swab inside.

Marissa smiles wide. 'Make sure to really get up in my fangs, it's been a while since they were properly cleaned.'

He pulls back before the swab can make contact, his hand shaking as he tucks the plastic tubes in the front pocket of his sweater. I'm kind of thankful she scared him from swabbing our mouths. I'm not exactly sure what Hedoness DNA looks like.

Ammon waves us forward. 'Take them to the holding cells. We can process them from behind bars.'

The officers push us into the precinct; the grip on my arm is too tight, but I'm afraid to complain. Ammon hurries ahead, disappearing down a corridor. The men guide us past it, stopping before a glass door. They hold their badges to a camera.

'He's seriously scared of two teenage girls?' Tucker says, not caring we can hear.

Mark laughs. 'It seems that way.'

There's a blond officer watching us through the glass divide, his big blue eyes glinting with mischief – something about him is familiar, but I can't quite put my finger on it. As we're buzzed through, he winks at me. I frown and glance at Marissa. She's smiling wide, and that makes me shake with anger – we could end up charged for something. Having a permanent record would affect my chance of getting into the social worker program, and she's getting a kick out of it all.

'He's been watching too many zombie shows on the space network,' Tucker continues. 'But he has rank on us, so it's to the holding cells.'

Their lack of respect for Ammon gives me hope that they might be persuaded to take a small detour from his orders. I hang my head and let the tears I've been fighting back freely flow. They come out much faster than I expected and it soon turns to sobbing; my whole body convulses.

'I . . . I . . .' I struggle to stop crying enough to form words.

'Don't waste our time,' Tucker says, shaking me harder.

'Easy now, just breathe,' Officer Mark says.

'I . . . I don't know what we did,' I hiccup out, taking another deep breath before wiping my eyes on my shoulder, 'but I would really like my ma here. Please can I call her?'

Mark glances at his counterpart.

'We're to process them from the holding cell,' Tucker says, firm, squeezing my arm tighter.

Marissa picks up on what I'm trying to do. 'And I need to call Mother Superior,' she whines. 'My mom's out of town, and she's my legal guardian.'

I glare at her, shaking my head for her to cut it out, but she doesn't get it – instead she spirals into the worst fake crying I've ever heard. She sounds like a cat in heat.

'Nice try, lady.' Tucker pushes us ahead.

I'm about to say something to Marissa but the doors swing open and we hear heart-breaking screams. And among them, a name.

'Marissa . . . Marissa, my love . . .'

It can't be.

My legs turn to jelly. I glance at Marissa to find her looking at me, eyes full of fear. She's figured it out too. The police have Nice-shoes and somehow they know Marissa turned him.

We round the corner to find Ammon waiting for us. He thrusts open a large blue steel door and shoves me into the room before him. The screaming increases, and this time it's directed at Marissa.

'My love, you've found me! I knew you'd come. Oh, my love . . .' Marissa's smart enough to not look at him. But this only makes the guy's desperation escalate. 'Marissa, please.' His hands reach through the bars, his face plasters against them, hoping to gain any distance that could grant him one touch of her arm.

Now that he's identified Marissa in person, it'll be hard to argue a case of a mix-up. I take in the officers and the cell-lined room, and notice an old computer monitor with a blurry image of Marissa and me in Central Park frozen on it.

We're screwed.

I nod in the direction of the computer, but she keeps her eyes down, trying to ignore Nice-shoes.

'My love, what have I done to anger you? Tell me, and I will make this right. Please, my love.'

He sounds like my father. They're always the same – desperate, weak, no longer themselves.

The officer is talking to me, saying words I can't hear over the cries. I'm afraid if I don't answer soon, I'll be back in Officer Tucker's iron grip.

Marissa spins around, her hair whipping past my face. 'Would you just *shut up?*'

Nice-shoes stops, slumping to the ground, arms still clawing through the bars for her. Officer Ammon's mouth hangs open and his eyes bulge through his thick red frames. Nice-shoes was probably a handful, a loud handful. I can't imagine it was easy getting him into the cell. I know what Dad's like when Ma's not around.

Ammon pulls on his collar and takes a deep breath before continuing. 'As I was saying, Benjamin Blake has been acting like this since his run-in with you.'

'Run-in?' Marissa asks.

Ammon motions to the monitor. 'No need for the charade. I was the reason he was at the park. I'd arranged for Benjamin to meet me there, and as I arrived I witnessed your altercation. Caught the whole incident on my phone. I brought him back for questioning but it was clear he wasn't going to cooperate, so we let him go this morning and he led us right to your school.'

58

'I would like to call my mother,' I say, trying to keep my voice level. 'We're supposed to get one call.'

'That's being arranged.' Ammon turns to the officers holding us. 'Empty their pockets, take their cellphones, take off their cuffs, then place them in the cell next to Blake. When you're done, join me in the Chief's office.'

Tucker's strong hand wraps back around my arm.

Seven

I'm worried about my entire future and Marissa cares more about her clothes. She's leaning against the back of the cell, scrubbing a dirt smudge from her skirt, instead of helping come up with a way to get out of this mess.

'A cop was filming us!' I shake my head. 'I told you not to turn him, but do you ever listen?'

'Shut up, Rach. Don't say another word.' She glances around like she's worried someone will hear.

'You afraid you'll get caught? Look at us, Marissa. We're already caught.'

She stops scrubbing and sighs, watching me pace back and forth on the left side of the cell – on the side as far from Ben as I can get.

'How was I supposed to know?'

I narrow my eyes and continue pacing.

'My love?' Ben pushes his face so far between the bars that his eyes and lips pull into tight slits. 'Is there anything I can do to make you happy?'

If we weren't in jail because of him, I'd be laughing at the scene. 'Oh, you've done enough,' I reply for Marissa.

'Leave him alone.' Marissa glares at me before turning to the guy plastered between our cells. 'And you can stay quie—'

The blue steel door opens, and Marissa holds up her hand, signalling for us to keep our mouths shut.

Ammon appears in the doorway. His sweater's half untucked and he's putting on a fresh set of white gloves.

'Can we have a phone call now?' I ask, as Marissa glares at me.

'That is why I'm here. You,' Ammon points to Marissa, 'go to the back and remain by the wall. I'll let your friend make the first call.'

Marissa jabs her finger into my collarbone. 'You better call Mother Superior.'

I'm done following her lead. It got us here. Still, I nod – it'll do no good arguing with her.

Ammon guides me out and slams the steel door behind us, locking it with efficiency. His bony fingers wrap around my arm, gripping tight. It hurts, but at least I'm not in handcuffs again.

Ben moves to the back, next to Marissa, and continues clawing through the bars as Ammon leads me past the row of cages and out of the cold concrete and steel room. As soon as we exit through the large blue door, there are photos of the officers and framed newspaper articles hung in neat rows down the halls. It's less cold than the cells, but every bit as intimidating. There are officers everywhere. We pass one officer guarding the door to the holding room, and Ammon directs me through the maze of corridors, stopping to signal through a glass window for entrance into a secure room with a phone and table. A buzzer goes off, and the door clicks open. Ammon tests the handle then pushes me inside.

'Make it quick.'

The door closes with a metallic screech, leaving me to myself.

I go over to the phone and pick up the receiver. My fingers shake as I punch in the numbers to Ma's cell.

She answers right away.

'Hello?'

'Ma, hi—'

'Rachel, thank the gods. I just got off the phone with the school. Are you girls all right?'

A sense of relief fills me. I find myself taking the first real breath since being arrested.

'Where are they holding you?' she asks.

'We're at the precinct on East 67th.'

'I'll be there soon.'

My mind fills with images of Ma in handcuffs, being shoved into the last empty cell, and my heart hammers away.

'Listen, Ma, don't try anything . . . anything funny. OK?'

'Don't worry. I'll take care of everything.'

'Ma, don't . . .' The static blips of a one-sided conversation fill the receiver.

Eight

Ma should be here by now. Instead I'm left alone in the cell beside Ben, as Marissa's away making her call. Our cellphones are bagged on a desk next to our school stuff, just out of reach. If only I had long enough arms.

I take off my blazer and use it as a cushion on the cold concrete floor. Undressing draws my attention to my upper arm. A bruise is on its way. I rub the spot and think back on the events of the day.

Ben slumps against the bars, his head leaning on his fist. He's saying Marissa's name over and over. I take in his stylish clothes: white v-neck T-shirt, under a denim jacket that's slightly worn around the cuffs and collar, like someone who takes care of his clothes but wears them hard. There's something about him, something unexpected. I can't figure out what it is, and I look, hard, from his bright blue eyes, his well-groomed dark brown hair, to his athletic form. My stomach tightens, and I brush it aside as nerves.

An eerie quietness overtakes the cells as he stops calling for her. He lowers his head into his hands, and

63

after a few moments looks up, catching me watching him.

I pretend to adjust my seat, so he doesn't think I was staring.

Despite my best efforts, my eyes keep wandering towards Ben. The next time I look his way, he shifts and straightens his back.

'Why am I here?'

I'm not sure if he's talking to me, or just out loud. 'Sorry?'

'Why am I locked up?' He stands and walks to the side of the cell nearest the door. 'Hello?' he calls.

Marissa's power must've run out already.

When he gets no response, he comes closer to me. 'Why are my shoes muddy?' His voice is husky but self-assured. It surprises me after having listened to hours of his whining.

'You don't remember anything . . . or anyone?' I lean forward, hugging my knees.

'I get these flashes of a beautiful girl, and then nothing.' He rubs his hand through his hair. He seems upset, confused, then suddenly his eyes light up with understanding. 'I was meeting a man named Ammon to talk about becoming an officer, and then . . .'

Then Marissa got to you. I quietly watch him try to process what happened.

He looks back up. 'And why are you here? They don't normally put kids in the cells.'

I cross my arms and lean forward. 'Kids? I'm sixteen.'

He holds up his hands and smiles. 'I didn't mean anything by it.' Something about the way he is without Marissa's power, that confidence, the strong posture, something about that draws me in. 'But seriously, why are you here? Did you steal from the Girl Scouts?'

I can't tell if he's joking or not. Either way, I've never had a guy talk to me like this. Granted, the guys I'm around are usually turned. But after today's events, I don't really feel like joking.

'I'm here because of you.'

'Me? That doesn't make any sense.' His blue eyes dart across my face, studying, analyzing, then something registers in them. 'Have we met before?'

I shrug and try to look natural.

'Everything's blurry. I don't remember . . . I couldn't have committed a crime during a blackout,' he mumbles and paces. 'Could I? I wouldn't. Becoming an officer is all that matters to me.'

He says *officer* like he owns that word, and it reminds me how far I am from my dream of being a social worker. Something about that gets under my skin.

'You mean Boy Scout not officer, right?'

He turns, caught off guard, fighting back a grin. 'Boy Scout?'

'That's what I said.'

He leans on the bars at the other side of the cell. 'Are you always like this?'

'Like what?'

'On the defence.'

I jerk back. He's right, I am on defence, more often than I'd like. We've only been talking for a few minutes and somehow he sees right through me. I sputter out, 'Only when I'm in a jail cell.'

'I see.' He laughs and it almost makes me want to smile.

I've never been around a guy like this before. It's refreshing to be challenged and to challenge back. It's almost enough to distract me from my current predicament and I'm not ready for this feeling to end. 'How old are *you*, anyway?'

'Seventeen.'

My smirk stretches over my cheeks. 'Legal drinking age is twenty-one. For someone so concerned with his record, you shouldn't—'

'I would never drink!' His head snaps to me, those blue eyes darkening.

Something about how he says those words catches me off guard. It strikes me that there's a sadness to him. My eyes flick back to those frayed cuffs and I pull my feet closer to my body. Maybe I'm reading him the wrong way. 'Sorry, I . . . I was just trying to lighten the mood.'

He's about to say something when the door to the holding room bursts open and Marissa hurries in, followed by my ma.

'Quickly.' Marissa waves her over to the cell.

'What's going on?' Ben asks.

'Ma?' I jump up.

'No time to explain,' Ma rushes, fumbling the keys in her gloved hands by my bars. 'You have to trust me.' The lock clicks over and she throws the door open.

There's no person I trust more. But I don't move. My legs stay cemented to the ground. My heart hammers so fast there's a ringing in my ears. 'What did you do?' I manage, my eyes locked on the keys in her grasp.

'Rachel, please?' Ma waves me out. 'Are you coming?' Her eyes fill with worry; she sees my turmoil, the churning indecision. If I leave the cell without police permission, I'll be in even bigger trouble. I'll be kissing any chances of becoming a social worker goodbye. And she knows how much that means to me, she's been there for the years of my declared hatred for the Hedoness ways. By asking me to trust her she's basically asking me to choose the Hedoness life, and one on the run at that.

I can only imagine what Ammon and Tucker would do to me if we got caught.

My breaths are thick, panicked gulps. I can't seem to get enough oxygen into my lungs. Marissa says something but all I hear is a mumble through the ringing in my ears. Ma reaches in and grabs my arm, tugging me hesitantly – I imagine Joan of Arc riding into the precinct and slicing her way to rescue me. It's not much different from what Ma's doing.

Her gloved hand outstretches, opening and closing as if willing my fingers to find hers. It's jail or Ma. My legs waver a hesitant step forward. It feels as though the fabric of Ma's saree is wrapping around me, pulling me towards her.

I step out of the cage.

'Oh, hell no.' Ben backs away from the bars. 'Help!' he yells. 'There's a jailbreak in progress.'

Marissa pauses, finally noticing Ben's change.

'He doesn't remember,' I say.

She ignores me and walks over to his cell. 'We're bringing you with us – isn't that what you want?'

His eyes narrow as he takes her in, trying to put the pieces of this puzzle together. 'You. I remember you.'

Marissa smiles. 'Of course you do, my love.'

'"My love?" Man, I don't know what the officer did to me, but when I find out . . .' He stops, realizing there's more going on. 'What are you doing?'

Marissa shrugs and flips a lock of hair over her shoulder. 'We're sort of starting a new relationship.'

I'd roll my eyes at her, but his bewildered look is good enough for the both of us.

'I get that you think that.' He lets out a long breath. 'I don't remember any of it. But I mean here . . .' he accentuates, pointing at my ma, who's trying to open his cell. 'What are you doing *here*?'

She leans into Ma. 'Maybe I should just turn—'

'Don't even think about it,' I say.

Ma glances at me, then turns back to Marissa. 'Do it.'

Before either Ben or I can react, Marissa reaches through the bars and pulls his lips to hers. He's stunned still at first, then he jerks back. She muffles a scream in her arm and presses her head. He slides down the bars to the floor, body shaking wildly.

This is the second time I've seen my best friend steal his will this week, and it doesn't get any easier to stomach.

Minutes pass. I glance between the door and him, worried we'll get discovered. Finally, he stops shaking. 'My love?' he says, looking up through the steel, eyes returned to the glossy haze.

I miss the perceptive boy already.

'Yes, now come on.' Marissa opens the door and grabs his arm, dragging him out.

'My—'

'Don't say another word until I tell you to.'

He nods and reaches for her hand. She lets him take it, and I can't help noticing how good her delicate fingers looked laced with his work-worn ones.

I grab Marissa's purse, my books and the bags with our cellphones and fall into line. Ma stops and motions us back against the wall. 'Shhh,' she says, reaching for the handle.

Before she has a chance, the door swings open and Ammon walks in. My heart races, the bruise on my upper arm pulses.

'What on earth?' He pauses, taking in the four of us lined up along the wall, his eyes stopping on my ma as he reaches for something behind his back. 'Mrs Patel, I presume?' He tries to look brave, in control, but his shaky knees give him away.

Ma lifts her chin and steps forward, slipping one of her blue gloves off. 'You will not unhook your gun.'

Ammon's hand stays behind his back and he steps away slowly.

'Let me rephrase.' Ma pounces forward with a predatory grace, shoving him into the bars. I startle, pressing my body as far from hers as possible. Marissa lets out a screech as Ma grabs Ammon by his neck. The man's eyes roll back and his body convulses. For a moment I forget she's my mother and my entire body fills with fear, my instincts telling me to run from the monster before me. I've never seen her use her power before. And now I wish I never had. My mind can't separate the gentle hands that once comforted me as a child from the hands that now squeeze the will from a man.

She replaces her glove and waits the agonizing minutes for him to stop, glancing at the door every now and again to make sure no one will catch her in the act. The rest of us try to calm our breathing, still pressed into the wall. It seems like for ever before Ammon slumps down the bars, eyes filled with adoration.

'My lov—'

She holds up her hand. 'Stop. Tell me, what evidence do you have on the girls?'

Ammon pulls a cell phone from behind his back, showing us that the camera's currently running. *Not a gun then, just a phone.* 'I have footage of this, and them with Benjamin Blake, my love.'

She pinches the bridge of her nose. 'You may only call me Mrs Patel. Not my love, not darling, nothing but my name. Can you delete the footage?'

'Yes, my – Mrs Patel.'

It's surprisingly isolating to stand against the cold concrete wall and watch my mother manipulate an innocent man. I step closer to Marissa, until our arms are touching, and thankfully she doesn't move away. Because right now, I need whatever comfort I can get.

'Good,' Ma continues. 'I want all surveillance cameras off, and any footage recorded today erased. That includes your phone. Do you understand me?'

'Yes, Mrs Patel.'

'Do it now.'

He pushes off the floor and wanders over to an older computer monitor on the desk where they had put our stuff. Ma watches over his shoulder as he logs in to the security system and taps in his password, overriding the footage.

'Does this please you?' he asks.

'It does, very much.'

This makes him smile, big.

'And now,' she says, 'I will be taking the girls and Benjamin with me. It brings me great sadness to see them behind bars.'

Ammon falls to his knees before Ma, clutching her saree.

'Forgive me, I did not mean to upset you. I will release them any time you want. Please don't be sad.'

'Stand up and act strong.' Her words are firm, and they snap him out of his trance.

He scrambles from his knees and stands before her, awaiting her next command.

'Good, I prefer you much better when you are not grovelling.'

He nods once, hard.

'If anyone asks, tell them the girls are innocent and you arranged for their release. Make sure you tell them – this is your command.' She pauses to flash a smile, which makes his eyes light up. 'This *is* your command, isn't it?'

'Yes. It is.' He clears his throat, deep, meaty.

'Good. What is your direct phone number?'

He writes it down and hands her the paper which she folds and tucks in the blouse of her saree. 'And one more thing,' she says, smiling. 'Tonight when you go to sleep, I want you to forget you ever met me and you will continue to forget unless I call on you again. Are we understood?'

Her gaze slices into his and a small smile slips over her lips. It takes everything in me not to grab Marissa's arm for support.

He puffs his chest. 'I would die for you, Mrs Patel.'

'I don't want your death. I want your understanding.'

'I do not need sleep and I do not want to forget you.'

She sighs. 'It's been so long, I nearly forgot how difficult the newly turned can be.' Ma claps and Ammon remains stiff as a board, waiting for her next command. 'You will sleep at precisely 11 p.m.,' she says.

'Yes, Mrs Patel,' he says. 'I will sleep at 11 p.m.'

'Good, now stay here for at least an hour, then go about your work as usual.'

'Yes, Mrs Patel,' he says.

Ma pushes open the door and peers into the hall. 'OK, quick.' She motions us in front, but we don't move.

'We don't have all day,' she says firmly.

'Can you teach me, *everything*?' Marissa asks as she slips out the door with Ben at her heels.

Ma ignores her and waves me to follow.

I take one last look at Ammon, watching quietly as we break out of his jail, before turning and following them down the corridor.

Nine

We come upon the exit controlled by an officer behind a glass window. It's a different officer to the one that winked at me on our way in. Ma calls for us to stop and goes ahead. My heart races – we're so close to getting caught I feel sick.

She pushes the intercom button. 'Open the door.'

The officer frowns, stands slowly, hand sliding to the holster on his hip. 'I wasn't notified—'

'No, you weren't. Call Officer Ammon in the holding room, he's released these three into my custody.'

I bite the inside of my cheek, shifting in place as we wait for him to page Ammon. Ma, on the other hand, is the picture of calm and that makes me even more uneasy.

The officer smiles as he lowers the receiver. 'Go on.' He buzzes us through.

We rush out the precinct doors into the glorious sunshine, taking refuge between buildings – three fugitives and a kidnapped boy.

'The taxi I ordered is over there.' Ma leans around a dumpster and points across the street to the black station wagon waiting by the pole. 'By ordered, I mean the driver's on an extended lunch break.'

Marissa elbows me. 'Your mom knows how it's done.'

I roll my eyes and dart from behind the green bin, running for the car. I glance back to see Ma and Marissa right behind me and Ben following them like a happy puppy. When I make it to the car I swing open the back door, waving Marissa in.

'Sit by me, Ben.' Marissa motions him after her as she takes her purse from my arm and slides in.

'He can't, he's driving.' Ma steps between him and the door. 'Hurry up and get in, Rach.'

'Why don't *you* drive?' Marissa snaps at me.

'You know I only have a learner permit.'

'So? We don't know that Ben has a licence.'

Ma clears her throat. 'We need to go. Now.'

Marissa registers Ma's annoyance and huffs out, 'Fine, he drives.' Which Ben takes as his cue, and he makes his way to the driver's side of the taxi. I slide over when Ma crams in, locking me in the small seat between the two of them.

Marissa wedges her gold purse next to the door and crosses her arms. 'Can't one of you sit up front?'

Ma smacks the Plexiglas. 'Go!'

Ben doesn't seem to get that we're in a hurry and takes his time adjusting the seat, the steering wheel, then the mirrors, both passenger and side view.

'Now,' Ma says, her eyes scanning the road to make sure we aren't being followed. My stomach's in my throat. I'm eager to put as much distance between us and the police as we can. But Ben keeps with his routine, putting on his seatbelt and adjusting it around his shoulders.

Ma leans over me and glares at Marissa. 'Speed this up?'

Before she can command him to do anything, he shifts the car into drive, and everyone lets out a breath. He sits stiffly in his seat, waiting for instructions.

My ma raps the divider again. 'What's your hesitation, son?'

He turns and looks at her, then looks to Marissa.

'I told him not to talk,' she says.

'Well, tell him to take us to 56th, and hurry.' Ma adjusts the saree's pallu over her shoulder, leaving her hand to rest on her gold and black beaded necklace, then sits back in her seat like what she just said is perfectly fine.

She can't seriously be suggesting what I think she is. 'You want to go to our house?' I lean forward and place my hand on the cool glass divider.

'Yes.'

'But we . . .'

'Oh please,' Ma says. 'It's the safest place, we're listed as a P.O. box upstate. The school doesn't even know where we live.' She cocks her head at Marissa. 'I don't need to remind you we're trying to evade arrest.'

Marissa purses her lips.

76

Ma taps over her glove, where most people wear watches, and glares at Marissa.

'You heard the lady,' Marissa says to Ben, 'head to 56th.'

Ma and I watch out the back window. There's police everywhere in the city, but none of them seem concerned with us. Still, every time I spot a patrol car my heart races into a panic. And the closer we get to my house, the clammier my hands become. I wrap my fingers in my skirt to keep them from trembling. I don't invite people to my house. Not even Marissa. It's embarrassing, with my dad and all. Marissa's lucky enough not to know who her father is. Now, a whole carload is going to meet mine. I can't think of a worse punishment. This is all Marissa's fault and she's too busy pouting to realize it.

Soon we're pulling up to the kerb in front of our brownstone. Dad comes running out before the doors are even open. He's wearing a red floral apron over his blue Chelsea Football Club tracksuit and a big smile of relief.

I slink lower in the seat. 'Oh great.'

He rushes to Ma's window, passing Ben, who's en route to Marissa's door.

'My dear, you've been gone so long. I was worried.' Dad flings open the door and helps, or rather pulls, Ma out.

'We're fine.' I force a smile, trying to lessen the awkwardness of the exchange. Ben puts his arm around Marissa, and she leans into his body with the casualness of long-time lovers. It would be a catalogue picture if it weren't for the glazed happiness in his otherwise sharp eyes. I miss the watchfulness that I saw briefly in the cell, the depth that hinted that Benjamin Blake is somehow more. Definitely more than this love-sick puppy. He doesn't notice anything but Marissa now.

It's Marissa's fixed curiosity on Dad that cracks through my fake composure. My cheeks burn.

'Yes, we're fine, dear,' Ma says, with a smile I know is forced, but it's pretty darn convincing. 'Why don't you go make our guests some tea and get started on dinner?'

'Yes, of course, anything you wish.' He kisses her and turns, rushing back inside. He doesn't even notice me.

'Is that your dad?' Marissa cringes. 'I didn't expect a—'

'Shut up, Rissa.'

'What? What did I say?' She holds up her hands, looking to Ben for support. Of course he'll agree with her.

My whole body tenses and I storm into the house, dumping my books and whipping off my blazer, skirt and blouse in our narrow front entrance. I head for the couch in the comfort of my under-tank and jean shorts, and collapse into the corner, running my hands over the familiar red suede. *Breathe, just breathe. Don't let her see you cry.*

The door opens and Marissa enters. She kicks my skirt out of the way and sets her gold purse on the mantle, Ben following after her. Awkward glances fling around the room and my heart pounds, wondering what they're all thinking. This is why I never invite her over.

'There are a lot of red things,' Marissa mumbles, picking up Ma's table centrepiece tapestry with a picture of the Vijaya Vilas Palace on it. 'You're, like, *really* Indian.'

Correction, *this* is why I never do.

'You know what, I don't make fun of your all-white house, don't make fun of mine.'

Ma enters the room and forces a smile. I hope she didn't overhear Marissa's words. She tries her best to preserve and share our culture. After almost thirty years in America she still dresses like she did in Gujarat. As much as she respects St Valentine's, I often wonder if she wishes she had never had to leave her country and her family for it. While my nani went to one of the Hedoness schools in India, disguised as a Hindu convent, she wanted Ma to experience other extensions of the global infrastructure and chose St Valentine's because many well-known Hedonesses come from there. She dropped Ma off and stayed only two weeks before rushing home, leaving Ma to board at school. Nani doesn't like America much. She says the women are too dreamy-eyed and the men act like boys.

I glare at Marissa using Ma's tapestry as a hand fan while ogling Ben. *Maybe Nani has a point.*

I stand. 'I need some air. I'm going to the garden—'

'You will stay here.' Ma flashes a weary look and I hesitantly reclaim my seat. 'I don't want anyone outside, even in the garden. I'm sure we weren't followed, but we can never be too safe. Now excuse me, I'll check on the tea.' She peels off her gloves and heads to the kitchen.

Marissa and Ben flop on to the couch beside me. 'My neck is stiff,' she says, batting her eyes at him.

'Let me massage you, my love.'

She flips around, grinning at me before removing her blazer, twisting up her hair and sliding her shoulders out of her button-up top. 'This is how it's done,' she says, leaning back into Ben's strong hands.

I search through the pile of magazines on the coffee table, picking *Runner Life* and a copy of *Femina*. I take turns flipping through for something, anything, to distract me from them. It doesn't work. All I can think about is Ben in a floral apron, rushing to attend to Marissa's every need. I can't picture him like my dad – I won't.

'You know what?' I slap the magazines on the table. 'I think we should release Ben. Tell him to forget you, us, all of this. Tell him to return to Central Park.'

'I will never forget, my love.'

I roll my eyes.

'Please,' Marissa says, leaning into his massage. 'Does it look like I'm ready to let him go?'

'He stays,' Ma says, re-entering with a tray of mismatched mugs and teacups and a pot of sweet masala tea in one hand and her gloves in the other. She takes in my glare and adds, 'For now. I'll just ask a few questions then we can send him on his way.'

'Fine,' I sigh.

'Fine,' Marissa says, crossing her arms.

The tea fragrance wafts across the room, and everyone retakes their seats as Ma busies herself filling the cups. When finished, she relaxes into her armchair, a teacup and saucer resting next to the gloves on her lap. 'Now tell me, Benjamin, what did this officer want from you?'

Ben glances at Marissa, who nods for him to answer. 'Ammon?'

'Yes, the man with the red glasses,' Ma says.

'I want to be a police officer.' Ben sits forward, cupping the steaming mug. 'He agreed to meet with me and answer questions about the job, maybe even give a referral to the academy. We were going to go over a missing person's case he's been working on. I was waiting for him at Central Park . . .' Ben blinks a few times and rubs his head, like he's trying to figure out how his words and memories don't match.

I try to imagine Ben as an officer and I can't picture him becoming like the men who handled us so roughly in the cells.

Ma lowers her cup. 'Who does he think is responsible for these abductions?'

'On the phone he mentioned something about aliens,' Ben says, as if it's something normal to say.

I practically drop my teacup. 'Aliens?' This confirms it, when Ammon said, *'I'm going to make sure you never*

81

reach the mother ship,' what he really meant was, 'you're one of *them.'*

Marissa giggles, leaning further into Ben, who wraps an arm around her and whispers something in her ear. All I make out is the word *love.*

'Of all the things I've been called,' Ma snorts from her perch on the side chair. 'This is a first.'

'Told you.' Marissa elbows me. 'There's nothing to worry about.'

I glance to Ma to find her fighting back a cheeky look, and it makes me smile. All the worry of them knowing our secret seems so silly now. Aliens are understandable. Offspring of Eros? That's just laughable. 'No, aliens is good.' I nod to Marissa. 'We're aliens, all right – some of us more than others.'

'Oh, please.' Marissa huffs. 'Do we look like aliens to you?' She flicks her long blonde hair over her shoulder and bats her eyes at Ben. 'We're so much more than extra-terrestrial beings – more like all-powerful ones.'

'Marissa . . .' Ma warns.

'What? It's not like he'll remember.' She turns to Ben and pinches his cheek. 'Besides, I'm thinking of keeping this one.'

Then the boy who looks and is just like Benjamin Blake in every way, except for his mind, says, 'Oh yes, my love, you should keep me.'

Ten

'What are we going to *do*?' I ask, leaning around Ben and Marissa's snugglefest to try and talk to Ma.

'I've put a call in to the school—'

'Ooh, that reminds me,' Marissa says, rubbing Ben's chest and interrupting Ma, 'get my purse for me, I need my phone.'

Ben jumps up and crosses the room, grabs her golden bag off the mantle and is bringing it back when his glazed eyes flick to the bag in his hands. He frowns, staring, blinking, trying to focus in a way someone does when they've forgotten a common word.

'Have a seat,' Marissa says, patting the couch beside her. Ben hesitates to listen; instead he releases the bag and squeezes his head.

Marissa's mouth drops. 'It's wearing off. How can that be? My last turning lasted two days.'

'Well,' Ma brings the teacup to saucer and sits forward, 'did you make good contact?'

Marissa crosses her arms. 'I did the best I could, considering the steel bars.'

Ben, still squeezing his head, lowers himself to the empty seat beside Marissa, and stares down at his socks, puzzling over a dirty spot he picked up from the fall at the park. Ma eyes me warily over him.

'Should I turn him again?' Marissa asks.

'What? No,' I say.

'Let's see how this plays out,' Ma says, louder.

He wobbles back, like he's being jolted into his body, blinking as he takes us in. I can only imagine what it's like being under Hedoness control and then suddenly released. Yo-yoing back and forth between sanity and delirium. He looks lost, confused, and I feel awful for him.

'What's going on?' he asks, glancing around the room, his eyes never settling in one place. He stands quickly. 'Who are you? Where am I?'

Marissa tugs on his sleeve, ushering him back to the couch. He sits, keeping his weight suspended by his legs, like at any moment he might bolt for the door. 'You're fine, we're here to help,' she says.

'You.' He looks at her, really looks, then his blue eyes shift to mine and I'm relieved to see that curiosity in them again. 'And you,' he says, 'I recognize you, at least I think I do. My head's kinda foggy.'

Ma takes a sip of her tea. 'Marissa, why don't you tell him why he's here,' she says, less in a *tell him the facts* and more in a *you made this mess, you clean it up* kind of way.

Marissa forces a smile and looks about, not focusing on any one thing. I've seen this shiftiness many times. Part of me wants to say something, but the other, larger part can't wait to hear what wild story she comes up with. When her eyes trail past the pile of books strewn by the door, they spark with an idea. She sits up straight.

'We found you passed out in Central Park on our way to school this morning. We didn't know if you had health insurance so we called Rachel's mom and she brought you here.'

He looks at me, then at Ma in a way that hints he's trying to gather his own evidence.

'Passed out?' he repeats, as if he doesn't believe it's true.

When no one answers, he stands and tugs on his coat. 'Well, thank you for your help but I should get going, I was supposed to meet someone and he's probably wondering where I am.'

Ma sits forward, shifting her teacup and saucer to the table and gripping her gloves in her other hand.

'No,' Marissa says, tugging him back. 'I mean, you hit your head pretty hard when you fainted. We called the precinct and they said Ammon's coming to get you.' She glances at Ma as if to ask if she did OK. Ma responds by refilling her teacup and sitting back in the chair. Marissa smiles.

'Oh yeah, Ammon, eh?' He frowns. 'How did you know to call Ammon?'

Ma's back stiffens.

Marissa crosses her legs. 'Well, we, uh—'

'We called the police to report finding you,' Ma says. I choke on my mouthful of tea. 'We gave your description and they connected us through to Ammon.'

He relaxes at this, in a way that a person relaxes in a room full of strangers, uncomfortable and forced, and he rakes a hand through his dark hair. 'I never thought of myself as the fainting type.' He grins at Marissa, a real grin, one he wants to give her, not the dull forced grin of a turned man. He just got jolted back into his body and doesn't really remember anything, and yet he's poised and confident in the midst of all this confusion. I can't remember a single time my dad looked that self-assured.

Marissa's ears flush. I've never seen that happen before either. She likes it, him. I don't blame her; there's something about him, something disarming.

'Thank you for helping me,' he says again, making intentional eye contact with each of us. 'I should probably call Ammon and find out when he'll be here.'

Both Marissa and I look to my ma. If we don't let him make a call, he'll know something's wrong. If he calls, he'll definitely know something's wrong and, worse, the police will know where we are.

'Let me go get the phone,' Ma says, setting down her cup and standing.

Marissa and I share a look.

'I could just . . . you know,' Marissa offers.

'There's no need for that,' Ma says, firm, a warning as she leaves the room.

Ben fills an empty mug with chai and shifts further into the side of the couch, away from Marissa. She flops back and crosses her arms, leans to me and whispers, 'I liked my plan better.'

'Be serious for once,' I whisper back, shifting to face her. 'It's your fault this is happening.'

'My fault?' Marissa whips around, bumping Ben, who almost spills his tea. She points over her shoulder at him, her whispers getting louder. 'If he wasn't hot, I wouldn't have stopped to turn him. So blame him. You know what? Actually, you're the one who pissed me off. If you hadn't been late, none of this would've happened.'

'You're not seriously trying to put this on me?'

'Then blame Ben's hot face if it makes you feel better.'

I slap the magazine on the table and sit hard into the couch. 'Don't you mean his *nice shoes*?'

The sound of Ben clearing his throat causes us to stop. We slowly turn. 'So, what are we talking about?' he asks, a large grin spreading across his face. 'Whose fault? What plan?'

He's newly returned to his mind, but it's probably still broken because the amount of flirt he's offering Marissa is disgusting. I hide my groan.

'It's nothing,' Marissa says, narrowing her eyes and cocking her head like she's accepting some unspoken challenge. 'We missed a big test at school today and Rach is a bit upset about that. Or maybe she's jealous I met you first. I dunno.'

Another quick lie.

He consents to that with a smile, before leaning back. The last thing I want is to see Ben's mischievous grin directed at her. I push myself off the couch and head to the kitchen.

From behind me I hear, 'So. You like my shoes, huh?'

When I reach the kitchen, I plop down on to a stool.

'Has your ma sent you? Does she need more tea?' Dad trips over his feet running to the stove to grab the kettle.

'No, she's fine.' I use my arm for a pillow.

'A snack then?'

'I said she's fine.' I whack the table with my knee.

'Don't talk to me like that, young lady!'

'Wha— ?' I'm pretty sure I just got in trouble, which means – Dad actually paid attention to something I did. My heart quickens, and I sit up straight.

'Your mother doesn't like it when people raise their voices,' he continues.

And just like that my heart sinks. Every time I fall for it. You'd think I'd learn by now that he doesn't care about me, not even enough to get mad. But once, just once, I let myself hope he'd be different. This is why I want to be a social worker. No one should have to feel this way.

I have nowhere to go so I just stay there, resting my chin in my hands, and staring out into the garden.

That's when I see Ma out there, on the cordless phone. I glance at Dad, head over a steaming pot, so focused on cooking dinner for Ma he's already forgotten I'm here. I slip over to the door, and crack it open enough to listen.

'Ammon, it's me . . . yes . . . listen, I need you to tell Benjamin Blake that he was injured and that he is to stay with us until you come to get him. Is that clear? . . . No, you don't need to come, just tell him . . . Good. Now that that's done, tell me what the police know about the escaped prisoners . . . OK . . . You freed them, yes? . . . Hmmm . . . OK . . . if anything changes, tell them you received an anonymous tip-off that they've gone to Canada . . . Good. When you're finished with Ben you will forget me and this conversation. Am I clear?' Ma straightens out her saree, whips her pallu over her shoulder and presses the receiver to it, then spins on her heel and heads for the door. I rush back to the kitchen, leaning awkwardly on the counter, hoping she won't notice me. But of course she does, so I smile, trying to look natural as I follow behind her into the living room. She marches up to Ben and holds out the phone in her gloved hands. 'Here. It's Ammon.'

Eleven

Ben hands the phone back to Ma when he's done and smiles anxiously. 'I hope it's not an inconvenience if I stay a little longer. Until Ammon picks me up?'

'Of course not,' Ma says, taking the phone from him and resting her free hand over her black and gold beaded necklace. 'Now, how about I grab us all a little something to eat? Rachel, will you help me?'

Ma's tone is enough to silence any potential argument from Marissa, who shrugs and slides closer to Ben on the sofa. He smiles at her and I quicken my pace out of the room.

Dad looks up from the stove as we enter the kitchen.

'My love, what can I do for you?'

'You are doing more than enough,' Ma says as she takes a seat, smoothing the dyed tablecloth out of habit. I tap my foot as I wait for her to explain – the whole table shakes from it.

Despite what Ma said, Dad brings her a mug of masala chai. She thanks him with a smile before turning to me.

'What's going on, Ma?'

Ma sighs, takes a sip of her tea and sets the mug down

hard. 'As I'm sure you're aware, after graduation every Hedoness is encouraged to sign on to a seven-year commitment.'

'Yeah, but I'm not planning on it. Why are you bringing this up now?'

She glances at me. 'You are told the work years are voluntary, but they are mandatory.'

'Mandatory? But . . . university?' I say, feeling the loss pour out of me with the word. No wonder Ma tried to encourage me away from it.

'Yes,' she says, not making eye contact. 'It was a difficult revelation for me too. But my hope is that they'll find you a job similar to being a social worker.'

I want to tell her that any job involving working as a Hedoness would crush my soul, but now hardly seems the time.

'As St Valentine's is now closed—'

'What? Wait? Closed? When did that happ—'

'I spoke with Mother Superior before I spoke with Ammon. The police were poking around, they've taken some of the Sisters in for questioning, so the Committee intervened, as they often do,' she says, so offhandedly that it makes me think there's a story there. 'Anyway, students are being transferred immediately.'

I sit forward. 'Transferred? To where?'

'They've arranged for them to go to Committee head-quarters in Athens. You're to continue your education there.'

'What's with this Committee?!' I explode. 'Why do they think they can dictate my whole life?'

'Rachel . . .' She cocks her head.

'I'm serious, Ma. What's their deal?'

Ma slides her cup away and leans in. 'There was a time when gods and man lived and interacted together,' Ma starts, sounding a little too like one of the Sisters reading from a textbook. 'Things went awry, as they normally do, and the pact was made ensuring the gods would never again leave Olympus and interfere in the ways of man.'

'I learned all this in school.'

Ma ignores me and continues. 'That pact established the Committee – a group of mortals tasked with the responsibility to govern and oversee the demigod offspring, where the gods couldn't. The Committee soon learned of the difficulties of rearing young Hedonesses, and established the interfaith programme, mimicking various religious establishments to guard us as they assist in training.'

I let out an exaggerated sigh. 'I know all that. But what I don't know is if I'm going.'

'Of course you're going,' she says, in a manner that makes me realize she has no clue her words just shattered my heart. 'Like it or not, you need to complete your training. And if they want you at headquarters for that, then we're all going to Athens. No way I'm letting the Committee take my only daughter to the opposite side of the world without me.' She chuckles, but it isn't her usual warm laugh – there's hesitation in it. After a moment of silence, Ma clears her throat and takes in the room with a long sigh. 'I guess we'll need to sell the house.'

'Ma, please. I don't want this.'

'I'm sorry, Rachel. This is our way.'

'Why? Why does it have to be?'

'Rachel—'

Suddenly this hand-dyed tablecloth I helped Ma pick out on our trip to India, this small kitchen where I've eaten every meal, these brick walls chipped by my chair from years of being whacked with my book bag – it all means so much to me. This is my home. It's all I have. I'm tired of losing everything because I'm a Hedoness. 'I won't go,' I say, a whisper.

'Excuse me?' Ma crosses her arms.

'Ma, the last thing I want is to fight with you. But the Hedoness way isn't my dream.'

'Dreams are a luxury,' she says, her eyes distant.

I reach across the table and grab her arm; she tenses beneath my touch. 'Please, this is important to me. Is there any other way?'

'What would people say if we go about disobeying the Committee?'

'I don't care what people say – this isn't their life!'

Ma lets out a long breath and leans back. I can see the thoughts swirling in her eyes. But I have no clue what they are.

'You said you want me to be happy, Ma. New York makes me happy.'

She pulls her arm free and spins her cup, but doesn't take a sip.

'Ma? Please, talk to me.'

She looks up. 'This isn't my first choice, either.'

My heart speeds. 'We can just wait a little while. Until this mess all gets sorted and St Valentine's reopens.'

She quirks her brow. 'You begged me yesterday to leave the school.'

'That was before it meant leaving our home.'

She's quiet again and I know I have to say something to make her see things my way. 'I don't have much, Ma. I don't get to have friends I choose, I don't get to pick my school, or my clothes. My future is outlined for me like some bad screenplay. But this home, this city, it's all I've ever known. Please don't make me lose it too.'

She takes a long swig of tea, sets her cup down perfectly in the centre of a large dyed flower, and looks back up. 'I suppose it doesn't hurt to gather more information before uprooting the house.' She frowns into her cup. 'We'll need to find someplace else to stay for the time being.'

It takes everything in me not to squeal *thank you, thank you, thank you.*

'Don't get excited just yet. This is temporary, Rachel. I don't doubt we will be heading to Athens soon.' She stops, her expression shifting to a more serious one. 'That said, I don't trust what's happening here. It seems strange to uproot a whole school.' She takes another sip. 'It feels too similar to an incident I had with them before you were born. Getting all the facts will help ease my mind.'

'Incident?'

She pauses for a long beat before answering. 'Incident may be the wrong word. I'm not sure if it was a coincidence or not, but they once approached me and offered a position at headquarters. At the time, I was assigned to the consulate for my work years. I loved it there so I turned the Committee down.' Her eyes fill with something softer, colder. Sadness? Anger, maybe. 'Anyway, two weeks after I turned them down, a mysterious budget cut cost me my job placement.'

'Seriously?'

'It wasn't for nothing,' she continues. 'The consulate is where I met your father and instead of continuing my work there, I continued with the greater calling we Hedonesses have. I had you.' She says it almost as though she were a normal ma telling a normal kid how their parents met. Almost.

I lean against the table and puzzle over her words. 'So what now?'

'Now I make some phone calls and—'

She's cut off by a high-pitched giggle from down the hall. Ma sets her cup on the table, tugging on her gloves out of habit. 'You shouldn't leave those two alone together too long. I don't trust that friend of yours.'

Twelve

I enter the room and flop down on the couch next to Ben. I'm not sure if I'm the third wheel, or if he is.

'I can't believe I'm still wearing this filthy uniform,' Marissa complains, scratching the spot on her skirt that got dirty at the precinct. It looks clean to me, but she sees some phantom stain. 'Can I go home and get a change of clothes?'

By the smile on his face, Ben's enjoying her whiny meltdown. 'I'm stuck here until Ammon comes – it's only fair you are too.' He leans back on the couch, stretching his hands behind his head.

Marissa huffs, crossing her arms and pouting. 'This isn't funny.'

He tosses one of Ma's throw cushions at her. 'It's pretty funny.' Ben runs his hands through his hair, taking extra care to make sure it all flows the same way. Marissa steals the moment to smooth down her previously perfect eyebrows after the pillow assault.

Ben notices me watching and cocks his head.

'You two have a lot in common,' I say, earning a glare

from Marissa. I return it with a smile. 'Borrow something from me.'

'Great.' She doesn't even attempt to hide her sarcasm. 'I prefer my dirty clothes to your clean ones.' Marissa curls her nose and stomps down the hall in search of my room.

'Second door on the right,' I call after her. A part of me feels guilty she doesn't know where my room is, that I've kept her from coming here all these years.

'Is she always like that?' Ben asks.

'Worse.'

His smile is contagious, and I can't help returning it. He picks up a magazine and flips through it. 'So you're a runner?'

It catches me by surprise – I'm not used to people noticing things about me. 'Yeah,' I squeak out. 'Well, I was.'

'I did track in school,' he says. 'Long jump.'

I would, if St Valentine's offered it. 'Elementary was my last team, and really we just ran after each other and everyone got participation ribbons, so I don't think it counts.'

'Sounds too communist for me.' He shows a cheeky grin, a different version from the one he gives Marissa – it's more transparent, real, and it's the first time a guy's ever looked at me like that.

A slamming door causes us to jerk towards the hall. Marissa, with an armful of clothes, comes storming into the room. She dumps the clothes on the coffee table and starts sorting through them. Pinching each item in her fingertips like it's infected. 'On second thought, do you have any of those fancy dresses your mom wears?'

'A saree?'

'Yeah, I want one that shows off my flat stomach.'

Ben flashes me a sympathetic look and mouths, '*Wow.*' 'I think I'll check in on the bathroom. You two play nice.' He stands and excuses himself.

He's not even in the hall before Marissa starts on me. 'Seriously, Rach, no wonder you don't have a boyfriend. Look at these clothes.'

'How can I even have a boyfriend?' I mutter, glancing down the empty hall after Ben.

'It's the principle.' She flings my Wonder Woman T-shirt at me.

'Last I checked, you don't have a boyfriend either.'

'Yeah, but it's not because I can't – it's because I don't want to be tied down.'

My anger rises, so I close my eyes and imagine Joan of Arc, with her sword and her horse, riding into the room and kidnapping Marissa. Even that's not enough to calm me.

Marissa holds up a white tank top. 'Guess I'll try this,' she sighs.

'Do you hear yourself? All you care about is what you're going to wear. Take some responsibility for once.'

'Responsibility? You don't know anything about responsibility.' Marissa cocks her head and drops the tank, placing her hands on her hips.

'Excuse me? I'm not the one who got us in this mess.'

Marissa laughs. 'Haven't you figured it out yet? I seriously thought you were smarter than that.'

My expression must give away that I have no clue what she's talking about because she rolls her eyes.

'Back in first year when we were told to pick accountability partners, I picked you because the Sisters asked me to. They noticed your resistance and wanted me to show you how a real Hedoness acts in the hope that you could live up to your mom's potential. But even I couldn't help with that.'

I stare back, not sure what to say. I always knew we were required to be each other's friends at the pair-up, but I thought it was a mutual thing. It turns out she was actually forced. Somehow that hurts more.

'It's why I tried to get you to turn Ben. Mother Superior told me to. But you failed and I had to deal with it, like always. We don't have long until graduation and the Sisters were getting worried about your lack of ability. If you would've just attempted it, once, this wouldn't be a problem. But for some reason you refuse to accept your truth.' Her head bobs as she animates her words.

The self-righteousness is too much and I snap. I jump off the sofa and shove Marissa back.

She stumbles, catching her foot on the table, and falling into the pile of clothes.

'You did not just—' Marissa dives for my legs, knocking me to the floor. We wrestle on the pile, pulling hair and pushing each other's faces. All the years of pent-up frustration come rushing out and I don't hold back.

The commotion brings Ben running from the hall. He slides to a stop. 'What the . . .?' He runs his hands through his hair and watches the fight. Finally, he tries to pull us apart. It takes a few tries to grab one of us, but he lands a good grip on Marissa's arm.

'Stay out of this, Ben. This is because of you.' Marissa clings to a handful of my hair as Ben lifts her.

'Me?' He drops her arm and stumbles back, a smile spreading over his face. 'You're fighting over me?'

'It's not what you think,' I manage, between laboured breaths.

'It looks like what I think.'

I pull Marissa's fingers, trying to loosen them from my ponytail. 'It's not over you . . . she can . . . just have you.'

'What's going on in here?' says Ma, bursting into the room, her going-out gloves gripped in one hand. From the tone of her voice she doesn't sound impressed.

Marissa drops my hair and scrambles to her feet. I spring up beside her, taking in the room, which looks like a laundry war-zone.

Marissa scowls. 'I'm leaving.'

'Maybe I should call and check in with Ammon,' Ben says, looking awkward.

'No one's going anywhere.'

'What?' Marissa's hands rest on her hips and her eyes widen. 'Why? This is so unfair.'

'I don't care if it's unfair. I'm the adult and you're all under my roof. Until I know more, you're staying with me. We already have enough to worry about. I just got off the phone with Cassandra Turner, Paisley's mother. The mothers are gathering to try to fix the mess you girls made.'

'Ma!' I motion to Ben. She shouldn't be talking like this in front of him.

'It's fine, I'll deal with him if I have to. This *thing* is bigger than him,' she says.

Ben takes a step back. He's starting to look really worried now.

'*All* the mothers?' Marissa asks, shifting her stance and glancing at me.

Ma's face softens. 'I'm sorry, Marissa, they couldn't get in contact with your mother. I'm sure she would come if she knew.'

Marissa slumps into the couch.

'We don't have time to sulk. We need to get going. A plane with St Valentine's girls has already left.'

'Left for where?' asks Marissa.

'The school's closed. Your training is being transferred.'

'What?' Marissa says.

'But we're not going, right?' I say.

Ma puts a hand on my shoulder; there's something more, something scared in her eyes.

'What is it, Ma?'

'The Committee,' she says. 'They said they're coming back for you two.'

Thirteen

While Ma goes off to wipe down the taxi we stole and find another car for us to use, I pack myself a carry bag. Now we know the Committee is coming for us, we need to get going sooner – as in, as soon as Ma gets back – otherwise we won't have any chance at a normal life. I return to Ben and Marissa on the couch, my overstuffed bag resting beside me. Marissa scrolls through her phone, showing me every photo she finds of our classmates en route to Athens. Even though they're posted on our school's private platform, Quiver, and not something like Facebook, it still makes me nervous. We don't know who's watching us right now, and we can't be too careful.

Ben's next to her on the couch, flipping through my magazine – I know he's not reading it, because half the time it's upside down and his eyes are everywhere but the page.

'It's getting kinda late,' Ben says anxiously. 'Ammon must've forgotten about me.'

Ma comes in with an armload of bags in her gloved hands. 'Nonsense, he's probably just held up.'

'Maybe I should call.' Ben stands and tugs his jacket.

Marissa and I share a look as Ma glances over. 'Do you have somewhere to be? Family that will worry if you're late?'

'No,' he chokes. 'No one. I—'

Just then there's a knock at the door.

I look at Ma, who seems just as confused as me.

'Finally, Ammon.' Ben stands, kicking out his leg like it's fallen asleep.

'Actually, it's my pizza,' Marissa says, hopping up.

'What?' I practically shout.

'Are you dense?' says Ma.

She frowns. 'No one knows this address, right? The P.O. box upstate and all that. I didn't think it would be such a problem.'

'Exactly,' says Ma, whipping around in a wild fury. 'You didn't *think*.'

Marissa cuts in front of Ben and swings open the door. There's an elderly gentleman there, dressed in a red pizza vest and visor. He smiles and holds out the box. 'Pizza delivery?'

'Yes, come in,' she says, opening the door, and shoving Ben back as he stands on his toes and looks over her, still hoping to see Ammon. 'Let me get my credit card.'

Ma stiffens, tension pulling at the small lines of her face. She smooths out her saree, her eyes never leaving the delivery man.

I know that look, that's the *something bad is going to happen* look.

Before I can stop her, she walks past the driver, pulls off her glove and slides her hand across the bare flesh of his neck. His eyes roll back and he starts to convulse.

'What the . . .' says Ben. He jumps forward and catches the man, lowering his shaking body to the ground.

'Grab some pillows!' Ben shouts at us, clearing the area around the man. 'He's having a seizure!'

But Marissa and I don't move. We're frozen, shocked, staring – not at the driver, but at my ma.

'Pass me those cushions,' Ben repeats, with force. When we don't respond he rips off his jacket and places it under the man's head, then drags my pile of clothes over. 'At least call an ambulance.' This time when we don't move he follows our gaze to my mother, and a sweatshirt slips from his fingers to the floor. 'What did you do?'

She lifts her chin, staring him down. 'What was necessary.'

'Necessary?' He stands firm, his fists clenched at his side.

I can only imagine what he thinks after witnessing a Hedoness turning. It worries me that he looks ready to fight. I like this Ben, the stubborn, challenging Ben. I'm not ready to see him return to the snivelling shell of a man he was under Marissa's control.

'Ma, please can we—'

She holds up her bare hand and jerks her hardened eyes to me. 'Marissa needed a reminder of who's in charge, and we needed a car. I did what was necessary.' She attempts to step around Ben, but he holds his ground, blocking her from the man. 'Stop acting like a child and watch what it is we do.'

'Ma?' I reach for her but she pulls back. 'We aren't supposed to show anyone.'

'He's just a boy. If he acts up, I'll deal with him.'

Ben's face turns an ashen hue and he hesitates to step out of Ma's path.

'I don't need you to move,' she says, glaring past Ben to the man convulsing on our rug. 'Stop shaking and get up.'

'Ma!' I gasp. 'You're crossing so many lines.'

Instantly he stops and rises to his feet. 'My love, what is it you want of me?'

'First off, I want you to have a seat on that box over there.' She points to her antique dowry chest.

'Yes, my love.' The man hobbles over and sits. It's apparent by his limp that he was injured in the fall, the bent pizza box still in his grasp.

Ben's jaw drops, and his eyes turn a frosty blue as memories flicker and spark behind them. Finally, he looks at me and says, 'Ammon isn't coming, is he?'

Fourteen

Ma steps between Ben and the door. 'We don't mean you any harm but you got caught up in this and you're here now. We can't let you go.'

'I won't become . . . whatever you did to that man,' Ben says, nodding to the delivery driver, reseated on the trunk, waving at Ma.

Ma pats down her saree and steps closer, bare hand raised.

'Stop.' I step between them. 'You're not doing this. It isn't right.'

'Either he stays on his own, or I have to force him. I'm sorry, there is no other way. I must keep you safe.'

'I'll keep you safe, my love,' the driver says.

'If anyone is turning him it should be me,' says Marissa.

'No one is turning him,' I say.

Ben glances around the room, his eyes alight with whatever he's processing. By the way his legs lock, ready to run, and his hands clench, I know he isn't about to go down without a fight.

'Please,' I say, gently touching his sleeve. He tenses beneath my hand. I don't blame him so I pull away. 'I'm so sorry you're wrapped up in this. But my ma's right. We don't want to hurt you, we never did. Right now, we're just trying to get someplace safe, then we'll let you go. I promise. My family, we're different; we can do things other people can't. But we're not bad people. Please, work with us here and I promise neither of them will do to you what they did to that man.'

His eyes wander to the driver and something in him shifts. 'What she did to him . . . that was done to me, right?'

'Yes,' I say, ignoring the sharp inhale from my mother. 'He isn't permanently hurt, just confused. It won't last long.' I don't go into more detail and I can tell this bothers Ben. He wants to know. *Needs to know*. His shoulders stay tense but his fists uncurl and something shifts in his eyes. He nods once and steps back from the door, picks up my magazine and sits rigidly on his claimed corner of the couch.

I breathe a sigh of relief.

'What now?' Marissa asks, picking her nails and kicking her leg at the air.

Ma adjusts her pallu and slips her glove back on. 'Now we pack the car, and then we go.'

The driver stands and salutes Ma. 'I can pack for you, my love.'

'Why is he calling you "my love"?'

Ma whips around, her hand fluttering to her chest. We were so focused on Ben we didn't hear Dad enter.

'It's nothing, dear, go back into the kitchen.'

'It's not nothing. I love you,' the pizza delivery man says.

'No, I love her.' Dad takes a slow step back.

The driver puffs his chest and steps in front of Ma.

My father takes another step back, tears forming in his eyes as he looks around the room before coming to rest on Ma. Always Ma. 'I'm going to the kitchen as you ask.' His bottom lip quivers. 'Please don't replace me. I'll try harder to make you happy.'

Despite the bitterness I feel towards my dad, even I can't stand to see him like this. And after everything with Ben, I snap. 'Enough of this, Ma, let one of them go.'

Ben's eyes shoot to mine, so full of curiosity, worry and something I don't recognize. It only makes this worse.

'It's not so simple.' Ma keeps her eyes on Dad, who as slowly as possible slinks away. 'Not for your father, anyway.'

I don't like this new version of Ma. Especially since I know it isn't new – it's just new to me. I cross my arms. 'Can't you just tell him to—'

'Rachel!' Ma warns. 'One day you'll understand.' Her voice drops and for a brief moment a deep sadness fills her eyes. Then she squares her shoulders and says, 'Now is not the time to explain.' She marches over to the pizza man and holds out her hand. 'I need your keys.' The man stands immediately and sets to fishing them out of his pocket. Ma turns back to us. 'You girls have everything you need?'

I grit my teeth and nod, holding up my backpack. Marissa hugs her purse and mumbles, '*No*.'

Ben watches everything.

'All right, let's grab the last of the groceries and supplies, and load them into the car.'

We file into the kitchen, fill our arms, and file out to the dusk-lit street in front of the brownstone. Ma carries only one bag and wears only one glove. Her bare hand follows inches behind Ben at all times.

Fifteen

Dad leads us up the street a block to a vintage two-door Civic hatchback with a handicapped decal hanging off the rear-view mirror and a Tupperware box tied to the pizza light-mount on the roof. It's not *adorable* vintage, either; it's *amazing that it's still running* vintage. The entire trunk is stuffed full. Dad peels open the door, ignoring the scream of bending metal, and waves us in.

Marissa doesn't even try to hide her scowl. 'There's no way we're all fitting in *that*.'

'We don't have a choice,' Ma says.

Ben hands over his armful of packaged dinners and absent-mindedly rubs his arms.

'Cold?' I ask.

'I'll be all right.' He tucks his hands in his pockets, wary at the way we watch him. 'I must've forgotten my jacket.'

Ma reaches into the car and pulls out a blue sweatshirt with a picture of a smiling pizza. 'Here, wear this. We don't have time to go back for it.'

He slips it on without argument and slides in the back. Marissa turns up her nose at the shirt before

111

following him, and I shove in last. Ma struggles with the passenger seat, trying to get it to click into place so she can sit. Metal groans as it finally pops back. She stops, surveys the area, then steps away, closing the door and trapping the three of us in.

'Ma?' I say, panicked.

She doesn't answer; instead she circles the car to my dad. 'Take the kids and continue with the plan.' She puts the keys in his hand and shoves him towards the driver's door. 'I'll make sure they don't follow you.'

'I'm not leaving you, my love.'

'Show me you love me by protecting Rachel with your life. Follow the plan. Now go.'

'Ma, no!' I try desperately to find the chair lever so I can get out of the damn car.

'It's OK, Rachel. I'll catch up with you.' She puts her glove back on and starts down the street towards the house, turning back to add, 'I love you.'

My fingers wrap around something sharp at the base of the chair, and I pull. It pops forward. I stretch through the narrow gap, reaching for the door handle, but Marissa tugs me back. Dad's already in the driver's seat, the key in the ignition, engine running. He starts off down the street.

'We can't leave her!' I twist to watch out the window.

'If anyone can find us, it's your mom,' Marissa says.

And that's when we hear the sirens.

112

Three squad cars whip past us with lights flashing. Two others drive up the street from the opposite direction and come to a screeching stop before our house. Ma's trapped.

I try again for the door, managing to get a good grip of the handle, but it won't open.

'Are you kidding me right now?' Marissa grabs my shirt and yanks me back, the flimsy plastic handle breaking off. I toss it on the floor and spin around, watching between stacks of food and bags as the cops surround my mother, guns drawn. I hold my breath as she turns to face us. She puts her gloved hands up, drops to her knees, her saree billowing out. It seems like the whole world is shaking as the glass vibrates from the rattling engine. An officer pulls my mother with force, handcuffs her, drags her to her feet. Another group cautiously approaches our house, guns drawn and ready.

I glance at Ben, hands clenched – no doubt wanting to smack the window and scream for help but he doesn't. *Why isn't he?*

I'm not as strong.

My fists make first contact. 'Ma!' I yell, eyes pooling with tears as I pound the glass. 'I'll get you out of this.'

The rickety old car screams around the corner, my mother disappearing out of view.

Sixteen

Even though she's gone, I keep watch out the back, one hand pressed to the glass. I can't find the energy to turn away.

Hours pass like this, the car engine filling the silence and the world blurring by in tear-streaked colours. I don't know how far we've driven, but the sun's setting, and the wide-open spaces tell me we're no longer in New York. The shock of Ma's arrest still consumes me, and the back seat becomes more suffocating the further away from her we get.

When I can't take any more, I crawl over Marissa, ignoring her protests, and flop into the empty chair beside Dad. After a few calming breaths I turn to him. 'We have to go back.'

'We're sticking to the plan.' He doesn't take his eyes off the road.

'And what about Ma?' I choke out.

'Follow the plan, go to Nashville, keep Rachel safe. I'm doing what makes your ma happy,' he says.

'Nashville?' Marissa says, sitting forward. 'I want to go to Athens with the school.'

I don't want to argue with Dad, especially in front of Marissa. Besides he's right, we do need to get to a safe place. Then I can figure out a way to help Ma. So instead I ask, 'Why Nashville?'

'My sister-in-law's.'

'What?' Ma never mentioned other family. This is a sucky way to find out. 'I have an aunt?'

Dad nods. 'Joyce, she married my brother.'

'Your brother?'

Dad's eyes stay on the road, his grip rigid on the wheel. 'He died before you were born.'

There's a dozen new questions springing to mind, but one screams louder than the others. 'How will we save Ma from Nashville?'

He hesitates. 'We're sticking to the plan.'

I'm getting nowhere with him, so I turn to the back seat. 'Can you pass me up my bag? I want to call Paisley, see if her ma's heard anything that can help us.'

Marissa begrudgingly hands me my backpack. 'Use Quiver. We can't be too safe.'

'I was planning on it.'

This grabs Ben's attention enough for him to tear his eyes from the window he's been glowering out since we left my block.

I hold up my phone. 'We have a special site for communicating with others like us. An untraceable place online where we can talk freely.'

115

'It's supposed to be secret,' Marissa says.

'Yeah, well, Ben knows a lot of things that are supposed to be secret.'

He holds my gaze for a beat, those blue eyes trying to read my soul, then turns back to the window.

I log in to find Paisley's online, and call her immediately.

'Rachel? Oh my god, are you OK? Where are you?'

'Hey, yeah, we're OK—'

'Oh good. Listen, my mom's here and she wants to talk to you about her A.P.'

'I hoped she would.'

There's shuffling, then Mrs Turner comes on. 'Rachel?' Her voice is full of worry. 'I heard about your mother. Don't worry. I've made some calls, asked around. So far nothing, but I'll keep trying until we have something to report.'

'Thank you, Mrs Turner. Your help means so much.'

'Of course, it's what any A.P. would do. We stand up for our own. And listen, don't come near New York, don't go to any airports. Just get yourselves somewhere safe. We are on it. Once your mom is free, and your names are cleared, we will let you know. For now, just stay out of sight and out of trouble.'

I can't help glancing in the rear-view at Marissa, wondering if she'd do for me what Mrs Turner is doing for my ma.

When I don't reply, Mrs Turner clears her throat. 'Well, here's Paisley again, you two should probably keep this short. Even with everything going on, we want to prioritize the rules.'

I bite my lip to keep from saying something I'll regret and glance again at my A.P., who's digging through her gold bag for something.

There's another shuffling and Paisley takes back the phone. 'Did you hear they arrested some of the Sisters, and the Committee wants us to go to its headquarters?'

'I heard, yeah. Do you know what's going on?'

'Nope. Mom says I don't have to go to Athens. Not yet anyway. And there's a protest for the Sisters. Mom and a bunch of the other moms are helping. They're hoping to make a big enough scene that the police let the Sisters go. We went down earlier to join the picketing and reporters are lining the block filming everything. Thanks to Marissa, a group of enthusiasts are there, upset over the lack of police response to the alien vampires in New York. Everything is off the rails right now. Have you seen the news reports of your mom's arrest? It's running on almost every channel.'

'What? No! I'll call you back later.' I hang up, and search for the *City News* livestream. The video loads and I nearly drop my cell when I see a reporter standing on the street in front of our home.

'Oh my god, that's your house,' Marissa says, leaning forward.

I hold out the cell so we all can see; even Ben turns from looking out the window to watch.

'. . . police report states a traffic camera captured a group of women escorting a kidnapped boy into a taxi moments after a suspected jailbreak. The police managed to grab the plate number off the footage and track the vehicle to this house behind me. One of the officers recognized a suspect and an arrest was made. We have no further information on the arrest at this time. Our contact at the hospital came forward with information about the police admitting an elderly man who claims to have been squatting in this house. The background check reveals he is a food delivery driver. He was very disoriented and taken for psychiatric assessment. One can't help speculating that these women are responsible for the other disappearances. And if so, are the rumours true? Are they vamp—'

I shut it off before I have to watch any more and shove my cell into my pocket.

Marissa sits back hard in the seat and huffs. 'I play one little prank on a ginger kid and the whole world takes it seriously.'

'You did a little more than a prank,' I say.

'Whatever.'

'Not whatever.' I twist to face her. 'They know about the driver, which means they'll be looking for this car soon. If not already. We need to find another ride.'

'We stick to the plan,' Dad says. 'We're going to Nashville.'

I roll my eyes, and am about to argue him, when my phone dings. I smile when I see a message from Paisley.

PAISLEY: *Mom says they have your mother in custody as they investigate what happened to the evidence. There doesn't seem to be any leads on you three, other than Benjamin Blake's name and the officer's memories of a video. They don't even know what you look like. The arresting officer apparently buzzed you out when you escaped the precinct. But he suddenly can't remember anyone but your mother. So she's probably got her hand in that. You should be safe now. I'll let you know if anything changes. Don't worry, my mom's on it. She's determined to get your mom out. Oh, and tell Marissa I'm pissed at her. I can't turn on the TV without seeing something about the vampire aliens – she made my favourite show go viral! And took my necklace and all. Though the one good thing is, watching news with Mom isn't boring any more. Gotta go check my blood sugar levels. Talk soon.*

I read it out to the car.

'See, we're fine,' Marissa says. 'And Paisley can suck it.'

'My ma, not so much.'

'Rachel is safe,' Dad says.

Ben doesn't say anything.

I type a quick reply.

ME: *Thank you. Please let us know the second there's any updates.*

ME: *I owe you.*

119

Messaging with Paisley leaves me with some relief. We are safe, and hopefully Ma will be safe soon too.

Despite my protests to find a new ride, we drive through the night in the rusty old bucket stopping only for fuel and restroom breaks. I try to sleep, cricked over, using my arm on the window as a pillow. Even though I'm exhausted, sleep never comes. Instead I listen to the sounds that break the silence – a spring's squeak when someone shifts in their seat, the rattle of the engine, Ben's deep breaths, Marissa's quick shallow ones – it's deafening.

Halfway through the night Marissa stirs. Through the rear-view I watch her slide her head on to Ben's lap. He wakes, but doesn't move away like I expect.

It seems odd, considering his circumstances. Then I notice how uncomfortably he sits, stiff and angled away, and his breaths are no longer low and deep. He doesn't want her that close, but he's not stopping her either. I turn back to my window, and shut my eyes. It's the closest I'll come to rest.

A short way down the road, Dad pulls into a gas station and parks the car. 'Stay safe here,' he says, exiting. 'I'm getting us coffee.' He locks the car from the outside before heading into the store.

I twist in the chair, back pressed into the dash, about to say good morning when Marissa shoves the seat forward, trapping me between the glovebox and chair-back.

'Um?'

'I'm gonna freshen up. Keep an eye on Ben,' she says, bypassing the broken handle by unrolling then reaching out the window, and opening the door from the other side.

When she closes the door, Ben pulls the chair down for me.

'Thanks,' I say, unfolding my body.

'No prob.' He half smiles and rests his head on the driver seat's back, looking up at me through his choppy bangs. He studies my face, finding something there that makes his smile slip into a frown. An awkward silence passes between us. I think of a thousand things to say but none of them seem right.

Ben finds something. 'I'm sorry about your mom,' he says. He watches me with his whole body and the car is so stuffy I can't breathe. I lean to the open window for some air.

After everything we've put him through, he cares enough to acknowledge I'm hurting. It doesn't make sense. 'Why are you being nice?'

'Don't let it go to your head,' he says, with a halfhearted chuckle. He pauses, and by the way his breathing changes I can sense his walls coming down, and that stupid swishing feeling returns full force. When he next speaks, his voice is soft. 'I don't know. Maybe because I'm freaking out over Ammon's whole alien thing, and being

kidnapped, and what your mom did to that man, and . . .
I don't know what to believe any more. I thought the
aliens were a joke, but now . . .' He clears his throat.
'Anyway, you seem the most level-headed and I could use
someone to talk to and help me understand all this mess.'

'Oh.' *Oh? Can't you think of anything better to say?*

'So, like . . . what are you?' He asks it softly, a whisper,
but he might as well have screamed it.

A monster – I want to say, but how do you tell someone
you're an offspring of a god? How do you change their
world? 'Maybe we should start with another question.'

He takes a deep breath. 'Ammon's disappearances.
Were those you, too?'

A part of me feels like I'm back behind prison bars
under officer interrogation, the other part of me feels like
a broken and confused girl before an equally broken and
confused boy.

'Yes,' I say. 'But not us, others like us.'

'Are there many others?'

'Yes.'

He's silent for a long moment. I count his unsteady
breaths as he tries to put this strange puzzle together.
Finally, he clears his throat. 'Am I really going to be OK?'

'Yes.' I sit up. 'I promise you, I won't let anyone hurt
you.'

He lets out an airy laugh. 'Is it weird that I
believe you?'

122

'Probably,' I say with a smile. We're quiet for a moment, our eyes often meeting. I can't help feeling guilt for what we've done to him. 'And your family too,' I say. He sits back, confused. 'They're probably worried sick and missing you right now. I'm sorry you got dragged into this.'

He looks away, but the window's reflection shows me how sad his eyes are. 'They aren't,' he says, 'but I do miss them.' He clears his throat and runs his hands over his face before turning back. He's about to say something more, when his attention redirects and he nods to the windscreen. I glance over my shoulder to see Marissa and Dad – Dad carrying an uncomfortable number of bags and Marissa carrying none. I have so many questions for Ben, so many things I still want to say, but mostly, I want to see the sadness leave his eyes.

Marissa yanks open the door and I offer her the front seat. She chooses the back, with Ben. They pile in, stuffing Marissa's purchases into every last spare space. Ben's more engaged now, starting conversations, helping with directions. Though he never fully seems as relaxed as he did back at the house, before he knew what we're capable of.

We follow the big lit-up highway signs shaped like giant yellow arrows – I hate every one we pass – and fifteen hours after we left New York we're in Nashville, pulling up to a double-wide mobile, decorated with scrolling shutters and light yellow paint.

Being far away from the school, and the troubles with the police, almost gives me the breathing room to be excited about meeting my aunt. Almost. If Ma were here, I'd be ecstatic.

We grab our things, leaving most of the stuff in the car, and follow my dad to the front door. There's a note taped to the handle, with turquoise loopy writing that reads, *'Gone to the store, let yourself in. xo – Joyce.'*

The inside is decorated in a vintage style, with light blue appliances and black and white checkered floors. It's cluttered with pawnshop treasures, and smells of coffee and baked bread, not spices. I wonder if this is how most American homes smell. And in this moment, standing in a strange house, with strange smells, my entire body aches to return to the cumin and masala chai and perfumed scent that is my home. All of me aches for my mother.

Seventeen

Joyce leans back in her chair and sips her coffee. If someone were to see us side by side, they wouldn't think we're family. Joyce has faded bleached blonde hair, backcombed high on her head, vampire-pale skin, and she's wearing a blue plaid shirt and acid-washed jeans that are bejewelled down the sides and around the pockets.

I can't help wondering how much Joyce knows about us. Did the family keep the Hedoness secret from her, like they kept her existence from me?

Joyce sets down her *I Love Lucy* mug. 'I have to say it was a surprise to hear from your father after all these years.' Her southern accent makes it sound like she's singing.

'I'm just happy I finally get to meet you,' I say.

'Me too. It's such a pleasure having you here, and your guests. It's a shame your mother couldn't make it, though. I was looking forward to reconnecting with Priya. Send her my love, won't you, sweetheart.'

'I will.' I force a smile, shoving down the anxiety and fear and worry.

'Your father looks so much like my Tommy.' The glimmer in her eyes seems to fade. 'It sure brings back memories.' Joyce's smile is warm and caring. I like my new aunt. 'I can't wait for you to meet my Kyle,' she says. 'You two will get along smashingly.'

'Kyle?' Maybe Joyce remarried.

'Your cousin,' she says, as if it's something I should've known.

'My cousin. Right, yes,' I quickly add. 'I'm looking forward to it.' And I am. My family is growing by the second.

'Look at you, Rachel, my, how you've grown.' She leans across the polished chrome dining table to squeeze my hand. As soon as our skin touches, there's a shock. 'Static one, you are.' She flinches back and laughs. 'Your father sent me a picture of you when you were just a babe. I've often wondered what you grew up to look like. You're quite pretty – must get that from your mother.'

'He sent you a picture?' All along my aunt knew about me, even thought about me once in a while. And Dad sent the picture? A stray tear threatens to escape. I rub my eye before she notices.

'It's over there.'

I glance to where she points, and sure enough, a small gold-framed baby picture of me on my dad's lap hangs beside various other family portraits. I go to it, and gently run my fingers over the image.

'That's grandma Rachel in the photo above.'

'Grandma Rachel?' I glance up at the photograph of a curly red-haired woman with a cheerful smile.

'Your father's mother. They named you after her,' she says, unsure why I don't know this. It becomes near impossible to hold tears back. I had no clue that I was named after someone who meant a lot to my father.

Aunt Joyce slaps the kitchen table. 'When Kyle gets back from baseball practice, I'll have him take you and your two friends out. Show you the town. There's a ton to do in Nashville.'

For the first time in my life, I'm beginning to feel normal-ish – I have a cousin and an aunt, a paternal grandmother I'm named after. Everything in me wants to go with Kyle and enjoy a typical teenage night on the town, but then I remember our current predicament.

'I'm not sure that's a good idea. We just got here. We should probably stay in.' I force a smile and return to my seat across from Joyce at the kitchen table.

'You have nothing to worry about,' Joyce says, refilling her coffee. 'My Kyle knows his way around town. He'll take good care of you.'

With Marissa, anything could go wrong. But Paisley did say the police have no idea who we are. So even if they are looking for us, they wouldn't know who to look for, let alone where to look. And I'd so like to get to know my only cousin. A fun night out sounds like just the distraction I need right now, so given there's nothing I can do until I hear back from Paisley and her ma, surely it wouldn't hurt to go while I wait, would it?

'All right, that would be nice,' I say, instantly second-guessing my decision.

'Oh good.' Joyce clasps her hands and stands. 'Why don't you go tell your friends while I make some ice tea.'

I hug her, then head towards the attached garage where Marissa and the guys are assembling Joyce's bunk beds. We plan on staying here until Ma's free. Hopefully that's sooner rather than later. At least that's what I'm doing. I don't know if Ma's original plan goes any further than that. Dad hasn't hinted at anything beyond coming here.

'Hey,' I say, pushing through the door to find Marissa leaning on a freezer-chest, ogling Ben, who's busy laying out the wood panels.

She glances up when I enter, crinkling her brow. 'What's with the smile?'

'Freedom,' I say, which makes her more confused. 'My cousin's going to take us out tonight.' I can't remember the last time I felt this normal; visiting family, hanging out with my friends and a cousin – this sort of stuff doesn't happen in my life.

'You have a cousin?'

'Yeah, I guess I do.'

Bored with our conversation, Marissa skips over to Ben. He whispers something that leaves her giggling in a voice so high-pitched it makes me wince.

Ben flashes an awkward grin and runs his hand through his hair. 'Can you hand me a hammer, Riss?'

I roll my eyes as she rushes over to the toolbox in a flurry of heel clicks. Although it's a small task, she acts like he needs her, like he can't survive without her help.

'Here you go.' Marissa presses her body against Ben's as she hands him the tool.

He offers a half version of his grin. 'Thanks.'

Their whole exchange is making me nauseated. I walk over to Dad in the far corner. He's diligently sorting the bunk bed panels and stacking pieces together, tears streaming down his face as he cries quietly to himself.

I don't dare ask him what's wrong. I know the answer. *I just miss your ma so much.*

'Man, it's hot in here,' Ben says from behind me.

'Let me help you with that,' Marissa replies.

My curiosity gets the better of me, so I look as Marissa grabs the edge of his shirt and tries to pull it off. It's the most desperate and ridiculous thing I've ever seen her do. I want to manifest something witty or sharp to say, but I'm stunned stupid by Ben's athletic body. It's like I've never seen a hot guy before.

He pulls down his shirt. 'I was hinting for a glass of ice-water or something.'

Ben leaves Marissa and walks over to the wood pile,

sidestepping my dad, who is oblivious to the fact that there are others in the room.

Marissa catches my frown. 'He was hot.' She shrugs.

Ben glances over his shoulder, acknowledging me with a genuine smile as he heads to Dad. I'm not sure what my dad was like before he met Ma, but in his current state he couldn't be more different from Ben. Dad crying into his work gloves, and Ben managing to wrap Marissa around his little finger. Something about seeing the pair of them, side by side, has me frozen, staring, worried that after everything Ben will end up just like him.

I step back. I don't know what I'm thinking, or why I feel the sudden urge to join Dad on Team Cry. All I know is that the happiness I felt moments ago is replaced with an overwhelming defeat, by Ben and Marissa and Dad and, well, everything. I rush out of the garage, shutting the door behind me and leaning against it for support. It's as if I'm still in there with them – I hear everything, every shuffle of their feet on cement, every awkward breath, the sound of Dad sorting piles of wood.

'Shouldn't you go check on your friend?' Ben asks.

'She's fine.' Marissa doesn't even try to hide the scorn from her voice.

'Didn't look that way to me,' Ben says.

Marissa sighs. 'I'll go.'

Not wanting her to find me just yet, I rush from my spot behind the door and outside into the garden, for some fresh air.

♥

From where I'm hiding on my perch on the swings, I watch Marissa push open the side door with her hip, carrying a tray of ice tea and cookies. She takes slow, careful steps, making sure her heels don't sink into the dirt, and stopping every time the tea splashes over the rim.

'Here.' She sets the tray on a tree stump and holds out a glass.

'Thanks,' I say, taking the drink, the cold sending a shiver through my palm. 'Where's Ben?'

'I told your dad to make sure he stays in sight. I said it was important for your safety.' She sits on the empty swing beside mine with an air of romance, and rocks in circles. 'Is everything OK with you?' Marissa's eyes dart longingly towards the garage.

My first instinct is to tell her I'm fine, and to pretend that I am. My mind replays my new Joan of Arc mantra – *fighter, fighter, fighter.* But I'm not fine. Not that she really cares how I feel. All along I've put up with her attitude problem because I understood it comes from a place of brokenness, and I guess I hoped that at the heart of it she cared for me, like I do her – in a sisters type of way. When she picked me to be her accountability partner, I was so happy. It felt like things were different from my elementary school days where being half Indian meant getting chosen last or always being grouped with other biracial kids. My classmates didn't even know my heritage. Most of them thought I was a Pacific Islander because of the freckles and wild waves I got from my dad. I should have known when I was picked first by a popular girl it wasn't because of me. I was just a notch on Marissa's Hedoness belt. Just like now – she only pretends to care because someone asked her to.

'Rach?' She waves her hand in front of my face. 'You're doing that thing where you stare cross-eyed into space.'

'You don't want to know what I'm thinking.'

'Try me,' she half-heartedly replies.

I take a deep breath. 'I'm wondering if we're really friends, or if the last three years was only because you were told to pick me.'

'Woah.' Marissa's forced smile drops. 'Seriously?'

'Seriously.'

'OK. Well, at first it was because they asked me to be your friend. I mean look at us, we wouldn't normally travel in the same social circles.'

I set my glass down and kick at the dirt.

She sighs, 'But of course we're friends,' and nudges my side. 'You're the only one who puts up with me.'

I glance at her, taking in her blue eyes, almost the same shade as Eros's in the painting. She looks so much more

132

like him than I do, it's easy to make their connection. And right now those blue eyes are the most genuine I've ever seen them, almost pleading with me to believe her. Knowing that she actually cares brings a small sense of relief.

Marissa pushes her swing closer. 'I'd be your friend even if you painted on your eyebrows, and you know how I am about eyebrows.'

I laugh.

'What's going on in that head of yours?' she asks.

'I guess ... I'm having a hard time adjusting to everything. I met my aunt and I have a cousin who I didn't know about until just now. My ma's in jail having god knows what done to her. And that's not even all of it ...' I clear my throat, taking a deep breath, trying to decide how honest I'm going to be. 'I'm starting to realize there are things I want that will never happen.' It's the closest to the truth I can give. The truth is – for some stupid reason I'm attracted to Ben and it's hard to see the connection he shares with her.

'Don't I know it!' Marissa whistles through her teeth.

'Oh please. You could have anything you want.'

She stops swinging. 'Not really.'

'What do you mean?' Then I remember her ma. All these years I've known Marissa I've only met her mother once. She spends most of her time away, living out some mid-life crisis, flirting and turning men instead of being here with her daughter.

Marissa smooths her hair over her shoulders. 'I mean, we can't really have love, can we? I know I always bug you about the *true love* stuff. But lately I've been thinking . . .'

This isn't about her mother. 'Ben?' I ask.

Marissa blushes.

And my heart sinks all over again.

Eighteen

The loud rumble of an engine pulling into the driveway causes me to jump up and run to the front of the house.

'Where are you going?' Marissa calls after.

'To meet my cousin.'

I swing open the side gate and skid to a stop before a dark red truck with raised tyres. The driver's door opens and a tall, muscular guy hops out wearing a baseball uniform. Unlike Joyce, Kyle looks like he could be my family and that makes me smile. We both have brown skin and black hair, though the tips of his hair are dyed the same bleached blonde as Joyce's. Kyle doesn't notice me, instead he puts on his hat and walks to the back of the truck and grabs his bag out of the truck-bed. It looks like it weighs fifty pounds, but he effortlessly slides the large sack over his shoulder.

He starts for the house and then he finally sees me.

'Oh, hey there.' He flashes a perfect white smile, his dark brown eyes glistening with mischief. 'Can I help you?'

I blush, realizing I'm staring at Kyle the same way Marissa stares at Ben. 'Oh, uh. Are you Kyle?'

His expression changes. 'Yeah, that's me. Listen, if you were put up to this, I appreciate you coming, but I'm not interested in dating—'

My nervous laugh cuts him off. 'No – it's not that. I think I'm your cousin.'

'Cousin? You must be Rachel!' He winks. 'I was surprised when my mom told me you were visiting out of the blue. After all these years. You on the run from something? Or finally felt it time to meet the fam?'

'On the run? No . . . I, we—'

He smiles. 'Whatever the reason, it's nice to finally meet you.'

There's a rustling from behind and I turn to see Marissa push her way through the gate. She dusts off her skirt, pausing when she sees Kyle.

'Woah.'

'Marissa, this is Kyle. Kyle, this is my friend Marissa.'

He tips his hat. 'A pleasure.'

Marissa giggles.

It doesn't seem to faze him any. But my guess is he has no shortage of female attention. He smiles and walks past, into the house, leaving us staring after him.

'I hate to see him go,' Marissa says. 'But damn, I love watching him leave.'

I roll my eyes. 'Yeah, OK.'

'OK? He's more than OK. He's hot. Like sexy hot.'

A laugh-snort fusion escapes my throat as I shake my head at Marissa. 'Come on,' I say as I head back into the house.

Marissa follows, a little too eagerly. 'I'll go wherever he goes.'

♥

'Bunk beds are ready to go!'

Marissa, Joyce and I turn from where we're sitting at the dining-table to see Ben and Dad stumble in from the garage. They enter the kitchen covered in wood dust and sweat.

'That was fast.' Joyce smiles. 'Want some sweet tea while you wait to meet my Kyle?' She holds up a frosted pitcher.

'That would be nice, thanks.' Ben sidesteps Marissa and grabs a glass. Dad takes the last empty seat at the far side of the table, so Ben heads to the couch in the adjacent room.

Before Marissa can hop up and join Ben, the door to the bathroom opens, sending out a cloud of steam. Kyle, with only a towel wrapped around his waist, strolls into the hall. His wet hair hangs around his face, perfectly framing his sharp jaw and broad shoulders. Water droplets cause his skin to glisten. Marissa and I can't help but let a gasp escape our lips as he walks into the kitchen. Me out of shock and her out of intrigue.

'Hey, Mom.'

'Kyle? What in the . . . go put some clothes on.'

He flashes her a grin, then turns his attention to my dad sitting quietly in the corner and extends his hand. 'And you must be my uncle.'

Dad looks at his hand but doesn't take it. 'Hi,' he says.

Kyle grins, though openly confused by my father, and kisses his mother's cheek before turning to Marissa and me. When he sees Ben sitting in the other room, he stops and smiles, raising his hand in greeting. 'Hey, man, I'm Kyle. You are?'

'Ben, nice to meet you.' Ben nods, returning his attention to some paper he pulled off the counter.

'And you are someone's boyfriend?'

'He's a friend,' I say, before Marissa or Ben answer with something that shouldn't be said.

'Ah, cool.' Kyle looks me over, head to toe. I fidget under his confident gaze. Where Ben has this relaxed confidence, Kyle has a bold one, and he's almost predatory with it.

'Our family is too good-looking,' he says.

Marissa's smile drops, and she runs a finger over her eyebrows in such an offhanded way, I'm not even sure she realizes she did it. 'You're hitting on your cousin?'

Kyle smirks. 'I'm not hitting on her. Merely telling the truth. And it wouldn't matter anyway because we're not blood relatives.'

Ben raises his gaze from the paper.

138

'What do you mean?' I ask.

'Joyce adopted me. I was born in the Philippines.' He winks at Ben and saunters away, his towel riding lower with every step.

Marissa sulks off to the room we're sharing. I get up from the table and slump on the couch beside him.

'Big day,' he says, folding the paper.

'Weird day.' I smile, turning to him, swallowing when my eyes lock on his. There's a certain intensity he has whenever he takes me in. Like he's studying, analyzing, trying to read my brain. It's intimidating, mysterious, and I wish I knew what he was thinking.

Ben undoes and refolds the paper. 'He's right about you, you know?'

I struggle to breathe. 'What?'

He smiles and rests his arm on the top of the couch. My hair falls over his hand and he flicks the ends of my ponytail.

'Oh, sorry,' I say, sitting forward.

He smiles. 'Nothing to apologize for. I like your curls.'

My whole body stiffens, and my cheeks heat up.

'You all right?' he asks

'I'm just . . .' I stop. Ben smiles and leans towards me. I'm suddenly very aware of our proximity. Even the hairs on my arm stand alert.

'You have freckles,' he says, staring at my nose. 'They're cute,' he finishes, flopping back into the couch.

I don't respond. Instead I cross my arms to keep from rubbing the fire from my nose, and I tap my foot at the air.

'You're not used to getting compliments, are you?'

His eyes tunnel into me, watching, analyzing. He'll make an excellent cop one day. Those eyes pierce straight to my soul. Everything in me wants to tell him the truth, all of it, just so he'll stop looking at me.

'No, not with a best friend like Marissa around . . . which suits me just fine.'

He laughs. 'She's beautiful, but so are you.'

Marissa spends two hours getting ready to go out. I swear she carries a whole cosmetic store in that gold bag. A good fifteen of those minutes were spent pencilling in her eyebrows, and from minutes eight to fifteen they looked the exact same to me. Now her hair's perfectly curled, her make-up precisely layered, and her outfit's meticulously pressed and worn in such a way that makes it seem like she just walked out of a store display. My clothes didn't even look that good on the mannequins.

Marissa twirls back and forth in front of the mirror before returning to the pile of clothes she's dumped out of my backpack. 'I could wear this instead.' She holds a white T-shirt up to her body, checking how it looks with her pleated skirt.

Where's Joan of Arc and her trusty sword when I need to stab someone? 'For the last time, Marissa, you look perfect.' I exhale noisily and check my chat thread to see if there's any updates from Paisley's ma. She hasn't replied yet, which worries me.

'It's not like I have better clothing options.' Marissa spins one last time, taking herself in. 'It's the best I can do, given my situation.'

It's another dig at my clothes. Her passive-aggressive levels are at an all-time high. Which is a little disappointing – I thought we'd shared a moment outside earlier, but she seems to have already forgotten. And right now, I really can't deal with any more drama.

A notification pings and I check to find a message from Mother Superior requesting Marissa and I follow Committee instructions and head to Athens at once. Just as I'm about to close it, I notice a list of suggested accounts to follow. One of them is someone named Surrender2Love, with a profile picture of a human heart and arrows crossing through it.

Suddenly I hear Ma's words from earlier in my head – *If you surrender to love, Eros will find you.*

It couldn't be . . . could it?

My curiosity drives me to send a request. They accept immediately. My heart races as I open the chat and click the message box.

ME: *Hello?*

The chat bar shows someone's typing a response. I pull my knees tighter to my chest and fixate on the screen.

S2L: *Hello, love.*

ME: *Who is this?*

S2L: *You know who.*

If there's any chance this is actually Eros, I need to know. He could help my ma.

ME: *I was hoping you could help me.*

S2L: *Is this about your mom?*

My hands shake, I nearly drop my phone. I glance up at Marissa to find her applying another coat of mascara. She's not watching me.

ME: *If you are who I think, can you help me save her?*

S2L: *You don't need me for that. Try embracing your gift.*

If Marissa wasn't standing right next to me, I'd think this was some sick prank she's playing. But she is, so that leaves who? Mother Superior? One of my teachers? I'm furious – did they just get my hopes up as a ruse to get me on Team Hedoness? I'm also mad at myself for being desperate enough to believe that the god of love would actually accept a friend request from me.

ME: *Whoever this is, it isn't funny. And you know what? I'm not interested in being a Hedoness. As far as I see it, it's the cause not the cure. I'm sick of being bossed around by Eros and his stupid arrow curse. Because of him my ma's in jail and I've lost my home.*

S2L: *Maybe it's time you stop complaining about Eros and follow your own damn arrow.*

ME: *Huh?*

S2L: *Bye for now, love.*

'Rach?'

'What?' I look up to find Marissa glaring at me.

'You ready?'

I glance down at my screen – S2L is now offline. I sigh, slip my phone in my back pocket. 'I've been ready for the last hour and forty-seven minutes.'

Marissa rolls her eyes and grabs my hand, pulling me from the bed. 'You're not seriously wearing that, are you?'

I look over my Converse, knee-high black socks, cut-off jean shorts, white Wonder Woman T-shirt and a long black cardigan. It's my staple going out outfit. 'Looks like I'm wearing it.'

Marissa crinkles her nose. 'Can I at least do your hair? I hate how you always wear ponytails.'

'Nope.'

'Oh come on, no one is that dedicated to ponytails.'

I cross my arms and glare.

'What about your eyebrows?' She reaches for them and I bat her hand away.

She rolls her eyes and grabs her gold purse, digging through it for cherry-red lip gloss. After applying two coats, she heads out the door, leaving me in her shadow.

143

I follow her into the living room, where Ben and Kyle stand awkwardly with their hands in their pockets looking like they've run out of things to talk about. Ben looks so out of place in the smiley pizza sweatshirt next to Kyle in a leather jacket. He sees me grinning at his sweatshirt and gives himself a once-over before turning to Kyle and looking him up and down.

'Dude, I can lend you a jacket,' Kyle says.

'It's all good.' Ben takes the sweatshirt off, flips it inside out and puts it back on.

'Somehow that's better,' Marissa says.

Joyce sits at the kitchen table pretending not to watch the whole exchange. I feel like those girls in the TV shows, the ones like *My Vampire Alien Life*, where they get dressed up and go on dates with guys who are too hot to be real. For a moment I forget about Ma, then the fear and worry come rushing back, this time with a side of guilt. It's hard to pretend everything's OK, no matter how much I want it to be.

Ma's words flit through my mind, *Your happiness is more important to me than my own,* and something about that memory makes it feel right to go. She wouldn't want me moping when there's nothing I can do for her right now, anyway. She'd want me to get to know my cousin. I check my phone again just in case. Paisley's still offline. I slip it in my back pocket and am just about to head out the door with the boys when Dad blocks my path.

'Rachel, you can't leave me. I have to keep you safe.'

I point at Kyle and Ben, both of whom are quite a bit bigger than Dad. 'They're going to make sure I'm safe. And if they don't, I have Marissa.' Truth is Marissa can do more damage than either of the boys could.

'Your ma wouldn't want this.'

'Ma said it's fine.' It's a white lie, she never said it, but my imagined version of her did.

'OK,' Dad says. 'I just miss your ma so much.'

'I know, Dad.' *Me too.*

'Be safe,' he says again.

'We'll be fine,' I say, squeezing his hand before following Marissa and the boys.

Kyle offers me his arm and that TV-show-girl feeling returns.

As we're about to step out the door, Ben turns back to Dad. 'Mr Patel, we'll behave, scout's honour.' He puts a hand over his heart. Marissa smiles at this, but I frown. Ben's acting too normal for someone who was just kidnapped. He looks at me and I wish I could read his brain and figure out what he's thinking.

Why hasn't he tried to escape?

Nineteen

In the rear-view I watch Ben fidget in his seat, turning around every few minutes to stare out the back, his eyes always returning to mine with that familiar questioning gaze. Marissa's been awfully quiet. She's spent the last five minutes thumbing through her phone. I'm wondering if there's any new info on Quiver. I'm about to ask her, when Ben leans into the front seat, his arm so close to brushing mine, and our faces so near, that it makes my whole body buzz with the tension. As I pull back I notice a black SUV trailing the truck. Kyle turns on to another street and the SUV turns too. My heart races. I thought Ben's body language seemed weird, and this confirms why.

'We need to find somewhere to pull over,' I say, looking at Kyle. 'Somewhere with a lot of pedestrian traffic.'

'That's oddly specific.' Kyle smirks.

I lean in, lowering my voice. 'I think we're being followed, and if I'm right we'll need to blend in.'

'I've never been good at blending in.' Kyle nudges me,

expecting a laugh, but I'm too focused on watching a black SUV and trying to keep from freaking out.

'What am I missing?' Kyle pulls into the parking lot of a strip mall and kills the engine.

The black SUV continues on. Ben's shoulders slump and a strange look passes over his face.

'Guys?' Kyle asks with more force.

'Some police officers think we're aliens,' Marissa cuts in, not even looking up from her phone, 'and a bunch of nuns were arrested trying to protect us. Rachel's worried we'll get arrested again too.'

Kyle's eyes widen and he looks from her to me. He starts to laugh, head back, chest rattling. After a few minutes he rights himself. 'Fine, don't tell me.'

He's right, our truth is too outlandish to believe.

Ben's focus fixes on the dashboard. 'Is that a radio scanner?'

'Yup,' Kyle says, picking up the mouthpiece.

Ben reaches over to scan through the signals, every once in a while stopping to listen to the line. I keep my eyes on the road in case the SUV comes back.

'Do you maybe just want to come up front?' Kyle asks.

Ben ignores him and keeps twisting the dial, his ear trained towards the speaker. He's only inches from me. The way he smells – paper and the ocean – it fills my head to bursting. The hair on the arm closest to him begins to rise and an electrical sensation pulses under my skin. I brush it off as nerves until Ben's arm grazes mine and my entire body surges.

He screeches into the back. 'You shocked me.'

Marissa snaps up from her phone, her eyes locking on me in warning.

'Sorry, I—'

'Did you just try to . . . to? You know?' He stumbles over his words, his eyes alight with fear.

'No. I didn't. I wouldn't. It's static from the seat belt or something.'

Marissa shoves out of the truck and storms over to my door, whipping it open and pulling me out. She drags me to the back of the car and pushes me down to the bumper so the guys can't watch us.

'What was that?'

'I don't know – my arm felt funny and then I shocked him.'

'We both know that's not what happened.'

'It can't be. I've never before—'

'You know very well the Patel bloodline is strong – that's why your mom can turn by touch. You probably can too.' Marissa starts to pace.

'No. It can't be.' I stare at my arm. *Please don't let it be that.*

Marissa stops in front of me and grabs my shoulders. 'Have you ever felt anything like it before?'

I don't look her in the eyes, I don't want to see what's waiting for me there, so I drop my head and mumble, 'No.'

'Shit. I can't believe you almost turned my boyfriend. Like we need any further attention on us.'

'B-boyfriend?'

Marissa glares.

I don't know what's worse, thinking about Ben and Marissa as a couple or that I might've just manifested Hedoness powers on him. 'When did you two start dating?'

'I figured it was obvious.' She slides her gold bag off her shoulder and searches through it, pulling out her phone. She turns on selfie mode and inspects her teeth, then sets to smoothing out a rebellious lock.

'When did he ask you?' *Who asks their kidnapper out?*

'He doesn't need to ask. I *know* he likes me.' She gives up on the hair, tucking it behind her ear, and dumps the cell in her purse.

'So, he doesn't know you're dating?'

Marissa sighs, and rests her hands on her hips. 'You are so oblivious to relationships. Everything doesn't need to be defined to be real. Why do you think he isn't trying to escape? It's because he likes me.'

'It's just—'

'What's the big deal?' Marissa's practically shouting and I'm worried the boys can hear. 'It's not like you like Ben. Right?'

'Yeah . . . right.'

She flashes me a weird look. 'Let's get back. And watch yourself. If you feel that way again, leave the truck or something.'

Ben and Kyle are chatting when we re-enter, and since Ben's hopped into the front, I'm stuck in the back with Marissa. She leans against the far wall, glaring at me.

'I'm telling you, man . . . it's not about the gun.' Ben forces a laugh, but his tone is insistent.

'Yeah, right.' Kyle glances at us in the tension-filled back seat. 'I was just asking Tough Guy here why he wants to be a cop. He's claiming it's *not* because he'll get to power trip with a gun.' Kyle snorts.

'It's not why,' I mumble.

'Oh, yeah?' Kyle asks. 'Why then?'

I flick my gaze to Ben, who has spun round in his seat, watching me intently.

'Um.' It's hard to think over Marissa's glare and Ben's curious eyes. 'It's, uh, because he cares. About people and stuff.' When I glance back at him he looks away.

'Cares?' Kyle wags his eyebrows. 'How can you tell?'

I gulp down the sneaker-sized knot forming in my throat. 'He, uh, he takes the time to ask people how they're doing, you know . . . like he's actually interested.'

'Aww, you're so sensitive.' Kyle elbows Ben, who uses it as a chance to face the front and flop back in his seat.

150

'Just the type of man we need carrying guns around. I think sensitive guys should be someone's boyfriend, not a cop.'

Marissa giggles, which only encourages my inner Joan of Arc to press through. 'Sensitivity isn't a bad thing,' I say crossly.

'Oooh, seems I pushed someone's button,' jokes Kyle.

Ben shoots him a look and sits forward. 'Leave her alone, man.'

'I see what you mean, Rachel.' Kyle laughs. 'He is sensitive.'

Something inside snaps. Maybe it's because I'm still frustrated at Marissa, or perhaps it's something else, but either way I open my door and get out.

'Was it something I said?' Kyle calls after me.

I don't know him enough to know if he's being serious. And everything that's happened today has me on edge. So I freeze, my back to the truck. 'Yes, it *was* something you said.' I'm yelling, I can't seem to control it. People across the parking lot turn and stare. 'And how you said it. My whole life I've had a dad who treats me like I don't exist, like my feelings don't matter. So when someone asks me how I'm doing, whether they're a guy or a girl, I'm thankful. I don't think that's a sign of weakness. I think it takes strength to put someone before yourself. He'll make a great cop. The kind of officer this world needs.'

'At least you *have* a dad,' Kyle says.

My heart sinks. Kyle and Marissa have no fathers and here I am complaining about mine.

People gather on the sidewalk, and when I look at them they glance in the other direction, attempting to hide the fact that they're watching. I take another breath, check my cellphone's in my pocket and walk away. 'I need some time,' I say.

'Rach, wait,' Ben calls after me. 'It's getting dark.'

I ignore him and march on.

When I pass the strip mall, I start into a run. The familiar rhythm of my steps syncing with my heartbeat helps calm me a little. Before long I'm a few blocks away, passing rows of houses neatly organized like keys on a piano. The sun's nearly set, casting the last of its glow over the chimneys and through the trees. I turn on to another street and see a faint outline of a steeple. I follow it down the road to find myself catching my breath at the steps of a church. The irony is not lost on me as I walk to the door. I reach for the handle, my hand still shaking and heart still racing from my sudden burst of anger at the truck.

It opens and I'm enveloped in a cloud of incense – a familiar smell that brings me right back to St Valentine's blue-striped halls. A strange part of me longs to return to them, to return to before Marissa kissed Ben. Maybe then the ache in my chest would leave.

Hesitantly, I push inside, peering in. A priest, dressed in a traditional long black robe, hears the squeak of the old hinges and turns.

'Hello?'

'Oh, hi. I was just seeing if you're open.' I flinch at my awkward wording.

'Of course, come in. Do you need someone to talk to?'

I hover in the door, not quite sure what I want or expect from the priest. But from years at St Valentine's, I feel comfortable around people who look like clergy and I could use a listening ear. 'I guess so.'

He smiles and motions towards the confessional booths in the corner.

'Oh. Right, confessional.'

He holds the door for me and waits until I'm comfortably seated on the wooden bench before he closes it and enters his side. His door shuts with a silent click and then the wooden divider in the wall slides open. Beautiful latticework blends with the colourful shadow of the priest.

I tap my knees together, trying to work up the courage to speak. This is my first time in a confessional, even though I go to St Valentine's and there's a really good replica of a chapel. But I'm here, he's here, and I'm done feeling all alone. Talking to him is my best and only option.

'Father, uh . . . I'm not sure what I'm supposed to say. I went to a kinda Catholic school so you'd think I'd know.' I air-laugh and bite the inside of my cheek, fidgeting in my seat as I wait for his response.

'Just say whatever is on your heart, dear.' His voice is so calm that I feel myself relaxing.

'OK.' I take a deep breath. 'Forgive me, Father, for I think I've sinned. I'm angry at the gods . . . uh, I mean God, for giving me a gift I don't want.' I take a deep breath, hoping he didn't catch my mix-up. I wait for his reply, staring through the wood slats that separate us, trying to get a better look at his reaction to my confession.

'What gift, my dear?'

'I'm not supposed to talk about it.' I'm sweltering in this stuffy little box. I wipe my brow, thankful for the privacy of the booth.

'Everything you share here stays between us,' he prompts.

The idea of a stolen confession, one with no consequences, feels darn enticing. 'All right, I guess, well . . . I don't know if you've ever heard of this, or know what it means, but I'm . . .' I pause, remembering every single warning drilled into me over the last three years. But what harm could come of telling a priest? He wouldn't know what it means, anyway. Besides, he just said everything stays here. 'I'm what some people call a

Hedon—' I stop when an image of Mother Superior's stern eyes fills my mind.

An awkward silence falls between us, then the Father clears his throat. 'Sorry, dear, I don't know what you mean. But nonetheless, God only gives us that which he knows we are strong enough to handle. I'm certain you will take this gift and make it something you are thankful for.'

A distant knocking sound interrupts us. 'Will you wait here a moment?' the Father asks. 'I should check the door.'

I don't have anything else to say but I don't want to be rude. 'Oh, uh, sure.'

There's rustling from his side, followed by gentle steps as he heads to the door.

I have a few minutes to kill so I grab my cell and bring up the school site to see if I can call Marissa through that, but she's not registering online. Neither is S2L or Paisley. But after what just happened in the truck, I add another question to our chat thread.

ME: *Hey Paisley, can you ask your mom about my ma's power? I didn't get the chance to clarify things before . . . well, you know. Ma told me what to look out for. But this seems different. Can you ask if she remembers anything from back when they were A.P.s and it first started. Thx!*

I wait a few minutes, willing Paisley to come online. She doesn't, so I slip it back in my pocket. There's a

155

rustling outside the confessional, followed by a click, but the Father's colourful shadow doesn't appear on the other side.

I assume we're done and reach for the door. It's locked. 'Father?' I knock on the carved wooden panel. 'Hello, Father. I seem to be stuck.'

He doesn't answer, so I shake the handle with more force. Still no movement. 'What the . . .?' I slam my shoulder into it but only manage to split some wood from the frame. 'Shoot.' I grab the broken piece and try to put it back.

'Hello? Help! I'm trapped in the confessional!' When no one answers, I flop down on the bench.

And that's when someone calls my name.

Twenty

'Rachel?'

This time it's loud enough for me to recognize the voice.

'Ben! Over here.' I shake the confessional door. 'I'm stuck.' My heart pounds fiercely at my ribs. Just knowing he's here makes everything better.

'What the . . .? How did this happen?'

I rest my head against the door and groan. 'It's embarrassing – I don't know.'

'It's pretty funny.'

His attempt to mask his laughter is poor. I shake my head, a smile forming on my lips. 'It's not *that* funny.'

'Apparently, there aren't many curly haired Indian girls in this part of town. Almost everyone I'd asked knew which way you went. I never would've guessed I'd find you locked in a confessional. Nothing is boring with you, is it?'

'I guess not.'

The door rattles from the other side.

'It's locked. Is there a latch?' he asks.

'I'm not dumb – if there was a latch, I would've opened it.'

'You could've just said no.' He pries the top corner a few inches and I look out at his cheeky grin.

'Oh, you're loving this,' I say.

'I am. I really am.'

I roll my eyes, preparing my next witty attack. But his face gets serious and he leans into the door.

It reminds me exactly what our situation is. He's not my friend, he's a prisoner. 'Where's Marissa?' If Ben's here she must be close.

'Back at the truck with Kyle,' he says.

'You could've escaped,' I gasp out. 'Just now, you could've run off.'

'I thought about it,' he says, 'every new street, every new turn. But for some reason I ended up here, saving your ass.'

My heart knocks through my chest; I ease off the wall in case it raps at the wood, giving me away.

He smiles. 'I still can . . . it's not like you can come running after me.' He glances around, rubbing his arms, his smile slipping into something sad. 'And I don't want to stay here longer than needed.'

'Not a believer?'

'No, it's not that.' He laughs. 'After meeting you and seeing . . . well, you know. I have no clue what to believe any more. I'm trying to figure that out.' He looks back through the crack at me. 'It's because I don't like churches. They remind me of funerals. Too many people I love have died.'

My heart aches for him, and I wonder who he's talking about. But before I can ask, a whacking sound similar to the old forced-air system at St Valentine's fills the church. It's so loud I can barely think.

After a few moments it suddenly stops.

'That was strange,' I say.

'Yeah.'

The doors to the sanctuary open. Ben turns from me and I peer out of the space he's made to see three people dressed in black suits running towards us.

'Hey!' One of them points at Ben. 'Get away from there.'

'It's OK, my friend's got herself stuck.'

They keep running, and one of the men reaches into his jacket and pulls out a gun.

'Rach, get down.'

I can't believe my eyes. The room echoes with the blast and Ben dives to the ground.

'Ben!' I scream. 'What's going on?'

'Rach, on the count of three I'm going to slam into the door. Get ready to run.'

I don't remember the counting but soon the whole confessional rocks against his attack.

'Stop!' one of them yells as they weave their way through the pews, just a few yards away now.

Ben throws his leg into the door with force. The wood buckles and crashes off the frame. He reaches in, grabs my shirt and pulls me after him. My blood buzzes, sensing his touch inches away on the other side of my shirt, and I'm too busy running to stop it.

'Don't shoot!' one of them yells. 'We can't hit the girl! The Committee wants her alive.'

The Committee? My insides become ice.

Ben shelters me with his body, pushing me forward one electric shove after another. The men are so close but we're running hard, faster and faster. As we zoom by one of the altars, Ben kicks it over, scattering the candles and stone statues to the ground.

'There, that door!' He shoves me towards it.

I push down my fear and focus on sprinting for the exit, Ben's hand is on my back, urging me forward.

For a moment it seems like we might get away from them.

As I burst through the door, my foot catches the ledge and I tumble to the ground, hands scraping over the stony concrete. Ben's momentum drives him past. He skids to a stop, running back to help me. Heavy footsteps charge behind.

The men are upon us now.

I push up, pausing mid-motion, my arms shaking from the strain of holding my weight. But I can't move, fear freezes my entire being – a gun barrel looms, inches from Ben's face.

Twenty-One

'It's OK, Rachel,' Ben says. He's like a deer in headlights – frozen, still – except for a hand motioning me to keep back.

'Stop resisting or your friend gets hurt,' the man tells me, jerking his gun at Ben.

My head spins, my heart hammers in my ears. The back of my throat fills with a phantom metallic taste. This is it. He's going to die. And it's my fault.

An arm reaches out, from one of the other men, and a new kind of horror rises in me. My insides twist at the thought of what I must do. 'Ben, look out!' I jump up and dive for Ben, slamming my shoulder into the gunman. Our bodies fold together, a tangle of limbs. Steel flashes in my vision as I wrestle for the gun.

'Grab her!' someone shouts.

My fingers slip over the cool surface as the gunman secures his grip on it. He knocks me to the ground and I curl into a ball, expecting to hear the blasting resound of a bullet rocketing from the gun. Instead, there's a hollow click. The man growls and tosses the empty pistol at my head. I manage to block it with my forearm. The blow stings, but I ignore it and push up, running for Ben, who's running for me. We meet halfway, he grabs my hand and I feel a surge of electricity. One of them lunges, holding me by my cardigan, trying to pull me back. 'We're not going to hurt you,' he says.

'Let go!'

Without hesitating, Ben punches the guy in the face. The man stumbles. Ben takes it as an opening to move me behind him. He raises his hands, ready to fight off the next assault.

People exit their houses, some pull out cellphones, others run over, stopping on the street, not sure what to do, who to help. It's not every day you see a gun fight at church.

'Hand her over and no one will get hurt,' one of them says.

Ben reaches back, resting a protective hand on me. The men form a line before him.

Even if we get out of this, we'll be found. The neighbours are taking pictures, probably calling the police. Maybe the Committee is a better option than jail. Maybe if we stop fighting they won't hurt Ben. Maybe.

A rumbling engine comes up the street. I turn to see Kyle's big red truck.

'Over here!' I wave and jump, stepping closer to the road, taking my first real breath in a while.

Kyle pulls up behind us. 'What's going on?'

The men charge, seeing our newfound escape route.

'Go!' Ben pushes me towards the truck then runs at them.

The men circle as he kicks and hits, blocking their attempts to get to me. It's three on one, and Ben takes a lot of blows.

I teeter in the in-between. Do I go to the safety of Kyle and Marissa, or stay with Ben? The thought of losing him makes me ill. 'I'm not leaving,' I say, glancing around for something, anything that can help us.

'Rach?' Marissa calls. 'Get out of there.'

'Not without Ben.' I turn back in time to see one of the men get past Ben and rush at me. I have nowhere to go. I raise my fists, prepared to protect myself, when large arms grab me and shove me back. Kyle appears in a blink, pushing over the man and heading into the fight.

'Get in the truck,' Ben yells again. He ducks in time to avoid a fist to the face, and one of the men grabs him from behind.

'Oh. My. God. What's happening?' Marissa says as I hop in the back, looking for something to help. I pull a wooden bat from under the seat, gripping it tight, eyes fixed on the boys.

Kyle rips the guy off Ben's back.

Ben turns from his current match, slamming his knee into the stomach of the guy Kyle's holding. He spins back in time to block a fist and smash his palm into the jaw of the other man. The man's eyes roll back and he timbers to the ground.

Marissa sits up. 'Whoa.'

'Dude,' Kyle says, surveying the scene.

There's a wake of unconscious men at Ben's feet.

'Let's get out of here.' Ben rushes to us, and Kyle's right behind.

I cling to the bat, knees tapping impatiently on the seat. My gaze bounces to the church doors, hoping no new attack comes rocketing out.

The boys dive in the front. Ben first, pressing Marissa into the corner to make room for Kyle behind the wheel.

One of the men manages to get up and get to the truck. He's inches from grabbing Kyle.

'Watch out!' Marissa warns.

Instinct takes over and I spring over the seat, using Kyle's shoulder for leverage, and strike the attacker. He falls to the ground with a humph. I throw the bat after him, and Kyle slams the door.

'Drive!' Ben says, slapping the dash.

Kyle slams the gas, sending me flying into the back. Tyre smoke clouds the parking lot as he peels on to the street.

We drive past a blue-and-yellow helicopter on the church's front lawn. It wasn't there when I went in. The door opens and a lady in a trousersuit steps out. She pauses, watching the truck speed by.

'What's going on?' Kyle says, cutting off a station wagon going school-zone speeds.

Ben turns and looks over the seat at me. I don't know what to tell him.

'Whatever that was . . .' Kyle continues. 'Dude!' He smacks the steering wheel.

'Just keep driving,' Ben says, wiping blood off his fists and holding out the seatbelt for Marissa to put on. 'You should've stayed in the truck. I had things under control.'

'If you call getting beat up in a church under control.' Kyle scrunches his nose when he sees Ben's hands. 'Try not to get any blood on my seats.' He reaches under his chair and grabs an old T-shirt. 'Clean yourself off.' He hands it to Ben. 'Where to?'

'Just don't drive home,' Ben says, taking the shirt, dabbing his lip and wrapping his hand. 'We have to make sure we don't have a tail first.'

I spin in my seat. Far down the road, a few men run after us with their phones raised, trying to capture our getaway as Kyle turns on to the next street and out of view.

'What happened?' Marissa asks.

I shake my head. 'I don't even know.'

'It's a little cramped up here,' Ben says. 'I'm going to slide into the back.'

'Want me to pull over?' Kyle asks.

'No,' Ben says, 'put as much distance between us and that church as possible.'

Marissa sulks, clearly not wanting him to leave her side, but luckily Kyle starts into a wild recount of the fight and she gets caught up in the drama. Ben crawls over the seat, making himself comfortable on the back bench beside me.

He puts his seatbelt on then leans over, keeping space between us, and lowering his voice to a whisper. 'Thank you.'

It's suddenly very hard to catch my breath and the buzz under my skin surges. The combination of the two makes it difficult to form words. 'Th . . . thank me?'

He lowers his eyes to my hands, clinging fiercely to my stomach, hoping to hold my gift in.

'For what you did back there,' he says softly. 'I could've been shot.'

And I could be a prisoner of the Committee if it wasn't for him. 'I had a feeling they wouldn't shoot me,' I say, pushing further against my door, away from him, so I can catch my breath. 'And that thanks goes both ways.'

Ben's face twists with conflict. 'Listen, Rach.' He hesitates. 'We need to get back to your dad and pack the car and leave, right now, tonight.'

'You think the men will find us?' He's scaring me. I don't want to leave Kyle and Joyce – we just got here.

'I have to tell you something,' he says, taking a deep breath. 'I left my jacket on purpose.' Ben's face shows no emotion. 'At your house, for Ammon to find.'

'*What?*' I gasp out, my heart hammering at my ribs.

He looks at me but his eyes never connect. 'Then when Marissa left me in the garage with your dad, I used the cordless to call him.'

I'm too shocked to reply.

'He's probably here already, looking for us. Maybe what just happened was because of me.' I don't correct him – he doesn't know about the Committee. And then he looks at me properly – his eyes filling with something similar to how he looked at the elderly pizza driver, a sort of *I will protect you* look – and it makes my stomach flip.

'I was doing what I thought was right,' he confesses. 'Becoming an officer is something I take seriously. I thought if I went along with you that it would help the police. You know, leave clues and collect info on you girls. I thought, maybe, it would secure me a slot in the academy. But now . . .'

My stomach sinks. Because of us he might lose the chance to live his dream.

Then I realize what he's telling me and my heart sinks too. That's why he didn't scream and pound the glass, that's why he's been friendly with Marissa, that's why . . . 'You being nice to me, that was all just trying to win favour with the cops?'

He raps his head against the back seat. 'No. That wasn't fake. I pride myself in being a good judge of character and when I look at you I don't see a villain.' He shakes his head, brown strands falling over his eyes. I don't respond, so he adds, 'I'm not sure which side is the good guys, what's right and wrong in all this. All I know is saving you felt right.' A spark of mischief flashes in his eyes and it fires up my blood. 'Plus, there's no telling what your family would do to me if I let you get caught.' He exhales an airy laugh then glances out the window, his mind wandering to another world. When he looks back at me, he's a reflection of the lonely boy with the frayed cuffs that I first met in the cell. 'Your family fights so hard to stay together,' he says, softly. 'There's no denying you love each other. It's been nice to be around that again. It's been a while.'

My heart shatters. I glance up to see if Marissa is listening, but she's still deep in conversation with Kyle. I'm about to ask Ben what he means by 'a while', but he continues, 'Rach, if I'm going to trust you, then you need to trust me. I want to know everything.'

If I can't trust Ben after he just risked his life to save me, then I can't trust anyone. 'OK,' I say, feeling some of the weight of the years of keeping the Hedoness secrets lift from my shoulders.

'OK.' He smiles. 'First, we should let your dad know what's happened so he can make arrangements.' He sits back, pushing the hair from his face and giving me enough distance to try to get my power back under control. 'Does he have access to that Hedoness website thing? If not it's probably not a good idea to use your phone.'

'No, he doesn't. Do you think the cops are tracking our calls?'

'We can't be too careful.'

I glance out the back window as he says that, half expecting to see that we're being followed – luckily, we aren't.

'Kyle, can we borrow your cell?' Ben says, loud enough to interrupt the conversation in front.

I pat my pocket, wondering about my own phone, thankful to find it there. After everything we went through, it could've easily fallen out or got crushed. I pull it out, only to discover the battery is dead. 'Darn it.' I shove it in the seat pocket in front of me.

'Yeah, man – here,' Kyle says, handing his back.

Ben scrolls through call history for Joyce's cell number, putting it on speaker so we can all listen. It goes straight to voicemail. He hangs up and tries a few more times, always getting voicemail. 'What's your home number?'

'615-555-0140.'

Once again, Ben punches in the number and puts the call on speaker.

'Hello?' a shaky voice whispers over the line.

'Joyce?'

'Is Kyle all right?' she asks.

'I'm fine, Mom,' he calls back.

Ben sits forward, holding the phone closer to his mouth. 'We've had an incident, but we're all safe. What's going on, you sound upset?'

'Listen, you kids – don't come home. There are police officers asking questions. They handcuffed your dad, Rachel. I'm out in the shed. They don't know I'm here.'

'What?' I gasp.

'They arrested Uncle Daniel? Why? Wait, Mom? Are you OK?' Kyle reaches for the phone but Ben pushes him back.

'Son? I'm fine. Just a little shaken is all.'

'Turn around,' I tell Kyle. 'We need to help my dad.'

Kyle pulls on to the shoulder of the road, preparing for a U-turn.

'Don't you dare,' Joyce says, her voice cracking. 'You hear me? Do not come home . . .'

The line goes dead and we listen to the static for a few minutes before Ben ends the call and hands it back. I hug my stomach and try not to let the worry consume me, or the tears loose, *or my power escape*. My parents have both been arrested, separated from each other. All because of us.

'They found us,' Ben says, glancing at me, his eyes filled with an unspoken apology.

I can't blame him. I might've even done the same thing in his shoes.

Kyle slams the truck in park. 'Who found you? And why the hell has your dad been arrested – does it have anything to do with those thugs back there? If my mom gets hurt because of something you've done, I'm going to—'

'Kyle.' Ben cuts him off before he says something he'll regret. It's a kindness I don't think Kyle picks up on, because he glares daggers at Ben. 'Your mom will be OK. Do you know anywhere we can go? Away from cops. The girls have something they need to tell you.'

Twenty-Two

Kyle drives us to a grungy diner miles out of town, down a long dirt road, the type of road where things go to get lost. The first thing I notice as we pull up is a giant neon sign that flickers 'arrow iner' in a faded pink glow. It's supposed to say Sparrow Diner, but some of the letters are burnt out. I can't help feeling it's no accident. *Arrow iner* is a little too personal.

I go to exit the truck, but Marissa grabs my arm, stopping me and blocking Ben. 'Can the two of us have a minute?' she asks him.

He looks at me, I shrug.

'We'll grab seats,' he says, sliding out Kyle's side. 'Don't be long.'

I watch the boys enter the foggy glass door peppered with posters and tape residue.

'OK,' says Marissa, 'so what the hell are we going to do?'

I tug my cardigan closer to my body. 'I think we should tell the boys the truth.'

'I knew you'd have some stupid idea.'

'For one, it's not stupid, they deserve to know. Ben could've been killed tonight.'

'What's two?' she asks, leaning into the dash and crossing her arms.

'Two: you practically already told Kyle about us at the strip mall anyway.'

'Whatever. All I said is they think we're aliens. I'm happy to stick with that story.'

'I don't feel right lying to him any more.'

'Him?' She cocks her head.

'Them,' I say.

'Fine. But if we get in trouble for this, I'm blaming you.' Marissa makes a hand-washing motion and holds out her palms.

I roll my eyes. 'The Committee and the police are after us. My parents are in jail. No one can reach your mom. Who's left to get in trouble with?'

'Uh, the gods, duh.'

'Like they'll leave their perfect world to deal with us.' As I say the words, I can't help glancing at that neon sign.

Marissa sighs and leans over the seat, resting her head on her hands. 'Do you think he'll still like me?'

'You can't be serious.'

'I mean it, Rach.'

'Is that what this little talk is about? You're worried that if you tell Ben you're a Hedoness he won't like you any more?'

She shrugs, and a sly smile spreads over her face. 'I guess if he stops liking me, I can always *make* him like me.'

I smack her forehead.

'Ouch, what the hell?' She rubs her head and glares.

'Now you're the one being stupid,' I say. But something deep inside me realizes – it *is* that simple.

♥

'Can we try this one more time?' Ben says. 'I want to make sure I heard you correctly.' He speaks slowly, not letting any panic escape into his voice. But he forgets his eyes – they give away everything.

I take a breath and sit forward. Cupping my mug, ignoring the fresh nutty coffee smell and the plate of fries in front of me waiting to be devoured. I'm hungry, but I need to get this over with first. 'We are descendants of Eros, and he—'

'You seriously believe this?' Kyle throws up his hands. 'Is this a joke? My mom could be hurt and she's cracking bad jokes?' He turns to Ben for answers but is ignored.

'We're getting nowhere this way.' Marissa picks at the ends of her hair.

'Then explain it in a way that makes sense,' Ben says.

I shove some fries in my mouth, wishing they tasted more like New York street fries and less like cardboard. Even fries make me miss home.

Marissa drops her curl and smiles. 'I can do you one better. Watch.' She slides out of the booth and starts for a table in the far corner.

I try to grab her, but I'm not fast enough. 'Don't even think about . . .' It's too late. Marissa leans in, making lip contact with a leather-wearing, face-pierced, tattooed biker. 'Seriously?' I huff. 'Have you learned nothing from the last week?'

She glares at me and turns back to the biker, watching him slip out the side of the booth and fall to the ground, convulsing.

'What the . . .? What'd she do?' Kyle asks.

I excuse myself and go to the man. A scruffy waitress and two bikers from another table follow me over to help.

'He's OK, just a seizure,' Marissa says, waving them away.

'I know that man, he ain't been prone to no seizures afore,' the toothless waitress says.

The groggy biker starts pushing off the ground. Marissa's getting better at releasing her gift – his turning was only minutes long this time.

I sigh. 'Look, he's fine now.'

The man blinks at Marissa, opening his mouth to speak but she cuts in, 'Come sit with us.' It's firm, a command, and the man nods.

The waitress shrugs and continues with her work, and the other men wander back to their table.

We take his elbows and guide him to our booth in the far corner, but before we can get him seated he starts to cry.

'My love, I've found you.'

Marissa turns to the boys. 'See.'

'I don't know,' Kyle replies, with cynicism.

'Fine.' She crosses her arms and turns to the man. 'I want you to stand on the table and do the funky-chicken dance.'

Kyle snorts. 'I doubt *that* man will do any dance.'

'Just wait.' Ben groans.

Sure enough, the man gets on the table, kicking utensils and spilling coffee as he starts to dance. I grab my plate of fries before he kicks it too.

'And sing,' Marissa adds.

The large biker dances and sings, flapping his arms and knobbing his knees. Everyone in the diner is pointing and laughing. Some pull out their phones.

'I think he dun drunk his fill tonight!' the waitress yells from behind the bar.

I hide my face and flop next to Marissa. 'Get him off now. You're drawing too much attention.'

Marissa motions to the large man. 'Get down.' Instantly he stumbles off the table. I raise my eyebrows. 'And?'

Marissa sighs. 'And I want you to forget all about me and go on with your life. If anyone asks what just happened, tell them you're drunk.'

The man's face changes instantly and he looks at the group with confusion. 'What are you looking at?' He glares and walks away.

Kyle whistles. 'If I had that power, I sure as heck wouldn't be single.'

I giggle, I can't help it. It's the most bizarre response to what he saw. A large part of me is thankful that his humour can distract me from worrying about my parents. I'm not ready for this feeling to end so I tease back, 'I thought you didn't want to date.'

'Girls,' he says, winking at Ben. 'I don't want to date girls. Ben's much more my flavour.'

Ben chokes on his mouthful of coffee. 'Sorry man, you surprised me.' He grins and wipes his mouth. 'You're cute, but not my type.'

Everyone but Marissa laughs. 'Of course he isn't your type,' she says, lashes fluttering as she slides closer to Ben and leans on his shoulder. It merits a glare from Kyle.

Ben clears his throat and moves away from her. 'The priests, um, when they were shooting at us, they mentioned the Committee. Who are they?' It's an obvious attempt to change the subject.

'I'm not really sure,' I say. 'All I know is, they govern us, and make sure we don't let the Hedonesses' secret out or cause other problems.'

'They wouldn't be too happy about this conversation,' Marissa says.

Ben sits back in his seat. 'We need to come up with a plan.'

'Just like that?' I say.

'Just like that. We need a plan.'

'You believe us? No more questions?'

'I have some questions.' Kyle raises his hand. 'How do guy Hedonesses happen?'

'That's your only question?' I ask, shaking my head. 'After everything you've seen and heard?'

Kyle shrugs.

'They don't, is the simple answer,' Marissa says. 'Male embryos aren't strong enough to take the gift and they die.'

'Maybe they just know better,' Kyle says.

I ignore him and keep my eyes on Ben. Marissa returns to twirling her hair and flicking looks in his direction, but he seems oblivious.

He takes a sip of coffee. 'I've heard, and seen, all I'm capable of.' He glances at Kyle before settling his gaze on me. 'I've made my choice. Now we need a plan.' His shaky hand grips the mug, attempting another swig.

I don't understand. Ben's risked everything so far, and this is the point of no return. He's smart. He must realize that. 'You're still willing to help us? What about what you said in the truck?'

His eyes flicker between hard and soft.

'You can still go back,' I say. 'You can still be a cop. It's not too late.'

'This is so much bigger than that.' His eyes are only hard now. 'Besides, I can't go back. Aiding and abetting criminals — sound familiar?'

Kyle smiles. 'You're a badass.'

'Stop flirting with my boyfriend,' Marissa interrupts.

Ben spits out his coffee. 'What . . .?' Ben takes a deep breath and turns to Marissa. 'Let's settle some things here. We,' he says, releasing the mug and pointing between them, 'are not dating. Got it?'

Marissa doesn't answer, and I struggle to suppress my smile. Ben keeps his attention locked on her, eyebrow raised. Finally, she crosses her arms over her chest and glares. 'Got it.' Despite her confidence, her lips tremble.

I'm thankful when the waitress comes by with a fresh pot of coffee — we could use the distraction — but Ben waves her off. Kyle holds up his empty mug and frowns.

'We should get going,' Ben says.

I slide my plate to the end of the table. 'I'm gonna try Paisley again. See if they have any new info. Can I use your cell? Mine's dead and my charger's back at Kyle's.'

'Here,' Marissa says, pulling out her phone. She glances at the screen and frowns. 'Never mind, I'm at two per cent and I don't have a charger with me.'

For everything she carries in that gold bag, you'd think she'd remember a phone charger.

'We'll have to find a payphone or internet café,' Ben says. 'But first, we need to get off the road. They're probably looking up Kyle's info as we speak. It's only a matter of time before they have the make, model and licence flagged in the system.'

'What does that mean?' Kyle turns over his empty mug and starts a pyramid tower out of the creamers on top.

'Every traffic and highway cam could be tracking our movements. Do you know anyone we can swap vehicles with?'

Kyle thinks. 'My pastor. He might be able to help us find somewhere they won't look. He's kinda like a dad to me – he's the one that brought me over from the Philippines.'

Ben finishes the last of his coffee and stands. 'We don't have any other leads. It's worth a try.'

'Uh, after what just happened, shouldn't we be avoiding church people?' Marissa says.

Kyle reaches across the table for another bowl of creamers. 'Don't you trust me?'

'No,' she says.

'I do.' And I mean it, and not just because he's my cousin – anyone who cares that much about their family has to be good.

He flashes me one of his charming smiles. 'We can sleep in the church parking lot. It's sheltered by trees and a big rock wall. It should be safe. Pastor Ron usually gets in first thing in the morning.'

'Good idea,' Ben says. 'We can take turns keeping watch at the wheel. If anyone suspicious comes around, we'll drive away.'

'Oh please, I'm not driving.' Marissa slides out of the booth. 'Do I look like a chauffeur?'

Kyle nudges me. 'Hey, Rach?'

'Yeah?'

'Can you use your power thing to turn Marissa and make her nice?'

'Ha.' I smile, diverting my eyes from Marissa's glare.

'No seriously, you should.'

'I'm standing right here.' Marissa crosses her arms.

'I can't.' I shrug and stand, following them to the till. 'It doesn't work the same on . . . others like me.'

Marissa shakes her head. 'Hedonesses are immune to the gift. Women in general aren't affected like men cause we're the genetically superior gender. If we turned a woman, all it would do is make her pass out.'

'Oh yeah? That'll do,' Kyle says. 'Rach, can you turn her now, please?'

Twenty-Three

Kyle nudges me until I open my eyes. 'Yeah?' I mumble.

'Your turn to take watch.'

I nod and clamber into the driver's seat, rubbing out the crick in my neck. A couple hours of sleep isn't enough. I'm running on fumes. I could use some of Ma's strong tea right about now. Or better, my ma.

My leg starts to tingle. I stretch it as best as I can behind the wheel. When that doesn't work, I resort to punching it, trying to get the blood flowing. Ben shifts in the passenger seat and I realize he's awake. He nods to my leg assault in question.

'It's asleep,' I whisper.

He grabs the keys, his sweatshirt and the blanket Kyle gave him, and hops out, waving me after. Careful not to wake Marissa or disturb Kyle, who's trying to fall asleep, I slip out of the truck, slowly putting weight on my leg, and close the door behind me.

Ben tosses the blanket and sweatshirt on to the hood. 'Stargazing? We can stretch out.'

Sounds perfect. I nod.

I'm about to climb up when a car approaches, its headlights illuminating the entrance to the church lot. I hobble back to the door as fast as my leg will let me. I'm ready to dive in, start the truck and race to safety, but the car continues past us, its engine fading into a gentle purr.

'Phew,' I say.

Ben holds up the keys. 'We'll keep these close.' He hops on to the hood and spreads out the blanket. I steal the moment to properly stretch my leg. When he's done, he turns and offers me his hand. I'm hesitant to take it, feeling the swirling electricity waiting on the surface of my skin.

'I got it, thanks,' I say, stepping on the bumper and using the wiper to pull myself up. It's less graceful then if I'd let him help, but at least there's no accidental shock incidents. We sit propped on the windshield, the blanket wrapped over our legs, the keys in the small space between us. The night air is cool and I hug my cardigan tight, though the chill doesn't bother me – it's the nerves being next to Ben that make me shiver.

'You don't need to wait up with me. I got it from here.'

'I can't sleep anyway,' he says. 'Too much on my mind.'

'Oh yeah?'

He turns and even in the dim moonlight his blue eyes pop. 'I thought Officer Ammon was crazy for thinking aliens abducted those boys,' he says, his tone becoming more serious. 'Still, a small part of me hoped he was right. That there was something more than us out there. Now I know it's true – just not what I expected.' He pauses and smiles. 'It's probably why I didn't put up a fight when you guys forced me to come with you.'

'Not just gathering bonus points for police academy, huh?'

'Yes . . . No . . . I don't know.' He chuckles and rolls on to his back, staring up at the stars. 'So there are gods and stuff. Does that mean there's heaven and hell?'

'There are many different versions of those, yes.'

He glances over, puzzled by my words. 'Will I ever be able to see the people I've lost again?' The sadness is back, but this time there's something far more dangerous than grief in his eyes – this time there's hope.

'I don't know,' I confess. 'But we're taught about a utopia called Elysium. Anyone good who is remembered by the living spends eternity there. I like to believe that's true, and that one day I'll go there too.'

'Yeah,' he says quietly.

His sadness is becoming more than frayed cuffs and lonely eyes – it's thick and tangible and hangs off every part of him. Whoever it is he lost, he loved them dearly.

'Assuming someone remembers me,' I add.

He looks at me again, holding me in his stare. 'I'll remember you.'

I break eye contact and turn on to my back, hoping he doesn't notice how fast I'm breathing or how loud my heart races, because the beat is filling my ears. I lose control around him. And I can't risk that.

The hard glass hurts my head. I try finding a comfortable position using my arm as a pillow.

'Here,' Ben says, rolling his sweatshirt and sticking it under my head. Where his fingers touch, my skin burns.

'Thanks.' I take it without argument and slide away, giving myself some much needed space. His foot brushes mine and my body fills with fire. This is going to be a long night.

Another car approaches. We jolt alert. Dive for the keys. Our heads bonking before we make contact. When it continues by, I giggle and rub my forehead. Our faces are only inches apart. Ben's eyes lock on mine. At that moment, I don't feel the sting of a newly rising bump – I feel a fire from my soul. All of me heats and I'm afraid I'll explode. I pull away, hop off the truck, pacing and rubbing my arms.

'Your gift?' Ben asks, catching me off-guard and making me stop.

'I think so.' I turn back to him, feeling the burn of his stare. 'Or my arms could be asleep. Kinda feels the same.'

'Why does it do that?'

Because of you. 'I don't know.'

Once the surge calms, I return to the hood. We sit in silence, sharing the odd glance and smile, and watching the sun rise, painting the sky with the most beautiful pinks and oranges. For those brief quiet moments, everything is perfect.

A minivan pulls into the lot, and Kyle hops out of the truck and stretches. Ben and I sit up, on alert.

'That's Pastor Ron,' he says.

I flick a look at Ben and we catch eyes for a second, both realizing our stolen time together is over. As if on cue, we get down and set to folding the blanket. The lights in the church come on, and the three of us stand around the truck for a moment, waiting for Marissa.

Kyle stretches. 'What I would kill for a coffee.'

'Same,' I say, still tired from the last watch. Ben must be exhausted – he hasn't slept at all.

Finally, Marissa hops out. Somehow she looks refreshed, her clothes not even wrinkled.

'Shall we?' Kyle waves us after him and we follow to a side door. I stop in my tracks when I see the name on the glass – *Arrow Heights Pentecostal Church*.

'Everything all right?' Ben asks.

'Yeah, no, I'm fine,' I say, forcing a smile.

Maybe Ma's right – maybe the gods do give us signs?

We follow Kyle through the door and down the hall and right into the pastor's office, without knocking.

It looks like a mini library with packed shelves lining the walls and two small armchairs in the far corner.

Pastor Ron sits behind a desk covered in stapled-on crayon drawings.

'Kyle? I thought that might be you in the parking lot.' The pastor lifts his head from a yellowed PC, an old relic. There's a big Sprite sticker on the back and as we get closer I realize it says 'Spirit' but in the same font as the soda.

'Hey, Pastor Ron.' Kyle whisks around the desk and gives the man a huge hug, lifting him from his chair. The pair stay embraced, patting each other's backs and laughing.

'It's been too long.' Pastor Ron grins, holding Kyle back to look at him. It's then that he glances past Kyle to the three of us standing wearily in the back of his office. 'Who do we have here?'

'That's my cousin and her two friends. We came because we need your help.'

'Cousin?' Pastor Ron smiles as he walks over and hugs me with the same fervour. My entire body tingles with the excitement of being introduced as Kyle's family. Pastor Ron lets go and extends his hand out to the others. 'Any friend of Kyle's is a friend of mine. Call me Ron.' After the greeting, he turns back to Kyle. 'So, what can I do for you all?'

'Like I said, we need your help.'

'Go on.'

'The police are after the girls.'

'The police?' Ron stiffens.

'It gets worse,' Kyle says.

'I don't know how you can get much worse than the police.'

Kyle kicks at the old carpet. 'I think they have my mom.'

'Joyce?' Worry floods Ron's face. 'Why?'

Kyle glances at me. 'That's not important right now. The important part is – can you help us?'

We grab everything useful from Kyle's truck as we prepare to swap vehicles with Pastor Ron.

'Kyle, could you come here?' Ron calls, lifting his head out of the trunk.

I watch as Kyle jogs over with an armful of blankets, and leans on the pastor's van.

'Tell me, did they do anything to merit the police's attention?' Ron glances at us, and I bend down, pretending to tie my shoe so he doesn't know I'm listening.

'Wrong place at the wrong time,' Kyle says.

I hate that he has to lie for us. The only person in the wrong place at the wrong time was Ben. Though, if I'm being honest, I'm kinda glad he was.

'I don't like this, not one bit,' Ron says. 'But I know you wouldn't ask me if it wasn't important. Help these girls and make sure your mom's OK, all right?' Kyle nods and Ron reaches into his pocket and pulls out his wallet. 'Here,' he says, holding a wad of bills. 'It's not much, but it should buy you gas and food for the next few days.'

Kyle smiles and once again hugs his pastor. It's all I can do to keep from crying. If he knew what we are he wouldn't be helping us.

'OK, OK.' The pastor pats Kyle's shoulder. 'And take these,' he says as he removes two keys from the cluster on his chain. 'This one's for my van,' he says, holding up the larger key. 'And this one's for the river house. If you don't remember the way, I gave Ben directions. It's about a day's drive from here, but you should be safe there for a while.'

'The river house?' Kyle beams. 'I've been waiting for this day.'

Pastor Ron looks over his nose at Kyle. 'I trust you'll be respectful?'

'Yes, sir.' Kyle smiles. 'Thank you, sir.'

Ron grins. 'Besides, driving that truck is going to do wonders for my ol' ego. I may even take the missus out tonight.'

Kyle tilts his head, mimicking Pastor Ron. 'I trust you will be respectful?' He laughs and hands over his keys. 'Also, maybe wait a few days before taking the truck out. You know, cops and all.'

'Yeah, yeah,' Ron says, his face lighting up. 'Oh, and here.' He reaches into the trunk and pulls out a portable charger. 'Ben said you needed to borrow this.'

'Thanks, it's actually Rach who needs it.' He turns, catches my eye, and holds up the battery.

I hurry over. 'Thank you, for everything, Pastor Ron.' I nod to the van as I take the charger from Kyle and plug in my phone. Ron smiles back, but it never quite reaches his eyes. I don't blame him. We put someone he cares about in trouble.

Ben and Marissa wander over and soon everyone is watching and waiting. I fasten a seat on the bumper, power up my phone and use a private browser to log in to our school's site.

My heart plummets when I see Paisley's offline. Then I notice a message.

PAISLEY: *Hey Rachel, no update on your mum yet, but I talked to my mum about the touch ability stuff. She said that when your mum first discovered her ability, her limbs fell asleep a lot. She accidentally turned a few guys before she got it under control. Sorry I don't have more.*

My heart sinks – so it is my gift.

Even though she's not online to see it, I type a quick reply.

ME: *That helps, though. Thank you. For everything. Please have your mom contact me ASAP about my ma.*

I try to keep my spirits high, but with still no word on my ma, it's impossible. I'm about to slam the screen when

I notice an unread message in my chat thread with Surrender2Love. After our last interaction, I'm not exactly in a hurry to open it. But curiosity drives me to click.

S2L: *Your mother needs you.*

S2L: *You have what's needed to help her.*

S2L: *Remember, follow your own arrow.*

Whoever is playing this prank has gone too far.

ME: *Either give me specifics or leave me alone. I don't have time for games.*

My shaky hands close the laptop. *Your mother needs you* repeats on loop in my head. Who the heck is S2L? What do they know? I glance up at the group watching me with anticipation.

'Nothing,' I choke out. Nothing helpful, anyway.

Twenty-Four

The front passenger seat bangs into my knees as Ben turns to talk to us. He leans into the back and that familiar buzz of electricity radiates up my arms. I pull away, pressing into the sliding door, afraid of sharing another shocking touch. It's become more and more clear that the feelings he stirs in me are unsafe.

Ben pauses, taken aback by my sudden change towards him. 'Um, how are you two holding up?' he says to us, but he's looking at me.

'Well, for starters, minivans are lame,' Marissa says.

'This minivan is saving your ass,' I say.

'I hope nobody recognizes me. It'd be social suicide.' She crosses her arms and glares out the window.

'You want some water?' Ben holds a bottle out between us, probably trying to stop a fight before it starts.

I could use a drink but I don't want to risk touching him. 'No, thanks.'

Marissa grabs the bottle and turns back to the window, the glass reflecting the look in her eyes. It's the same wounded animal look she gave when I first asked about her mother being in London. Ben shutting her down at the diner must've really got to her.

'Hey, Riss?' I gently put my hand on her shoulder, letting her know I'm here if she needs me.

She snaps around. 'What?'

I drop my hand, the hope of a civil conversation fading. 'May I have a sip?' I say instead, reaching for the bottle.

She moves, pinning it to the door with her leg. 'Ben just offered it to you, and you didn't want it.'

'Well, I'm thirsty now.'

'Then get your own.'

'That was the last one,' Ben says, reminding me that he's been watching us this whole time.

Marissa crosses her arms, and Ben offers a shrug. 'We can pull over at the next store,' he says.

'It's OK, I can wait for the lake house.'

'It's no problem. We should grab food and supplies anyway.'

The more Ben's attention is on me, the stiffer Marissa's posture gets. The back seat feels like a cage. I'm trapped with a wounded animal, and she's about to pounce. 'It's fine, really, Ben,' I say, nodding to Marissa. 'I only wanted one sip.'

'Could be a while before we see a store.' Kyle turns to look at us, registers the tension and adds, 'Just give her some.'

'You give her some, I don't feel like sharing.'

Ben flops back in his chair, exasperated.

Kyle looks at him and shakes his head.

Marissa ignores them and soon the van returns to normal. As normal as awkward silence and forced small talk can be. I stare out my window, thankful that not much time passes before Kyle pulls into a small gas station and convenience store.

I didn't even know we'd left Tennessee but the hand-painted store sign reads *Mississippi North Gas and Grocer*. When Kyle opens his door the smell of old gasoline wafts in. On the far end of the building, a hodgepodge of shiny and rusted car carcasses form a line outside a greasy mechanics' bay. One of them is a black and white police car.

My heart stops. We need to get everyone back in the van and get out of here. If we're caught, we can't help my parents. I stick my head out the window, ready to yell for Kyle, when I notice the police car has no wheels and the decal on the side door is faded, some letters missing. I let out a big sigh and shake my head, collapsing back into the seat.

Ben hops out, heads to Kyle at the back for money, before coming to my side and opening the sliding door. I jerk away from him, hovering in the space between Marissa's and my seat, suspended by one leg.

He cocks his head. 'Uh, I'll grab water and groceries. Is there anything else you want?' He smiles one of his caring smiles and I'm too flustered to talk or to move. Ever since the shock incident, and with all the emotions he stirred in me last night, all I can think about is how dangerous Ben is.

He can make me feel.

I sense Marissa's eyes on me, stabbing into my back, then I catch her watching us in the window reflection, and I can tell – she's pissed.

I can't handle this space between them, Marissa's anger, and whatever it is I feel for Ben – it's suffocating me. I climb into the front seat and exit the van, taking deep, lung-filling breaths. My arms are still alight with the stormy sensation. They've never pulsated like this before and it's starting to hurt. I take a few steps away, breathing slowly, rubbing my arms, trying to calm the sting.

'You OK, Rach?' Ben calls after me.

I freeze, keeping my back to him. Every time he asks, those words pierce straight to my heart. I don't think I'll ever get used to someone being this aware of me. He makes me feel things I've only ever dared dreamed of.

The type of feelings my gift turns into nightmares.

'Yeah,' I say, turning around. 'My arm just fell asleep.'

'Sure,' Marissa says with a laugh. She turns from watching us and heads to Kyle at the back of the van, which Ben takes as a sign to walk towards me. He steps closer and I turn away, not trusting myself near him.

I rub the buzz from my arms, part of me wishing I could use my power and that doing so would drain it from me for ever. As I focus on it, it surges inside, the hair on my arms rising and moving in its current.

There's a crunching of footsteps on gravel. Suddenly I'm grabbed and lifted from the ground.

'Hey, cuz, Marissa said you were upse—'

My body explodes with electricity. I scream, crippled with pain as my gift tears through me. It's worse than the Sister described. This is no bee sting. This is acidic blood. Then I see him. Kyle. Convulsing at my feet and I scream again, this time for Kyle, for who he was, and for what I've stolen. I fall to my knees, holding him as he shakes uncontrollably. 'Oh my god, please no. Not Kyle. Please. I'm so sorry, I didn't mean to, please don't turn.'

Twenty-Five

When Kyle stops shaking, I release my grip and stand, turning my back to him. I can't bear to look, in case, just in case . . .

'My love?'

My knees buckle. *'No.'*

Ben jogs over and grabs my arm. 'What did you do?' I rip it away before my gift ruins him too. I can't handle his touch right now, or the look of fear hidden beneath the anger in his eyes. He's never looked at me like that. Like I'm a monster.

'Tell me, Rachel.'

I glance between Ben and Kyle – looks of disgust and love.

'I . . .'

'Do not hurt my love.' Kyle moves to step between me and Ben, but Ben holds his ground.

'She's not your love.' Those eyes return to me. 'How could you do this to him?'

Kyle shoves closer. 'She *is* my love.'

'It was an accident. I didn't know.' Tears pool on my

lashes, blurring him into a phantom. I hang my head, hiding my face in my hands.

'You've made her cry!' Kyle pushes Ben out of the way and rushes to me.

He tries to hug me, but I twist away from him. 'Stop.'

And he does, he drops to his knees.

Ben takes a hesitant step closer. 'What happened?'

'I don't know. I felt funny and then . . .' Kyle wraps himself around my legs. How could Marissa, or any of the Hedonesses, like it when guys act like this? It's breaking my heart.

'Oh, my love, I'm—'

'No, Kyle. I'm not your love, I'm your cousin.' My voice wavers as I try to shake him free. He tightens his grip. 'Stop, Kyle.'

'Stop what, my love?' He looks at me with those love-glazed eyes and my heart breaks all over.

'Clinging to me, calling me "my love".' I scan the parking lot for Marissa – she'll know what to do. I spot her leaning against the van, a grin across her face. 'This isn't funny. I don't know how to make him stop,' I say.

Marissa shrugs. 'Maybe if you listened in class.'

'Help her already,' Ben says. 'This is wrong on so many levels.'

'Geez, chill. It will wear off soon.'

'*Chill?*' Ben points to Kyle, straddling my legs. 'You've got to be kidding me?'

198

I'm shaking. 'I don't know how long this will last. It's not fair to leave him like this.'

Marissa picks at her nails.

'Do something!' Ben shouts.

'Fine,' she says, holding out her hand to inspect her polish. 'You can tell him to forget he ever loved you. If he doesn't love you, he can't be subjected to your commands. But I think you should wait it out, just sayin'.'

I should've thought of that. That's what she did with the biker, and Ma with the pizza man. A flickering fear for my parents rushes through me again. I shove it back down. I can't think of them now. I have to fix Kyle.

I take a deep breath and face my cousin. He's gazing at me with a dreamlike devotion. 'Kyle, I want you to forget you ever loved me.'

In an instant, Kyle pushes to his feet. I flinch when I see the changed expression on his face. It's mean.

'Out of my way.' He shoves past, nearly knocking me over en route to Marissa.

I'm stunned; my mouth hangs open and I grip my side.

'That was quick turnaround,' Ben says, stepping closer to me.

Kyle cocks his head, looking like I'm chewed gum stuck to the bottom of new shoes.

Marissa giggles into her hand.

All the years of bearing the brunt of Marissa's mood swings and letting her get her way bubble up inside me and when I close my eyes I see red. *Fighter red*. I clench my fists. 'This isn't funny!'

Kyle crosses his arms and glares.

'There's no need to be an ass, it was an accident,' Ben says.

He's protecting me again and I should find comfort in it, but I don't. I know what I'm capable of now. I'll only hurt him. If I care for Ben, I need to let him go. Seeing Kyle treat me this way is heartbreaking – but all of me would shatter if it was Ben reacting like this.

Kyle snorts, rolls his eyes and marches to the store.

Ben offers me a sympathetic smile and gestures after Kyle questioningly. I nod, and he jogs to catch up to him. Hopefully Ben can figure out what's happening. Something definitely went wrong. I've never seen this type of reaction before.

I need answers, so I head to the only person who might know. Marissa.

'How did that happen?'

She's inches from her selfie cam, picking at her eyebrows, making a face similar to the one she makes when she puts on mascara. 'I guess you should've specified *romantic* love.'

It all falls into place – watching me rub my arms, telling Kyle I was upset, Kyle thinking I wanted a hug, and this, tricking me to tell my cousin to stop loving me. I was played by my best friend.

'You did this on purpose!'

She glances up from her cell with a smug look. 'I did exactly as you asked. If your cousin doesn't care for you any more, it's not my fault. I'm not the one who turned him.'

'How could you?' I feel sick so I make my way to an abandoned bench seat pulled out of some old car. The last thing I want is for Marissa to see how deeply this is impacting me.

I flop on to the seat, running my finger over a tear in the leather, trying to regain a smidgen of composure. After a few deep breaths, I call back. 'Can I fix this?'

'Fix what? He's doing what you asked him to do.'

'I've just met Kyle. Please, Marissa. I can't stand to lose more family.'

'Don't be stupid, Rach. He's not really your family. He told you already, he's adopted.'

Typical Marissa.

I should be crying, heartbroken, feeling the loss of the last three years with her, but I'm not. I'm too empty to cry. I hang my head and mumble, 'I should've just waited for my power to fade. This is my first time, he'd probably be back to normal in twenty-four hours.'

'I told you to wait.'

She doesn't get it – twenty-four hours or not, one minute is too long to force someone's will away. 'I couldn't bear seeing him like that.'

'You're so selfish sometimes,' she says.

'Excuse me?'

'You just had to go and do something to appease your conscience. Even you should know that every instruction given to a turned man stays even after the ability wears off. He's going to be like this for ever now.' She drops her phone in her bag and heads after Kyle to the store.

My fists clench and unclench as I try to clear my head.

Whatever bit of relationship that may be reparable between Marissa and I can wait. My priority is Kyle. I never thought this day would come – I'm actually regretting not paying attention in class. The only thing I can think of is turning him again. I never wanted to use my gift, but it can't be wrong when it's helping someone. The niggly voice in the back of my head is reminding me that other than not loving me, he isn't broken. Is Marissa right – would it be selfish to re-turn him? I focus on taking deep calming breaths, when a shuffling of light footsteps approaches. It's followed by a gentle pressure on my shoulder. Ben's shoes slide into view and I shrug his hand off.

Those damn shoes – they caused all of *this*.

'What?' I say, a little too sharp. I don't look up. I can't. I don't dare look into the eyes of the one person left caring for me, the person I could hurt the most. Everyone else is gone.

'He seems to be his same old self . . . at least to me,' Ben pauses when he sees me stiffen. 'Can't you command him to go back?' His voice is so kind and I hate how it picks my heart up. Still the electricity fizzes through me and I'm left weaker than before. I slide further down the bench, claiming space from him.

'It doesn't work like that. Our power makes men love us, but without the love we have no power. The only way is to re-turn him. I don't know if it's the right thing to do for Kyle.' I rub my eyes and glance over. I've never intentionally turned someone.

And it feels wrong.

'But he loved you before – you'd be correcting that.'

'By retaking his will.'

'Yeah, that's not cool.'

'I won't turn him again, not just for my sake. I'll have to get him to like me the old-fashioned way: by spending time together and getting to know each other.'

Ben goes silent for a beat before asking, 'What is it you do when you turn someone? Does it hurt them permanently?' It's obvious he isn't asking for Kyle. He stares up at the clouds and continues, 'Because Marissa, she pisses me off, but I'm still drawn to her. Is that . . . that's the after-effect, right?'

My lip quivers and I struggle to hold back tears. I know I can never be with Ben. I know that with every fibre, but it still hurts to hear how he reacts to Marissa.

In the end she even gets Ben.

He must notice how my body hardens, because he sits beside me, pulling me into his arms.

I try to push away, but he doesn't let go. 'Ben, no. What if I—'

'You won't,' he whispers, his fingers brushing my hair.

I'm a torrent of emotion – being in Ben's arms, being held by him, it's so comforting. It doesn't concern him that I could turn him. He trusts me. I let myself relax against him, feeling his warmth, the steady beat of his heart. And for a moment I am completely and utterly safe.

Then the electricity returns, burning beneath my skin, threatening to steal the boy who's winning over my heart. I can't risk it. I can't risk hurting him.

It takes everything within me to push out of his arms and walk away.

Twenty-Six

My heart is on fire.

'Rach, wait up.' Ben runs after me and even though I can't trust myself around him, I stop.

'Hey.' He grabs my shoulder, spinning me to face him. I keep my gaze down and focus on fighting back the energy that surges with his touch.

'Rach, you can't let her win. That's what she wants.'

'She's already won.' I risk glancing up and quickly divert my eyes. Seeing the concern on his face isn't going to help control my feelings. 'She turned Kyle against me. I know I didn't know him for very long. It's just—'

'It's nice having family.'

'Yeah.' I choke over my words, trying to hold back the waterworks. 'I have my ma but it's not the same. She *has* to love me. But Kyle had a choice, and we were just getting to know each other.' A tear escapes down my cheek.

'I know what that's like.' Ben reaches to wipe it but I turn my face.

'Please don't touch me.'

He tries again, raising his hand.

I pull away. 'No – it's not worth the risk. Just . . . don't, OK?' I turn my back. Now more than ever, I hate being a Hedoness.

'Rach, is this about more than Kyle?'

I snap around, my eyes challenging him to ask what he's implying.

'It's about love, isn't it? Not family love, but . . . you know, *love*.'

He asked – I can't believe he actually asked *that*. Of all the people to ask. I try to hide the awkwardness by lifting my chin. If he wants the answer I'll give it to him.

'You'd think that being related to Eros would come with some perks. Like, I don't know, maybe a boyfriend, or a magical first kiss. Not my luck. Instead I get to be alone because if I so much as touch a boy, my power takes everything from him.'

I try to calm my breathing as I wait for his response, hoping he'll say something, anything, to make me feel better. But his blank expression gives away that he's as clueless about this as I am. Which is a first – Ben always seems to know what to say. Somehow, his silence takes me back to that police officer with those damn gloves, too afraid to touch me.

Back to feeling like a freak.

'Rach, that can't be the only—'

'Don't,' I say, taking a step away from him and closer to the store. I'm done letting my power run my life.

I'm done running. 'Do you have any money I can borrow?'

Ben blinks for a moment too long. 'Money?'

'Yes, money. I just, I have to get something.'

There's a sudden strain in his jaw, but he reaches into his back pocket and pulls out two crumpled bills. He unfolds them and hands me a ten.

I know what I have to do. That officer was right. I'm different and I have to do whatever it takes to keep others from being different too.

With the bill clutched in my fist, I march to the store and shoulder through the door. A chain of bells jingle from the handle. Marissa and Kyle are talking to someone at the far end of the first isle. I ignore them and walk up to the elderly man at the till.

'Afternoon, miss, how can I help you?'

'Do you sell gloves?'

'Let me check what we have.'

I tap on the counter until he comes back carrying a handful of options. I pick through them, finding two leather sets – one red and one black – and a variety of floral gardening gloves. My mind flashes to Ma's navy-blue going-out gloves. I never realized what they were for before. S2L's warning starts looping again – *Your mother needs you.*

'I'll take the red ones, thanks.' I force a smile and plop the money down. When his back is to me, I slide the gloves on. The soft leather protects me from myself. This won't stop people from touching my exposed skin, but it's a start. He slaps the change into my red leather palm, eyeing me with deep curiosity. Seeing as it's not exactly glove weather, I don't blame him.

I close my fist around the coins, noticing a quarter. 'Is there a payphone?'

He nods to the restrooms.

'Thanks.'

The gloves stick to my pocket as I slide the rest of the change in. I should be using Quiver to call Paisley. But I'm not sure when I'll have another chance to connect. I'm desperate to find out about Ma, so using the phone is a risk I have to take. I plop a quarter in and begin dialling when a scuffle comes from the store back. Both the teller and I turn to see Marissa and Kyle standing shoulder-to-shoulder, blocking the aisle. Between their legs, I catch glimpses of a man convulsing on the ground.

'He slipped,' Marissa lies.

I glare at her and slam down the receiver, storming out of the store.

I throw open the van door to find Ben reclined in his seat, listing to the radio. 'She's at it again!'

He raises a brow and turns down the volume.

'Marissa! She just turned some guy.'

Ben sits up. 'What?'

I climb into the front beside him and roll down the window, and we keep our eyes peeled on the door.

208

Minutes pass painfully slowly, until finally Marissa and Kyle exit the store with armfuls of bags.

Ben hops out and rushes over to them. 'What'd you buy?' he asks, glancing past them. 'There's no way Ron gave us enough to cover all that.'

'Ron?' Marissa's grinning at me. 'You should know by now I don't need money to get by.'

'What did you do?' Ben tries to step around them, but Kyle blocks him.

'It was awesome, man. She kissed some dude and he gave her everything she asked for. Check this out.' He holds up a set of keys.

'Tell me you're not that stupid.' Ben runs his hands through his hair, keeping them tangled at the base of his neck.

'They're for that SUV.' Kyle points to the black Tahoe with tinted windows, parked behind a rusted propane tank in the corner of the lot.

'You're in the wrong car,' she yells to me, and swaggers over to the vehicle, clicking the doors unlocked with the fob. 'I got us an upgrade.'

Marissa swings open the rear and is about to toss her bags in when she pauses. She peers inside, a sudden look of confusion on her face.

'What the hell?'

Twenty-Seven

Marissa slams the door closed again, leaning against the bumper.

Her reaction makes me feel uneasy so I make my way over to the SUV.

Ben's with Kyle a few yards away, but Marissa's odd behaviour catches his attention too. 'What's going on, Riss?'

Marissa says nothing, but she seems to be having trouble breathing.

'Riss? What's in there?' I reach for the handle but she raises the fob and clicks the doors locked again. 'What the hell? Just open it.'

Ben's almost at the SUV. 'Marissa, open the door.' His patience is dropping fast. 'Open the door, or I'll take the keys from you myself.'

She turns her back but he reaches around and grabs them from her death-like grip.

'Ouch,' she complains, overdramatically rubbing her hand.

He ignores her and presses unlock. I open the door, stand back, and look in.

There are no seats except for the front two. Instead, a computer station with various monitors and speakers flanks one side, its screens filled with surveillance photos of us at the church with Pastor Ron.

We stand there, staring, mouths agape.

Kyle comes up behind us. 'Oh shit.'

'It's official, you're an idiot.' I'm shaking. I don't care how mean it sounds. Marissa isn't exactly my favourite person right now. 'Seems you have a thing for turning cops.'

'Shut up, Rach! It's not like he announced what he was in the store.' Marissa stomps away, smoothing down her hair, trying to regain her composure.

'Even if he did, it wouldn't stop you,' I say, getting in her face. 'All you care about is your damn self.'

'How dare you! This whole mess started when Mother Superior asked me to help *you*. This is your fault.'

'*My* fault? I'm not the one who just turned a cop with James-Bond-level surveillance equipment. This is on you.'

Marissa lurches at me, fists clenched.

'Not again.' Ben steps between us. 'We don't have time for fighting. We need to fix this mess.' He pauses, letting us soak in the gravity of our situation. 'Where's the officer?'

When she refuses to answer, he grabs her face so she can't look away. 'Marissa, where is he?'

Jealousy washes through me. I hate that he can touch her without the same consequences as touching me.

211

Marissa diverts her eyes from Ben. 'I told him to go to sleep in the bathroom and not leave until someone told him to.'

I roll my eyes. 'Of course you did.'

Ben drops her chin and holds up his hand. 'Rachel, please. You're not helping.'

I ignore him, a wave of worry filling me. 'So that's it then. We've been found. We can't go to the river house, not now that they know about Ron. My parents are screwed!'

Marissa leans past Ben to glare at me. 'Oh goody, we live to flee another day.'

I clench my fists.

'Well,' Ben says with a deep breath, 'the good news is we've detained this officer and can throw them off our trail. Temporarily, at least.'

He's right, we still have a head start, and that's something. 'Marissa, you need to fix this,' I say, grabbing her arm to try and get her attention. 'Go in there and ask him if he was alone. If not we need to know where his partner is. And if he is alone, I don't know, tell him he isn't a cop or something. Last thing we need is him calling in reinforcements.'

'Fine,' says Marissa, glaring down at my red-gloved hand before shrugging it off her arm.

'Then let's get going,' says Ben. 'We shouldn't hang around. Kyle?'

Kyle strides over, a bag of potato chips in his hand. 'What's the plan?' he says to Ben, ignoring me completely.

I shrug off the wave of sadness and focus on how to get us out of this mess. We have two vehicles, and nowhere to go. The police know where we are. Shaking them off should be our priority. Then I need to get to my ma – and she'll help save my dad.

'We'll split up,' I say, realising it's the best way to lose the police. 'If Marissa and I take the Tahoe, you boys the van, and we both go in opposite directions, there's a good chance one group of us will get away. And if the police pull you over you can blame everything on us.'

Ben steps close. 'They'll have a GPS tracking system in the SUV.'

'Then we'll swap it out as soon as we can.'

His eyes dart over my face. 'I don't like separating. But it's a good plan.'

Marissa places her hands on her hips. 'I'm not being left with her.'

Ben takes a calming breath. 'If Kyle and I take the SUV, you two have the best chance to—'

'Nope.' She crosses her arms and turns her back to him.

Kyle laughs. He's acting so weird. 'No use arguing, man. Rissa's made up her mind. Let's split up. We can each protect one of the girls.'

'I don't need protection,' Marissa says.

Ben sighs, and runs a hand through his hair. 'We know you don't but we need to split up somehow.'

My plan is smarter, but unless I duct tape her into the Tahoe, she won't come with me, and at this point, I don't have time to waste arguing. We need to get going, now. Part of me wants to go with Ben. A huge part of me. He has this way of making me feel safe when no one else can. But I'm struggling with controlling my gift around him. The buzz grows stronger beneath my skin, and I'm afraid that soon looking at him will make me explode. My gloves can't protect either of us from that. Then there's Kyle. To say he's being a jerk is the understatement of the century. Jerk or not, he's my cousin, and I'm not going to give up on him. He doesn't like me now, but maybe he can learn to again.

I blurt out my answer. 'I'm going with Kyle.'

Both Ben and Kyle stare at me like I've lost it.

'Me?' Kyle points to himself.

All I can do is nod.

Marissa puts her hand on her hip. 'She does have a point.'

'What point?' Kyle throws up his arms. 'She's made no point. I don't want to go with her.'

'Rach, wait.' Ben grabs me and the electricity is palpable.

I yank away.

He blinks and steps back. 'Why, uh, Kyle?'

214

'He's my cousin.' I can't bear looking into those eyes, so blue and full of questions.

'He had you in tears.' He steps closer. 'Why do you really want to go with him?'

I hug my stomach, afraid I'll succumb to the need to reach out and touch him. Trust Ben to see through my motives.

Despite how much I want to tell him that being near him makes me want to lose control, I can't. Even saying it makes my powers well up inside me. But it's not easy to keep it in either. And it's not just about how hot he is, or how good he looks with his shirt off, or the way his dark brown hair makes his blue eyes pop. I wish I could tell him how I feel, how I love the way he protects people, listens intently, puts others first. The way he cares. Hell, he's risked his dream of becoming a police officer to help us. But wishes don't change the facts – I can't risk my power hurting him.

'I just do,' I say, avoiding his eyes.

'Fine, all right,' he replies in a clipped tone. 'Shall we?' He waves Marissa after him to the SUV.

'No way. We're taking the van.' She picks up her bags and heads across the lot. 'Right after I deal with this cop.'

Kyle runs after her, leaving me alone with Ben again.

Ben sighs. 'So where are you going to go?'

I'm done running. I'm going back to New York. I need to find a way to rescue my family and fix this messy web

Marissa's spun around us. I kick a rock and glance down the road. There's a blue highway sign with a big white arrow on top. My heart quickens.

It reads – *Vallecillo, NL, Mexico, 1180 miles, next right*. Perfect.

'You and Marissa take the highway right and head for the Mexican border.'

'OK,' Ben says. 'The police don't have jurisdiction there and we can probably find a way in without passports. I'm sure Marissa will be up for that challenge. But what about you two?'

'Don't worry about us. And be careful. You might lose the police, but the Committee could be there.'

Ben nods, and looks over to the gas station. Marissa and Kyle are coming out of the shop, making their way over to us. He looks at me – a goodbye hangs off his lips. Then it hits me. This could be the last time I see him.

I suck in a breath, staring back into those deep blue eyes. He saved my life, both literally and metaphorically, and I'll miss him more than I can bear. Benjamin Blake is the closest I've come to falling in love.

Twenty-Eight

There are times in life when you surprise yourself. This is one of them. I'm in a stolen SUV, trying to evade the police, looking for a vehicle to steal and a place to ditch the Tahoe. That's not something I would've ever guessed possible a few days ago. A strange part of me feels brave and capable and in control for the first time.

Still, it wasn't easy watching Marissa and Ben drive in the opposite direction; my eyes were glued to the side-view mirror until the van was all but a speck. The only good thing about this whole mess is that the farther I am from Ben, the less destructive my power is.

I try to think like Ben would. Going through every possible scenario of finding a way back into New York. I'll do anything to get my family out of jail. I glance at Kyle. Now that I know what I'm capable of, my family is all I've got.

I don't tell Kyle we're heading back for them, not yet. For now, I keep my eyes on the road. We've been driving for almost thirty minutes and haven't come across anything. We have, however, passed a large billboard of a

217

man biting a young girl's neck, featuring the cast of *My Vampire Alien Life*. I can't escape it, even here. I glance out the back again, checking no one is following us.

'Anything?' Kyle asks.

'Coast's clear,' I say.

He lets out a long breath, and I can't help noticing that he seems annoyed.

'We'll find something to swap with soon,' I say.

Kyle's grip tightens on the wheel, but he keeps his eyes ahead. 'When we do, I'm going to stay with the Tahoe.'

I frown. 'You want to split up?'

He doesn't answer.

'We should stay together.'

'Yeah, well it's not up to you.'

'I miss the old you,' I mumble, straightening my gloves and reaching for the radio. I flick it on to a rock station and leave it there. We can argue some more when we find a car, but for now I could use something to take my mind off things. I flop back into the plush seat, staring out the window and listening to the lyrics.

> *He could be your hero,*
> *If you let him try,*
> *Follow your own arrow,*
> *Let your heart fly.*

What are the chances? I lean forward and turn up the volume. 'Do you know who sings this?'

Kyle turns it off.

'I was listening to that.'

'I prefer silence.'

I spin to face him. 'We have to get past—'

'I also prefer you not looking at me.'

'Come on! This is getting ridiculous.' I turn back to the window. My shoulders stiffen. 'You know. I was really excited when I found out I had a cousin. I don't really have a big family. It's just me, my parents and my nani, but then you and Joyce—'

Kyle reaches forward and turns the radio on, cranking it full blast to drown me out.

'Really?' I turn the volume back to a normal level. Kyle pushes my hand away and cranks it back up. 'I don't want to fight with you, Kyle. This isn't who you are. Can we talk?'

The SUV hisses to a tyre-screeching stop. 'I'm done!'

'What?'

'I can't deal with you.'

When I don't move he grabs my cell from the dash charger and powers it up, searching through for Marissa's contact.

'Don't use that!'

He ignores me and presses call, leaving it on speaker. I try to grab it but he holds me back. After a few rings she picks up.

'The van isn't so bad after all.' Her obnoxiously happy voice cracks over the line. 'There's a cable I can use to charge my phone and it has satellite radio.'

'Tell Ben I'm finished,' Kyle says, glaring at me. 'She's annoying. I can't stand her.'

All I can do is stare, mouth half open.

'Kyle?' Marissa says, her voice low, a warning.

There's a shuffling on the other end of the line.

'Hey,' says Marissa, 'I was using that.' She isn't talking to Kyle.

'What the hell?' It's Ben, and just hearing his voice makes me feel safe. 'Wait there. We'll turn around.'

'We shouldn't waste valuable escape time,' Marissa says on the other side. 'The police are probably following us.'

'We're coming to you, meet half way,' Kyle says, cutting off Marissa. He tosses me back the phone, not bothering to hang up.

A large part of me wants to slip off my glove and reach across and touch his bare arm. It would be easy to turn him again, to make him care. Instead I grip my phone like a lifeline. 'This isn't you.'

He grabs my cardigan off the seat and throws it on my lap.

I sit there, blinking at him. This can't actually be happening. Something flares up inside me. 'No matter how you feel for me, I don't deserve to be treated like

220

this,' I say, grabbing my things and, even though I know I should go with him to meet Ben, I get out of the SUV. 'Tell Ben I'll wait for him here.'

I don't know what I was expecting, but Kyle doesn't hesitate. He pulls the truck into a U-turn and leaves me, all alone, on the side of the unfamiliar road.

Twenty-Nine

I kick rocks off the shoulder, replaying the fight with Kyle. I don't know what I could've done differently. One thing's for sure, not listening to Marissa would've been a good start. I shake my head and kick another rock, missing it and stubbing my toe.

'Seriously?' I pick it up and throw it at a tree.

Time passes painfully slow as I pace on the gravel shoulder. Other than the rustle of tree branches and the odd bird chirp, it's silent and empty. I plop on to a small boulder and dig through my pocket for the phone, pulling it out to reveal my battery's too low for a call. It's been nearly an hour since Kyle ditched me.

Ben should've been here by now.

The sun will set soon, and I can't help thinking he's not coming. If he isn't, I can't very well sleep here, on the side of the road, next to the woods. I stand up, slip my cardigan on and start walking, hoping that it won't be far to somewhere with a phone or a way to New York.

The walk is hard. My legs ache, my stomach rumbles. The evening breeze chills me. I hug my arms, but my knees are like icicles. I'm regretting wearing shorts. I'm not warm enough to last a night like this. And worse than the cold is the loneliness. It makes an awful companion. It whispers that I'm not good enough, I'm too freaky, I'm the worst daughter and granddaughter and friend, it tells me there's no point trying to help my family because I'll let everyone down – just look what I did to Kyle.

I imagine Nani on the other side of the world with no clue what's going on, Ma and Dad locked up in cells, Dad screaming to be near Ma. I used to pity him, but maybe his life isn't so bad. He has one focus, he knows what he wants and he goes for it.

My chest aches from how much I miss them.

In the end we all want the same thing.

Love.

Ma's words fill my head, 'Eros looks out for his descendants. If you surrender to love, Eros will find you.'

I glance up at the cloudless sky. Surrender to love. What does it even mean? I clear my throat. 'Eros, if you're out there, somewhere, I could really use your help right now.' I feel silly for even saying it. It's not like he's going to descend from Olympus to help me – the girl who hates what he's made her.

A revving engine booms down the road. I skip off to the side and hide behind a tree. I peek around the trunk and see Pastor Ron's van approaching. For the first time in an hour, I smile. I tug my gloves down and run from cover, waving like some wild woman.

The van comes to a screeching halt. Ben jumps out. 'Are you all right?' His voice is solid, with an edge of relief. He rounds the front and reaches for me. Instinctually, I pull back. Frown lines form around his eyes and I want to kiss them away, to ask him to hold me, to never let me go, but I don't. I can't. I step further back.

He backs off too, and opens my door.

'Thanks for coming for me,' I say quietly, and climb in.

'Yeah. It was hard getting away. Marissa wasn't exactly thrilled to be left with Kyle.' He smiles, but it never makes it to his eyes. 'I'm glad you're OK.' He closes the door and goes around to his side. It's warm in here and I start to thaw.

He waits for me to put my seatbelt on before starting the van. 'We lost a lot of time and need to make up for it. I'm going to need to drive as fast as this van will push. Is that OK with you? I don't like putting you at risk, but right now I think there's more risk of being caught.'

'Yes,' I choke out, still not used to the level of respect I get from Ben.

He turns on the radio and speeds off down the road. Every once in a while, one of us will brave looking at the other. When our eyes lock, I smile and return to looking out the window. Despite the burning beneath my skin, it feels right being back with Ben.

'We'll drive until we need gas,' he says. 'Then we'll find a place to refill and grab some food. Kyle only left me with forty bucks, so hopefully that can get us to the border.'

'The border?' I blurt, then realize he's still following our old plan of escaping the police in Mexico. He doesn't know about New York.

'It's a good plan and when we find somewhere to stop we can ask them to reroute us to the nearest crossing.'

I nod; there's no point arguing with him until I can come up with a way to get into New York that avoids all the traffic cams Ben warned us of. Besides, maybe there was something to Kyle's wanting to separate. Maybe I should leave Ben in Mexico and travel on, on my own. I hate the idea of being away from him again, but it's the only way I can think to keep him safe.

I grab my cell and plug it into the cord hanging from the dash. It flashes to life. I search to see if Paisley is online – she isn't, but Marissa is. My finger hovers over her name, tempted to press call and check in on them, but also not wanting to hear her voice.

The phone rings and for a second I think I accidently pushed the button until I realize it's her who's calling. I hold it up to Ben. 'Do I answer?'

He shrugs.

I decide to, just in case it's important. 'Hello?'

'Rachel, hi. Should we keep going to Mexico or did the swap change things?' Marissa asks.

'Say hi to Rachel for me, my love,' Kyle says in the background.

'Wait.' I fumble the phone in my shaky, gloved hands. 'Why did Kyle call you "my love"?'

'I dunno, Rachel. Do we continue to Mexico or not?'

I grip the phone tighter. 'Answer me. Why did Kyle call you "my love"?'

She sighs. 'I don't know . . . Maybe because you can't take a joke and I knew you wouldn't have the lady balls to fix it. I felt bad and did it for you. I turned him and told him to stop treating you like crap. You're welcome.'

'You what?' I should be happy that Kyle doesn't hate me any more, but I'm not. I feel selfish and broken and so worried for him. 'Promise me you didn't turn him. Marissa, promise me this is a joke!' All of me shakes now, not just my hands. When she doesn't answer. I bite my lip to keep from shouting. I put the phone on speaker, leaning back, not wanting to touch it and be any closer to her than needed.

'Don't worry, my powers will wear off in a couple days. Then he'll go back to his normal friendly self, but this time with his Rachel-loving side. It's not that big a deal.'

Ben shakes his head and offers me a look of sympathy. 'Where,' he clears his throat, 'where are you guys?'

'Hi, Ben!' Her voice picks up. 'I'm not sure – it's almost dark here so it's hard to read street signs.'

A loud thumping static comes over the line.

Ben frowns and leans closer to the phone. 'Can you turn down your radio? I can't hear over the bass.'

'It's not the radio . . .' The sound overpowers Marissa.

Ben frowns and pulls the van over, putting us in park. 'Hello?'

I grab the phone, checking to see if the volume's maxed. It is, but it beeps the low battery reminder, so I plug it back in.

'Riss? What's happening?'

'What is that?' she says.

'Marissa, what do you see?' Ben leans over to ask.

'There's a spotlight . . .' She pauses and the thumping gets louder. 'I can barely hear you guys. Speak up—'

A high-pitched scream interrupts, and it takes a moment to realize it's their brakes.

'Kyle, look out—' Marissa's cry blasts through the phone speaker.

'*Hang on, my love!*' Kyle yells.

I take the phone, ignoring the battery warning. 'What's happening?'

'Road block, police barricade, the noise . . . helicopter.' Marissa sounds frightened, confused.

'They found them.' Ben turns to me. 'We have to get out of here. Now!'

'Rachel, this . . . *Kyle, watch out!*'

There's a harmony of shouts, the squeal of tyres, popping metal. I glance at Ben, nearly dropping my cell when shattering glass and crunching bone come through the line too.

'Marissa?'

The speaker blasts an eerie hissing sound.

'Marissa! Marissa?' I try to breathe but my lungs refuse to cooperate, and my hands shake so bad that I hand Ben the phone.

He puts his ear to the speaker, holding a finger to his lips.

That's when I hear Marissa cough.

'Rach? Rachel . . .' Her words slur out. 'Rach? Oh god!'

I ignore Ben's look warning me to keep quiet. 'I'm here, Riss. What's happening? Are you OK?'

'Rach, we don't have much time. They're coming . . . I've done so much – Ben, Kyle, all the mean shit I pulled . . .' She wheezes in a breath. 'I was jealous of you . . . of your relationship with your mom and your strength and . . . I promise to do better, be better . . .' She stops to cough again, her breathing raspy. 'Rachel, you're my best friend. The . . . only one who has stuck with me . . .'

'Riss, just tell me what's happening, where are you? We're coming to get you!'

I glance at Ben, eyes full of worry.

'*My love? Are you all right, my love? Leave her alone!*' Kyle's voice is unsteady, but other than the fact he keeps calling Marissa 'my love', he doesn't sound injured.

I grab the phone back, holding it out so Ben can hear, and get out of the van for some fresh air.

'Rachel, we have to go *now*.' Ben waves me over. 'Hang up and get back in the van!'

'But . . .?'

'We can't help them if we get caught too.'

He's right. I hate to admit it – even more so, I hate to leave Marissa and Kyle. But all we can do now is get to a safe place and come up with a plan. 'We'll come back for you,' I say, hoping Marissa and Kyle can still hear. My hands tremble as I hold the phone out to him. I won't be the one to hang up. I can't be.

Ben takes it from me, turns it off, smashing it on the sill until it splits in two, then throws it out the window.

'What if they try to get in touch, or Paisley's ma calls with news?'

'That's exactly what I'm worried about. We've taken one too many gambles with the phones. I have no doubt the police will look up their last call. Listen, Rach, they're alive, that's all that matters.'

Everything in me wants to go after them, to help them, but Ben's right. We need to be smart. I'm surprised by how much I care about Marissa and Kyle after everything they've done to hurt me. Especially Marissa. I can't believe she turned Kyle.

'Why?' I mumble, as I put on my seatbelt and close the door.

Ben pulls back on the road. 'I don't know why, accidents happen . . .'

'I mean, why did she have to turn Kyle?'

He shrugs, his Adam's apple bobbing as he swallows. 'People do strange things when they're scared.'

I allow myself to make eye contact with him. His unbending eyes hold mine where his body can't, and somehow it's enough.

Thirty

We drive in silence down the deserted road for over an hour. Not one car passes us. Even though we're in the middle of god know knows where, the further we get from the police the more relieved I feel.

'I hope we find something soon,' Ben says.

I send him a quizzical look.

'We're low on gas, and I'm starving.'

'I'm hungry too.'

A couple hours ago I didn't even want to look at food. All the stuff with Kyle and Marissa left me sick to my stomach. But the safety of Ben lets me relax enough to feel the hunger. Last time I ate was at the diner.

Arrow iner flashes through my head.

That sign was an odd coincidence. I can't help wondering if it was a *sign* sign, the kind my mother spoke of. And if so, I wish I knew what it meant. Marissa would tell me it meant to embrace my gift, to be who I was created to be. I can't argue that it would be easier sometimes – if only my power didn't scare me so much. I glance at Ben, wondering what it would feel like to kiss him, and even just thinking about it alights my power within me. I'm burning up, so hot and fast that I have to take my cardigan off to cool down. I lean into the door, away from Ben, and any chance of my power erupting. The fear is too real.

I remember the frightened look on Paisley's victim's face, the red-haired boy, who freaked out on live TV and said otherworldly creatures took him. He was beyond fear, and the reporter believed him. Everyone in New York is probably still hunting for the alien that abducted their boys, which can't help our current predicament. I should be there too – doing whatever it takes for my parents. No matter how scared it makes me.

Fearing what I am has kept me from too many things. If only my ability could control fear, it would be a lot more helpful than the stupid love curse.

'*Control fear?*' I whisper, sitting up in my seat, suddenly knowing what to do to help my family.

'What?' Ben glances over.

'How much further to the border?' I ask.

He shrugs. 'We don't have GPS and someone broke your phone so we can't check.'

'Someone?'

He laughs. 'My guess is twelve hours or so, that's if we're going in the right direction. The sun's setting behind us so we're travelling east. Why?'

'I have a plan.'

'Oh yeah?' He smiles at me.

'I'm going to turn myself in.'

He laughs.

'I mean it. It's the only way.'

He falters. 'You're serious?'

'Yes.'

The van swerves a little. Ben rights it again and turns to look at me. 'Rach, you need to think this through.'

'I have.'

'I doubt that,' he says, eyes facing forward once more.

'What motivates you?' I ask.

'What does this have to do with your plan?'

'Just answer me, Ben.'

'I don't know . . . love?' he half-heartedly replies.

'This whole mess makes me realize, it isn't love – I mean yes, it's a factor, but fear is one too. For me anyway.'

'Fear?' He works his jaw, keeping his eyes on the road. 'So fear is your big plan?'

'I'm going to use it to get the police to listen to me.'

'Oh yeah, you're going to march up to them and tell them a scary story?'

It's a joke, he's smiling, but he won't be when he hears the rest. I'm not even confident it will work, or that I want to do it. But if there's ever a time to do something wrong, it's now. I take a deep breath. 'I'll turn myself in, tell them I'm one of those vampire aliens. I'll make a big scene of it, so there are witnesses.'

Ben looks at me, a little too quickly because he swerves the van again in the process.

'If I confess to all the other abductions and everything, my family and Marissa can go free. I'm going to say I forced them to do it, brainwashed them.'

'No one will believe you.'

'I have to try.'

He sighs, his eyes staring forward but never connecting with the road. 'Rachel, you can't—'

'What other option do we have?'

'What about you?' He glances at me, his eyes so full of determination that it makes me hold my breath. 'They don't deserve what you're offering. Did you even think of what they'll do to you when you're arrested? You're telling them you're supernatural. That's not something they'll ignore.'

He's right, I know it's a risk. I'm scared shitless about it. But what other choice do I have? 'It's my family, my best friend. I have to do something.'

His shoulders droop and he lets out a long breath. 'What about me? Where do I fit into your plan?'

I pause, taking in the weight of his words. What about him? I can't very well tell him everything – that he's the reason why I'm doing this. That he's the one who taught me how to put others first, even when it's uncomfortable, even when it goes against what I believe in. 'I'll drop you at the border and turn back.'

'Turn back?'

'I'm going to New York.' I lift my chin. 'There isn't another way.'

'You're just going to do this all on your own? Do you even know how to get there?'

'I'll figure it out,' I say, looking out the side window so he can't see the fear in my eyes. He doesn't answer, but I watch him in the reflection and the way his jaw flexes and his eyes dart across the road, I can tell he's thinking. And whatever he's thinking is causing him to grip the steering wheel so hard his knuckles blanch. I understand, though – it isn't exactly like going to jail is something I want. But if I can save them . . . one life for several – it's the only option that makes sense.

'So, you're just going to drive into New York and hope you don't get noticed?'

Drive, or turn someone to drive for me. 'It's not like I can hop on a plane. I don't have other options.'

He stares back at the road. 'If you had access to a boat, I could get us there.'

'Us?' I ask.

Thirty-One

We've driven for hours and the sun has long since set, so we don't even have that as a guide any more. Twisted shadows from the trees cast on to the road. It's creepy, the silence, the darkness.

Ben still hasn't answered my question – that, and the lack of conversation, is overwhelming. I try to lighten the mood. 'Do you like Mexican food?'

He glares at me. 'We'll talk more about your *plan* later.'

'So? Not a fan of Mexican?'

Ben doesn't laugh, doesn't even respond.

Before I press further, I'm distracted by a white blur between the trees – at first I think it's a person. Why would a random person be in the middle of nowhere? I twist in my seat, hoping for another glimpse. Ben's still driving like a racer, and I can't find it again.

I turn forward and catch Ben watching me, then his eyes dart out the window.

'What's that?' He points to his side of the road.

It's another white object. I sit up to get a better look. It's a statue of two people dancing placed precariously on the edge of the cement. Ben drives close enough for me to make out that the statues are adorned with hair and clothes. It's creepy how real they look. They hold a sign, but we pass too quickly so I can only make out the word *Little*.

'Why would someone leave that there?'

He shrugs and continues on. 'It's a weird one.'

A short way down, the road forks to the left but Ben continues on the straight route. There's another statue on my side. An archer, with her bow and arrow drawn and pointing to the left of the fork. A sign hanging from the arrow reads *That Way*. I gulp down the sneaker-sized knot forming in my throat.

When you focus on it, signs are everywhere.

Ben's about to pass the turn-off. I dive across and crank the wheel. The van screeches as it slides to the left.

'Rachel! What the hell?'

'We should follow the sign,' I say.

'Next time, just ask.' He straightens the van and turns down the road. We pass many statues – a child with a balloon, a juggler, a small crowd of tourists complete with hats and cameras, each illuminated in the headlights like frozen ghosts.

We drive a few yards further and come across a field full of statues and a big sign that says *Little Tokyo Sculptures and River Tours*. Ben slows, pulling to the shoulder. The moon's glow breaks through a patch of grey clouds, sending an eerie shadow over the figures.

'What is this?' I ask, reaching for the door and pressing the power lock button. Even though the statues don't move, I don't trust them. It's all too weird.

Down the middle of the field is a long dirt road, and for some reason – maybe curiosity or maybe madness – Ben turns the van down the path.

'What are you doing?' The dips in the road send me into further panic. I cling to the handle. 'I don't like this. Let's go back.'

'You're the one who wanted to come this way. Besides, it's a safe place to spend the night, off the road and out of view.'

'Spend the night?' It hits me. We're going to sleep in the van. Something about that makes my insides burn. It's going to be hard as it is to shut my brain off from worrying about my family. Being confined to a small space with Ben won't help me get any sleep. He catches my eye and grins like he can read my mind. I turn away, cheeks heating, heart pounding at the thought.

Ben pulls into a small opening between two statues and shuts off the engine. He hops into the back and sets to work folding down the seats, giving us a nice flat place to sleep. When the back seat is stored, he notices Kyle's blankets and tosses me one, making a sleeping-bag-sized bed for himself with the other, and using his pizza sweatshirt for a pillow. When I don't move, he pops his head into the front. 'You gonna sleep in that seat?'

'Oh, I—'

He pats the small empty space beside him. 'It'll be more comfortable back here.'

I push down my internal warning alarm and crawl into the back, spreading out the blanket and rolling my cardigan into a pillow. Ben's beside me, taking off his shoes, then his shirt, when he starts unbuckling his trousers, I turn around, waiting for him to get under the covers. My entire body heats at the thought of him, an arm's length away. Once he's covered by the blanket, I kick off my Converse, but leave my gloves on. I pull out my ponytail, letting my curls fall everywhere, and hurry under my blanket, holding it to me like a lifeline and feeling safer now that my body is mostly hidden.

He rustles in the makeshift bed until he's settled, then takes deep heavy breaths as his body relaxes.

'Goodnight, Rach.'

'Goodnight.' I adjust my cardigan pillow, tug down my gloves, facing the door so I don't have to look at him. Still, I count his breaths, wondering how on earth I'll sleep with him so close. The air between us buzzes with electricity. I can't be the only one feeling it.

I yawn.

'Can't sleep?' Ben asks.

'No.' *There's too much on my mind.*

'You worried about your parents?'

'Yeah.' *Them and you.*

'We'll find a way to help them.'

'We?' My heart skips a beat. This is his second time saying that.

'I'm not going to Mexico, not without you. And if you're still set on going back to New York, I'm coming too.'

I want to argue with him, to make him go to Mexico where he'll be safe, but I also want to dive across the van and hug him. Knowing that he's willing to be with me to the end, to help me save my parents, makes it less overwhelming somehow.

'Ben?' I roll on to my side, facing him.

'Yeah?'

'Why don't you ever talk about your family?' The van falls quiet as I wait for his response – an awkward amount of time passes. 'It's OK if you don't want to.'

'No,' he exhales sharply, 'it's not that. It's hard.' His breaths turn to quick shallow bursts, and he sits up, watching me in the low moonlight streaming through the window. And I watch him too, feeling the heat rush through me as I take in the way the light reflects the sadness in his eyes.

I roll on to my back, staring up at the domed ceiling, afraid if I watch him any longer I'll pull him into a comforting hug. 'Why hard?' I ask.

'They passed away a few years ago, my little brother and Gramps too.'

I suck in a sharp breath, remembering the sadness I first felt on him back in the jail cell. His frayed cuffs, his worn clothes – he's an orphan. No wonder he doesn't talk about it. I turn back on to my side so I can watch him again; watch those lips form his undoing.

'I got a call at school.' He speaks so quietly it's hard to hear. 'At lunch. I remember it like it was yesterday, the teacher coming to get me from the cafeteria.' He stares out the window, his eyes so distant. 'They were taking Gramps to a doctor's appointment. It was a hit and run. A drunk driver. At lunchtime, can you believe that?'

Tears form in my eyes. 'I'm so sorry.' I don't know what else to say. 'Is that why you don't drink?' I instantly regret my curiosity.

'Yeah . . .' He breathes an awkward laugh. 'It's also why I wanted to be a cop.'

I hate that he says *wanted*. It's my fault he might lose that dream. And now that I know why it's so important to him, I hate myself even more.

'Let's hope my plan works and you still can be.'

'Let's not talk about your plan right now.' He doesn't sound so hopeful.

I sit up, hugging the blanket to my body. 'Ben?'

He looks at me, his eyes roaming over my face, my hair, as if he's really taking me in. He reaches for a rogue curl, hesitates, and pulls back. 'Yeah?'

My heart's racing so hard I almost forget what I was going to say. 'Um, for what it's worth, I think you'd be an amazing cop.'

'Thanks.' He smiles and flops back.

'Rach?'

'Yeah?'

'What do you want to be, you know, if we ever get out of this mess?'

I pull my knees close. 'I thought about being a social worker. Helping kids with absentee parents. I even filled out my college applications.'

'Rach?'

'Yes, Ben?'

'For what it's worth, I think you'd be an awesome social worker.'

I smile. 'Thanks.'

He yawns and rolls over. I follow his lead and curl into the scratchy blanket. I lie there for a while, watching his back. Soon my body relaxes, and my eyes close from the weight of exhaustion. It doesn't take long for my mind to go blank.

Then the van wiggles and warm air blows across my cheek. My eyes flutter open. I frown, not trusting the image in front of me.

Ben?

He's right up close, his dark hair falling into his eyes. Those eyes. They flick to my mouth and a smile spreads

242

across his face. He brings his lips to my cheek. I suck in a breath as he presses them against my skin.

'Ben,' I groan. His kisses trail down my jaw, down my neck. He pulls my T-shirt, kissing the delicate skin on my collarbone. 'Ben, you shouldn't . . .'

He puts his finger to my lips. 'Shhh. I know what you're going to say, and I don't care.'

He holds my face. Brings his lips to mine. The moment they touch, my gift pulses feeling like magic. Then it erupts – jerking me up and pushing him back. 'Ben, no!'

He smiles, trailing my bottom lip with his thumb. 'I'm fine, see. Tell me to stop.'

I pant in mouthfuls, trying to regain my breath. 'Stop. I don't . . .'

His lips come crashing back.

He didn't listen. He didn't obey – he still has his will – he's kissing me, a toe-curling, heart-pounding, world-shaking kiss.

Relief floods through me like a tide, pushing and pulling, and melting me into his touch. I wrap my arms around his neck, tangle my fingers in his hair, pull him closer.

He can't be close enough.

Tears escape from the joy of knowing my gift doesn't work on Ben.

I can be with Ben.

Thirty-Two

Two strong hands grip my shoulders, shaking me. 'Rach? Rach!'

I jerk up, nearly bumping heads with Ben. My fingers trail my lips where the memory of his kiss still lingers. When my eyes brave finding his, he raises an eyebrow and takes in my weird expression.

'You OK? You were calling me in your sleep.'

'In my sleep?' I repeat the words, not wanting to believe them true. 'You mean you didn't, we didn't just . . .?'

He frowns. 'What's going on?'

I was sleeping.

'Oh god, it was a dream.' I throw the blanket aside, shoving Ben back as I pull open the door and run from the van, embarrassment fuelling my speed. The interior light illuminates all the freaky-looking statues. I weave my way through them, trying to get away from him. Dream or not, it was too real – too good. I'll never be able to shake the memory of his lips. If there was a chance at ignoring my feelings for Ben, it's gone now.

I stop by a statue of a girl on a bench staring into a vanity mirror. I sit in the empty space beside her, looking into her mirror. In the low moonlight my loose curls almost glow. They hang over my shoulders, and the light dusting of embarrassment is still warm on my cheeks. I'm not the same girl Ben met that day in the jail cell, the person he labelled a kid. Too much has happened. My face is different. Brave. Ready to embrace being a Hedoness and do whatever it takes to save my family.

Why don't I feel so brave?

My eyes flick to my freckles, remembering that time back at Joyce's when Ben first noticed them. The way he made me feel in that moment shifted my world.

I sigh and cling tightly to the vanity, aching for water to wash away the intensity of the dream, his touch, his lips. The night chill soon wakes me to reality, though. I'm a stupid girl with a crush. I've let myself get lost in the hope that he feels the same. I let myself think that his willingness to help me was something more. My dream was proof of that.

'Don't be stupid, Rach.' The words come out sounding too much like Marissa. I rub my face. 'He likes helping people. He wants to be a cop.' That's Ben. He helps the police, he helps the pizza delivery man, he even helps Marissa. He's a helper, that's all, nothing more.

The best gift I can give Ben is freedom.

I push up from the bench, standing in the darkness, taking one last breath before wandering back through the statues. This is it – when I return to the van, I'll leave any hope of him behind.

Ben's sitting in the open side door and when he sees me he jumps to his feet. I look at the ground, not wanting my eyes to linger too long on his body.

'Rach, you had me worried.' He rushes over and grabs my shoulders and as soon we make contact, my stomach flips and my hands heat, *and my heart breaks all over again*.

He escorts me back to the van, his hand on the small of my back. My gift pulses, aching to be released. It takes all my concentration to keep it in check. Ben must sense my struggle, because he stops a few feet away and watches me. 'You all right?'

I pull away from his hand, finding the strength to look into his eyes. His attention fixes on a curl, stuck to my lip.

'I'll be OK.'

He waves me back into the van. I step inside and get straight into my bed, pulling the covers over my head. There's a scuffle as Ben hops over and shuts the sliding door. Being back under these covers, with Ben only inches away, makes my lips tingle with the whispered memory of his kiss.

It was only a dream, I remind myself, tugging down my red gloves. My body is electric right now, and with Ben so close I can't risk accidently turning him in my sleep.

It was only a magical dream. What wrong could come from having another, though? I let myself drift to visions of what our normal life together could've been and soon my subconscious takes over. I dream of us in Central Park, spread out on a blanket, my head on Ben's lap as I study for a social work exam. Then Ben in his police cadet uniform, meeting me for lunch on my university campus. The first time seeing him drive a squad car when he picks me up from my job at the community centre, and as I lean in to his window to seal our hello with a kiss, it isn't him, it's me. Just as I'm about to pull away, a single drop of blood drips from my eyes, down the inside of my cheek, pooling on my lips.

I sit up in bed, panting hard. Trying to blink the strange dream from my mind.

The warmth of the morning sun streams through the van window, falling over us. I can't believe I slept the night away. It felt like only minutes had passed.

I glance at Ben. The blanket covers his waist and legs, leaving his chest bare. It rises and falls with his steady breath. The sunlight turns his skin a golden hue. He's so beautiful when he sleeps. Even the statues outside seem to stare. My stomach flutters and my breaths quicken. I need to calm my head. I slip out of bed, grab my cardigan, wrap it around my shoulders and open the door as quietly as possible.

A cool morning breeze greets me. I pull my sweater tighter to my body and stick my gloved hands in my pockets to keep warm. Taking in a deep breath of the damp air, I wander to explore the first patch of statues.

They're much less scary in the light. Something about them reminds me of New York; the vibrancy, the diversity. It makes me miss home. Every now and again I come upon one that's so beautiful or unusual that I stop to study it, but each statue is quite remarkable in its own way. It must've taken years to make them all. When I come across a mother and child, my heart breaks thinking about my own ma. I'm so powerless to help her, and that feeling makes me snap.

'Eros!' I yell in desperation. 'You're supposed to look out for your descendants. So help me get my family back.' I grab a fallen branch and whack it against a statue, over and over. 'Eros!'

A flicker of movement catches my eye. 'Ben?' I groan, worried I woke him with my racket. When I get no reply, I turn down a narrow pathway between the statues towards where I saw him.

'Rachel?'

Someone calls me, but it's so faint I can't be sure it's not just the wind whistling through branches and my mind twisting it into my name. I continue looking for Ben but all I find are new statues.

A shiver runs down my spine. It's probably just heightened nerves after the bad dream. Still, I'm aware of how far from the van I've wandered. I take a step towards the way I came and stop in my tracks.

There's a man watching me.

At first I think he's a statue, but then his head turns and his blonde curls dance in the breeze.

'Hello?' My voice shakes.

'Hello, love,' he says in an unrecognizable accent.

I shield my eyes from the sun, trying to get a better look at him. His unnaturally blue eyes lock on me as he steps forward. There's a strange familiarity about him. I'm sure I've seen him before. He's the kind of handsome you don't forget – regal, somehow.

Then it hits me. He was at the precinct – the officer that winked as we passed. I open my mouth to scream a warning for Ben when the man wags a finger. For some reason, I stop.

'I'm not a cop. I just pretend to be sometimes.' He smiles and leans casually on a statue.

A shaky hand rises to cover my mouth. I don't remember saying anything.

He laughs. 'I can hear thoughts.'

I step back, using a small statue of an older lady for support. I slip my fingers from the glove and pinch my wrist. I feel the sting. This isn't another dream.

The guy looks about a year or two older than Ben, but holds himself in a way that makes him seem much older. He's wearing jeans and a purple T-shirt, and though there's nothing odd about the clothes, they look weird on him. He doesn't seem to mind the cold air on his bare arms. He stands tall, shoulders straight, not slumped forward like most guys, and he walks to me with one hand behind his back, the other swinging by his side like a march for some military procession.

If he isn't a cop, what is he? And how can he read my mind?

'Are you with the Committee?'

'Do I look like a priest?'

I shake my head and cast my eyes down. The good news is, if he isn't a cop or with the Committee, I'm probably safe.

'You are safe,' he replies, once again answering an unasked question.

'Please stop doing that.'

'I forget how creepy it must be.'

There's something about him. I run through my memories, certain there's somewhere else I can place his face. The precinct wasn't my first time seeing him.

'Who are you?' I finally ask.

'You've given up guessing?' He smiles, amused, and runs a hand through his curls. 'I suppose you could say I'm your great, great, great – add some more greats – grandfather.'

My legs give out and I find myself sitting on the damp ground. The picture in St Valentine's, that's where . . .

'Eros?'

Thirty-Three

Eros offers me his hand. It's then I see a dark purple cloak and his golden bow, with its white-gold amethyst handle, leaning against a statue by his feet.

'I've got it,' I say, pushing myself up from the ground, trying desperately to hide the shake of my arms as I stand teetering before a god.

He drops his hand. 'My given name is Eros, but you can call me Grampa if you prefer.'

'I . . . I . . . you . . .'

'Not exactly the warm welcome I was expecting after you spammed my inbox and screamed for help baring sticks like some mad cave woman,' he says, with a grin.

'Surrender2Love? I can't believe that was you.' And I can't believe he expected a warm welcome from me. I've spent most of my life imagining what I'd say if we ever met, and none of it is warm.

'Ouch,' he says.

My hand shoots to my mouth. This whole mind-reading thing takes some getting used to.

His fingers find my chin, and the moment he touches me my gift ceases. No buzz, no tremble: it's gone. I take a deep breath, relishing how it feels. I never realized how much I sensed my gift, even when inactive, until now. The last time I felt like this I was twelve, when I didn't even know Hedonesses were a thing let alone that my own mother was one. He tilts my chin so I have nowhere to look but those bright blue eyes. 'Don't think I don't understand. I once loved someone I couldn't be with.' He releases me and the electricity returns like a smack.

I pull back from him. Feeling like a jerk for my thoughts. I shouldn't have been so harsh. It's not like he knew he was going to ruin my life when he put the arrow in Psyche. He was trying to save the woman he loved.

'I'm sorry, I . . .'

'Hush now. If I could've seen what my actions would do to future generations, I would've found another way. But as you know, love can be crippling and delusional.'

'Delusional?'

'You intend to offer your freedom for the exchange of your friends and family, do you not?'

My eyes widened and I lick my dry lips. How much does he know?

'More than I'd like.' He smiles again. 'You're planning to break into the police station and confess to their crimes.' A sly grin spreads across his face as he leans against a statue. 'May I suggest doing something to make them think you're violent? The bigger the threat, the more attention you'll get. A confession alone isn't really that impressive. They'll want a demonstration.'

A threat? Demonstration? Like turning someone?

'Yes,' he says. 'Though kissing a man isn't really that impressive.'

I'd never thought of that. He's right. I need to do something bigger, something fierce. But turning someone? I couldn't. It would be breaking everything I stand for. What would Joan of Arc do? My mind flicks to the billboard of *My Vampire Alien Life* we passed yesterday – a man with his fangs deep in some girl's neck.

'Don't get me started on Joan. What a mess that whole thing was. The Committee got to her before I could. They're always hunting down my prospects. I was sure she'd be the one . . .' He brushes a blond curl from his face and smiles.

'The one?'

'That's not important. What's important is your idea. It's smart, really. Playing into the whole vampire epidemic. People are so inundated with them these days they actually believe they're real.' He looks deep into my eyes, a firmness taking over his features. 'Though, we both know you don't need to kiss or bite someone to turn them.'

I suck in a breath. 'I can—'

'—touch,' he finishes. 'You're quite remarkable, you know? Yours is the only bloodline—'

'I don't think stealing a man's will with my touch is remarkable.' I'm shocked at how open I'm being to a god. A real, living god. 'I mean, I . . .'

'I appreciate your honesty. It's been far too long since a Hedoness has had your disposition. It was never the intention of the arrow to be manipulated for one person's will alone. The purpose has always been to bring *two* people together in love. Unfortunately, human nature has corrupted the arrow's gift. And the Committee's school system doesn't help.'

'Human nature?' I ask, leaning forward.

'More precisely, selfishness. But for some reason, you, love, do not possess that particular quality.'

'Oh yes I do.' I practically snort. What about all the times I wanted to steal Ben's attention from Marissa, or when I purposely fought Ma to get my dad to notice me?

'You mistake your own actions,' says Eros.

I lift my eyes in question, waiting for him to explain.

'Those acts were not done out of selfishness. Your love for your father makes you fight for any injustices you see befall him. It's not selfish to desire what's best for people, if *you* are what's best for them.'

'Me? Best?' I whisper the last part, casting my eyes back to the ground. It can't be true. This is that damn hope again. False hope. As long as I'm a Hedoness, Dad will never love anyone but Ma. *And I can never be with Ben.*

'You're wrong – there's always hope.'

'How?' I ask, squaring my shoulders and lifting my chin to challenge him.

His eyes tear through me like he's trying to decide if I have what it takes.

'The curse will be reversed one day. I promise you.'

'Reversed . . .' Blood rushes to my head, and my eyes take in too much light, making spots swim in my vision. So Ma was wrong. There *is* a way to undo the Hedoness curse. I can barely breathe. I force myself to suck back mouthfuls of air. My lips tingle with desire to turn the kiss of my dreams into a reality.

'You're a god,' I say. 'If it can be undone, why haven't you done it already?'

His smile becomes a thin line. 'I do not have the power to do such things.'

'Then who does?'

'Now that is a good question.'

'Well, who?'

He grins. 'You do, my dear. Any Hedoness, really, if the circumstances are right.'

'Circumstances?' I cling to the statue next to me, hoping whatever it is, it's something I can do.

'We'll get to that later.'

'If I can help reverse it, I will.'

'I was hoping you'd say that, I could use your help. But that would require you alive, and not arrested. You know what? I have a better plan. Leave Ben here. It's safe. Come with me, and I'll protect you from the Committee.' He spins on his heels and starts walking, waving for me to follow. I cross my arms and hold my ground. After a couple of strides he stops and turns back.

'Let me guess,' he says. 'Your family?'

'Yes, my family. I'm helping them before I do anything for you. Even if that thing is breaking the curse.' Which is the one thing I've wanted since I found out what I was.

'Very well,' he says. 'Then tell me, how will you plan your getaway? You know, after you free your family?' He takes a few steps closer and stops.

I cross my arms tighter. I never thought about getting away – I just resigned myself to being arrested.

'And if you confess with no demonstration, they'll order you a psych evaluation.'

'Fine, I'll turn someone. If the curse is reversed it won't matter.' As I say it, I regret it. I never want to turn anyone. Ever.

Eros leans in. 'It seems you haven't thought this all the way through. Have you considered what you will do if they shoot you? Like it or not, you'll have to attack one of their officers to drive home the stakes.'

Right. I hadn't thought of that, either. My arms drop. I'm not sure how I'll pull it all off.

Eros leans against the adjacent statue, ankles crossed, a big grin on his face.

'Help me,' I plead.

'Help you?'

I lift my chin, trying to appear brave. 'If you want my help to break the curse, then help me free my family.'

'Are we negotiating now?'

'Yes,' I say firmly. 'You're a god, you must have some magic that can keep me from being shot.'

'I see,' he says.

'Well, do you have something?'

'My power won't help with such things. What you need is spare magic.'

'Spare magic?'

'You know arrows, potions, spells, that sort of thing.'

'Do you have any?'

'Rachel,' he sighs, 'it's all very complicated. It's been a long time since I was allowed in Olympus, so what little I have left I will not be able to replace without going back, and I cannot go back. Not until the curse is broken.'

'I can help you do that once I'm done saving my family and then you can replace whatever you need.'

'You can. However, even if I can help you to not get shot, what's keeping the police from discovering they don't have a body?'

'I'll get a fake body.' As soon as I say it I regret how foolish it sounds, though we are standing in a field of lifelike statues, so I'm sure it's possible to fake a body, somehow.

257

'Let me get this straight – I help you fake your death and all that entails, and you will help me break the curse?'

'Yes.'

'How can we guarantee you will be shot?' Eros says. 'This plan is based on speculation. They may arrest you, and then you're stuck behind bars and of no use to me.'

'Well, then you shoot me. You've faked being a cop before.'

Eros frowns. 'I'd like to help, really. But we're not supposed to intervene with humans and your plan requires a lot of intervention.'

I want to yell, to tell him he's kinda late to be obeying that rule, having pierced Psyche with his arrow and created Hedonesses and all. But I don't. What's the point – he can read my mind anyway. 'I guess Ma was wrong about you,' I say instead. 'You don't care about me, or your descendants. All you care about is yourself.'

His face has a weird expression that makes me think he's fighting back a smile. After a long pause, he reaches into his pocket and pulls out a small glass vial that looks like it's filled with liquefied rubies. He turns over my hand and places it in my gloved palm, the red disappearing into the leather. 'I don't have long. As you know I'm not supposed to be here. Interfering,' he says with air quotes. 'But I like your spunk, love. You remind me of my mother. Well, the good parts of her. This will assist you if you are willing to pay the price.'

258

Of course there's a price. There's always a price. I pick up the vial, rotating it in my hands. The shiny red colour sparkles in the sun. How could this help me?

'It will make sure a bullet won't penetrate,' he replies. 'Any weapon, really.'

I frown, holding the vial to a beam of light. 'What's the price?'

'We were always supposed to meet, you know?' he says instead of answering my question. Still, I'm curious enough to let it slide.

'We were?'

He smiles. 'I've left you some signs, I've been guiding you to me.'

All the arrows.

He smiles. 'You see, I've tried for hundreds of years to undo the arrow's curse. There were other Hedonesses who had your potential. They were thwarted one way or another by the damn Committee.'

'The Committee,' I gasp, wondering about my classmates overseas. 'Wait, my potential?'

He smiles. 'They've been trying to stop me, and maintain control of you Hedonesses. Without your power, their infrastructure crumbles. They lose everything they've built. But unless the arrow's magic is reversed, I can't return to Olympus. It's a conundrum. So you see, I've waited a long time for you.'

'Waited for me? Why?'

His blue eyes lock on mine, looking deep into my soul. 'You have the circumstances needed to reverse the Hedoness curse.'

I nearly drop the vial, managing to trap it between my hand and stomach. I stare at him, opening and closing my mouth, trying to figure out how an inexperienced, ungrateful Hedoness can undo hundreds of years of *the gift*. There's a big difference between helping him, and having *what's needed*. I don't know how much time passes before I can form a normal word. 'M-me? How?'

'First, according to our deal,' he adds dramatically, 'you must perfect your plan to free your family, then I will find you and we will reverse the curse. It is very important no one knows about this. They must believe you are dead.' His eyes lock on mine and he lets that word hang in the air – *dead*. 'No one must know we will attempt to break the curse. Do you understand?'

'That's a lot of pressure,' I say, more to myself than him.

'Rachel, we cannot risk the Committee discovering us.' He reaches over and closes my fingers around the bottle. 'Be careful with that, it's my only one.'

I slip the vial into my sock. 'How do I use it?'

'Drink it at the time you need its help. But,' his voice turns low and cautious and he exhales loudly, 'the cost is high.'

My smile slips and I look at him. 'What if I don't like it?'

'You're the one that asked for my help.'

I fight the urge to roll my eyes. 'What is it?'

'The serum requires you to sacrifice your beloved. You will forget Ben and he will forget you.'

'No,' I gasp out. I can't breathe, my heart throbs, I feel like I'm going to puke. I lean my head on the stone statue and think over Eros's offer. Even with the Hedoness power reversed, I still can't be with Ben.

'There's got to be another way.'

'Not as far as I can foresee. You must fake your death, which requires the vial. We can't break the curse with you in jail.'

'But I can say goodbye, right?'

'I'm sorry, Rachel. He can't know. It will influence the magic and telling anyone puts us in risk of the Committee finding out our plan.'

'I'm supposed to just lie to him, make him think everything is OK?'

'Nothing about this is OK.'

I brave looking into his eyes – they're nearly the same colour as Ben's – and I know he's right. Letting Ben go gives him the chance to follow his dream, and freeing my family and reversing the curse is more important than my heart. But the cost of that is Ben. It hurts to even think of it.

'Your family's lives will be far better without the Hedoness power,' he says softly, but he might as well have ripped my heart out and bitten into it.

How can I deny my family that? All the Hedoness families. This is much bigger than me.

'OK,' I whisper. The words poison my lips, but I say them anyway, because I need to hear them. 'No more Ben.'

Eros puts his hand on my shoulder, and even with his touch easing my powers, I still feel sick. 'I know it doesn't seem like it now,' he says, 'but one day you will thank me for all this.'

'I doubt it.'

'Whenever it hurts, remember that your sacrifice will mean countless other girls can be with the people they love.'

I force a smile. Deep inside, knowing that all the girls from school, and the ones I don't know, even my parents, will have a shot at love – it does make me feel a bit better. It's just me who has to sacrifice, and I'm already used to that. Still, the desire to cry is overwhelming.

Eros puts his hand on my head and my sadness leaves. All that fills me is overwhelming love. It's the same as when my ma hugs me, or those brief moments my dad smiles for something other than Ma, or when Nani tells me she's proud of me for something other than being a Hedoness. It's every goodness, every joy, every warmth, all in one. Instead of dwelling on what I'm about to lose, I'm filled with what I will gain.

'That should help you cope for a while,' he says, reaching into his back pocket and pulling out a bank card. 'Here, take it.'

I grab the card, flipping it over. 'Olympus Gold Card? Really?' It's too cheesy to be real.

'Zeus's sense of humour.' He rolls his eyes. 'A while back he got those made for us. Don't lose it – it has no purchase limit.'

I flick the corner against my other glove. Marissa would love getting her hands on this. I can only imagine the damage she'd do on a shopping spree.

'I should leave now. You'll see me next in police uniform with a fake gun aimed at you,' Eros says as he pushes off the statue. 'Rachel, *valedico*.'

'Huh?'

'I bid you farewell.' He smiles, extending his arm in salute. 'And don't forget, you'll need a body.'

'Where will I get that?' I think aloud.

'You'll find a way,' he says, nodding with encouragement.

I glance down at the Olympus Gold Card, thinking about his warning. When I look back up, he's gone.

Thirty-Four

The sun crests over the trees, the newfound warmth keeping most of the cold away. I bite the inside of my cheek, flipping the card over in my hands, thinking about the conversation with Eros. I still can't believe he feels the same way about the Hedoness powers.

Footsteps approach, slapping heavy on the damp ground. Ben runs through an opening, his head darting from side to side, looking for something.

'Ben?' I pocket the card.

He stops, hands on waist, panting from the exertion of the run. When his eyes land on me a sense of relief floods his firm features. His shoulders drop and he exhales loudly. 'I was worried when I woke and you were gone.'

I start towards him and he jogs the remaining distance, standing a few feet away, staring like he's trying to read my mind.

Thank the gods he can't do that. I laugh, and he raises an eyebrow in question.

Then his gaze shifts, moving down my face to my lips, staying there for a moment too long.

My breath catches in my throat.

A breeze pushes a lock of my unruly curls in front of my eyes. Instinctively, Ben steps forward and reaches up, tucking it behind my ear and leaving his hand resting on my shoulder. A current of electricity burns where his fingers trail my skin. My heart knocks against my ribs.

Each time I breathe Ben's hand brushes my neck. The electricity surges in me. I find myself looking at his mouth. Questioning what a real kiss would be like. I try to push it down, ignore how my body aches for his, but it only continues to build. I've never let Ben this close, for this long. I bite my bottom lip and pry my eyes from his. Now is not the time to take this risk.

With the last of my determination, I step back. I can't bear looking at him, at his questioning eyes.

'We should probably leave soon,' he says. 'It's only a matter of time before the police start looking in this direction, if they aren't already.'

I nod and we walk back to the van, me thinking about my family, and Ben thinking about . . . I'm not sure.

'Ben?'

'Yeah?'

'Will the police take everyone back to New York?'

He runs his hand though his hair. 'If they follow standard procedure, they'll see to their medical needs and then, if the detainee is able, they'll question them before transporting them back to their state. But there's nothing standard about this.'

'Where do you think Marissa and Kyle will be?'

'I don't know how hurt they are.'

I pull my cardigan tighter, even though I'm not cold any more.

'Rach?' Ben asks. 'What's bothering you? Your whole face just dropped.'

His care-clouded eyes give me courage to ask. 'What if they haven't been moved? What if the police here don't let them go?' I shove my hands in my back pockets and my fingers brush the gold card. If everything works, I'll fake getting shot and go into hiding with Eros until we break the curse, which could take gods know how long – Eros didn't really give specifics. It might be my last chance to see everyone for a while.

'Is this about your plan?' He sighs. 'It's not right.'

He's right. It's wrong. Even more so now that I might have to turn someone. But now it's something more. With the chance to break the curse, anyone I turn will go back to normal. *Even Ben.* He can forget all about us and become a police officer. But I can't tell him that, so I stare at the ground. 'What other option do I have?'

'I can think of some. For starters, they can take responsibility for their own actions.'

'What about Kyle, Joyce, my dad? They were dragged

into this. Yeah, I have to do things I'll regret, I hate it. I hate it so much. But I can't think of another way.'

'You really want to spend your life in jail?'

Ben paces. His jaw clenches and his hands are in fists at his side. The vial burns against my skin, reminding me of what could be for my family.

He stops suddenly, and turns back. 'Their actions led to their consequences. While you, on the other hand, fight to be good, fight to never use your gift. Why should it be you who is punished? You who makes all the compromises? It's not right, Rach. You don't deserve this.' We reach the van and he hops in and starts the engine, putting it in drive before I even make it to the passenger side. I get in and close the door and he drives down the dirt lane, through all the statues.

'Shouldn't we head back to the main road?' I ask.

'We're almost on empty. This is the first sign of something that could point us in the direction of a gas station. I want to see where it goes.' He keeps his eyes carefully ahead.

'But . . .' I close my mouth when a small wooden store with smoke rising from a chimney and the warm glow of lights comes into view.

'Let's ask where we are,' Ben says. 'Plus, I really could use the bathroom.' He pulls the van next to a line of ballerina statues and puts it in park. The door to the store creaks open, casting warm beams of light on to the shaded porch. An elderly lady, with her grey hair piled in a messy bun, wearing a short floral dress and yellow gumboots, waves from the doorway.

'Welcome! Welcome to Little Tokyo,' she calls in a thick European accent.

Ben turns off the engine and opens his door, looking back at me. 'You coming?'

I wait, watching him walk over to the lady and shake her hand, before hesitantly opening my door. I pull on the edge of my red gloves and clutch tightly to my cardigan. The statues seem to press in – I can't even see the path we drove down to get to the store.

'Little Tokyo?' I repeat, remembering the road sign.

The lady smiles and motions me to follow her. 'My husband lived there for a few years working at a wax museum. When he returned home he felt uncomfortable in our isolation so he recreated the feel of Tokyo, people of every type and every fashion, everywhere.'

The name suits the place. Whatever place it is.

'What can I do for you this fine morning?' she asks. 'Not every day we get customers this far out. Most people order online.'

'We were looking for someplace to get gas,' Ben says.

'I'm afraid the only gas we sell is for boats.'

'Is there somewhere nearby we could go?'

'Our docks back on to the Mississippi river marshlands. There's not much around. If you continue east, you'll run smack dab into a swamp-logging mill. Nothing else's that way, except a couple of swamp squatters like us. There's a little gas station a couple of hundred miles back. Or you can reach the major highway and connect into Jackson. There's good shopping in Jackson.'

I had no idea we'd driven so far. What are we going to do? We can't stay in a mill and we can't go back.

Ben smiles. 'Any chance we could use your bathroom before we go?'

'Of course, follow me.'

Something about the lady's friendly disposition helps me settle. I return the smile and follow after her into the store. The front entrance has a reception desk and till with some fishing flyers stacked in neat displays. A large statue of a sailor holds a big sign that reads *Fishing Charters* and a cork board showcases pictures of various boats available.

'Heinz, put your trousers on,' the lady yells as she pushes through a worn blue door beside the desk. 'We have company!' She motions us after and we follow into a little kitchen behind the shop.

There's a grunting sound from a far room. 'No!' he replies, short and firm.

The lady's hand flutters to her chest. She offers a half smile. 'Heinz!' she tries again, adding a hint of warning to her tone.

'No!' the voice repeats.

I glance at Ben, nodding to the blue door, hoping he'll pick up on the hint and get us out of here. He smiles, big and cheeky. He's enjoying my discomfort way too much.

'Artists,' the old lady says, as if that one title pardons the fact that Heinz, whoever he is, refuses to wear trousers.

She motions us after her and Ben follows. I pause in the kitchen entrance, watching them leave before sighing, and following after.

When I round the corner, I freeze. Heinz sits on an olive-green couch that quite possibly could be older than him. His outfit isn't as bad as I expected. I mean, it's bad. But more it's just comical. He's wearing a white button-up that forms tightly to his beer belly, his grey hair's slicked back as though he spends too much time grooming it, black dress socks pulled halfway up his calves, and black suspenders clip on to his underwear.

My face flames at the sight. But for the absence of trousers, his outfit could've been considered Wall Street bests. I slip my hands in my pocket, wrapping my fingers around the gold card.

Ben extends his in greeting. 'Hello, I'm Ben and this is my friend Rachel.'

The man stares at Ben's outstretched hand and raises an eyebrow. He grabs his remote, pausing the show blasting out of a projection TV that's taller than me.

'You're not here to complain about my art?' Heinz asks.

'No, sir,' Ben says.

'Then we are friends. Don't mind me, I was catching up on the latest episodes.' Heinz points to the TV, frozen on an image of bloody fangs. 'Do you watch *My Vampire Alien Life*?'

'I wouldn't admit it if I did,' Ben says with a grin.

Heinz laughs. 'We saw a news report of what's been happening in New York and decided to check the show out. I'm not convinced it's real, like Frieda is, still – it makes you wonder if there's something bigger than us out there.'

Ben looks at me, and I shrug.

'Heinz!' Frieda tosses a dishcloth at him. 'You saw what the boy said to the reporter – he was abducted and marked with that necklace.'

The last time I saw Paisley she was wearing that spaceship necklace. So much has changed since then.

'Are you here to charter a fishing boat?' Heinz asks, determined to find out why we're standing in his living room. They really mustn't get many customers.

'As much as I miss fishing,' Ben says, 'we're hoping to get some directions to a place we can get gas and food. We have a long trek ahead.'

I glance at the TV screen, and squeeze the no-limit gold card tight. 'Actually,' I say. 'We want to buy a boat.'

Ben snaps his attention to me, eyes full of questions.

271

'Ha!' Heinz laughs, and grabs Ben's hand, using it as leverage to pull himself up. Once standing, the man yanks Ben into an embrace. 'Boats we have.'

It's hard not to laugh as Ben stiffens in the arms of the trouser-less man, his eyes fixed on me.

'Come now,' Heinz says, waving us all after him. 'I'll show you our inventory.'

Frieda hooks elbows with him and smiles at Ben. 'But first, a detour to the bathroom.'

We follow after the pair. Ben slows his pace to match mine, and leans in. 'We want to buy a boat?'

'We need to get to New York and avoid traffic cameras – you yourself said it was a good option. And you can drive it, right?'

'Yeah, but . . .' He stops mid stride and sighs. 'How will we even buy this boat?'

I pull out the gold card and hold it up. 'Eros. He gave me this – it has no limit.'

Ben frowns. 'Eros?'

'Long story, I'll fill you in later.' I nod to Heinz and Frieda, who've stopped in the kitchen to wait for us.

'Right. Fine,' he whispers, firm. I know it's not fine. He doesn't like being kept in the dark.

'The bathroom is there,' Frieda says, motioning to a door beside the worn blue one.

Ben frowns at me one last time before hurrying in, leaving the three of us standing awkwardly in the kitchen.

Heinz sways from his heels to his toes, his thumbs hooked on his suspenders. Frieda notices my unease and whacks him on the back of the head. 'Go put your trousers on and prepare the boats.'

'Yeah, yeah,' he says, waving her off, turning and wandering out another door.

Ben exits shortly after, shaking his hands dry, and I slip in the restroom behind him.

'Help yourself to anything,' Frieda calls.

I slide the Olympus Gold Card in my back pocket and notice a basket of ribbons next to a bottle of spray deodorant on the counter. It seems weird using someone else's deodorant, but we've been on the road for days, so I give myself a quick spray. Frieda said to help myself to anything, so I grab a black ribbon, tying it to the vial. I slip that around my neck and tuck it under my Wonder Woman T-shirt, patting it for good measure. My hair is everywhere. I finger through it, trying to get it to lay flat enough for a ponytail. There's a few bumps but it will do. I splash water on my face and wash my hands and arms. A shower and some clean clothes would be better, but still, I feel more myself than I have in days.

I open the restroom door, pausing when I hear Frieda and Ben's conversation.

'You two make a beautiful couple,' Frieda says. 'How long have you been together?'

I press against the wall and hold my breath. My heart thumps so loudly, I'm afraid they'll hear it and notice the door's propped open.

'Rachel and me? No, uh . . . we're just friends.'

The words come off his tongue so quickly that it catches me by surprise. He didn't even have to think about it. Now I know. It shouldn't bother me, especially not after I've committed to forgetting about him. Still, my lip trembles and tears threaten to come. The last thing I want is to cry over a boy. And if Ben saw me crying, he'd ask a hundred questions. I return to the sink and splash another handful of water on my face, letting the droplets fall down my cheeks like tears.

Thirty-Five

We wait for Heinz in the store. He comes back wearing trousers and plops a stack of pictures before us. 'We have two seaworthy boats we can sell, both for a special deal.'

'Price isn't a worry,' I say.

'They'd be around fifteen thousand,' he says.

I pull out the card. 'Do you take plastic?'

Heinz smiles.

I'm half surprised when the point of sale machine registers the transaction approved. Ben's even more curious, but he doesn't press further yet. Frieda and Heinz bring us back outside. We gather our things from the van then head through the twisted maze of statues and trees towards the boats. It's a long walk, and I half expect to see Eros pop out from behind one of them, but he never does.

When we finally reach a clearing, I smell the river before I see it. It reminds me of the musty plant smell of the turtle tank we had in my sixth-grade homeroom. Despite that, this place is magical. Lime green sludge-covered water carves a path away from us, winding through low-hanging trees; leaves and flowers float on the surface, and white birds fish from exposed roots.

'Here we are,' Heinz says, stepping down a steep path to the water. 'Careful,' he finishes, turning to help Frieda. A couple of boats are propped up on blocks on the bank, a few more are anchored in the marsh, and a giant weatherworn waterwheel is tied to a tree jutting out of the sludge, fallen white paint flakes floating around the hull like snow. 'It's beautiful,' I say.

'I plan to restore it,' Heinz says proudly. 'Come back some time and I'll take you for a ride.'

'I'd like that.'

We follow him down the steep path towards a small dock with two large boats. I have no clue how such a little dock can hold the bus-sized ships.

Heinz waves at the boats. 'Which one?'

Ben takes his time, looking them over, then points to the blue one. 'This one looks more ocean-ready.'

Heinz smiles. 'Oh . . . *Betsy*.'

Frieda lovingly slaps Heinz on the arm. 'He thinks this boat is his mistress,' she explains. 'We took *Betsy* out recently and haven't had the chance to clean it. There's a bit of canned food and some linen and things. They're yours to use. And there's a couple of good places along the river for groceries.'

'You'll have to refuel soon anyway,' Heinz says. 'She holds enough gas in her to get you around the Keys to Outlet Bay – you can grab food there too.'

As we near *Betsy*, water floods over our feet. Heinz and Frieda back away, allowing the dock to float up. Ben hops in and holds out his hand. I hesitate, adjusting my gloves before reaching for him. In an effortless motion he lifts me on to the boat, holding me until I stop swaying. But even when he lets go, my insides still rock.

Heinz comes back, unhooking the ropes. 'You sure you know how to drive it?'

'Yes, sir,' Ben replies with a smile. 'I used to fish the ocean with my dad every summer.' His smile drops and his eyes grow distant. All I can think about is what he told me last night. His dad's dead.

I lean into Ben. 'Can I have the van keys?'

He frowns in confusion but hands them over.

'Here,' I say, holding them out to Heinz. 'We don't need this any more.'

Ben's eyes quickly find mine and he shrugs.

'Thank you. This will help move my statues.' He smiles and finds his place next to Frieda. He puts one arm around her and tugs on his suspenders with the other. 'Just follow the arrows, they lead to the ocean.'

Of course they do.

Thirty-Six

Despite the narrow swamp-banks, Ben expertly manoeuvres the large steel boat through the twisting bends until we reach the river. I sit on the bow, wincing at every white-weathered arrow we see hidden beneath hanging branches or propped on stilts out of the water.

We come to a section of trees so low I have to duck. I pluck a leaf as Ben guides *Betsy* past.

He smiles at me. I hop down and open the door to the bridge room, popping my head in and handing him the leaf. 'So you've done this before?'

'My dad taught me a few things.' He tucks it behind his ear and smiles.

I want to ask more about his dad, but he faces front, his grip tightening on the throttle. It doesn't seem the time to pry, so I return to my seat, enjoying the breeze and the comforting rock of the wake. We pass a big boat and I wave at the passengers – some return the gesture, and for a moment, in the sun, on the water, en route to save my family, with Ben here, everything is perfect.

After an hour or more of this, I leave my perch on the bow and go to him inside the small bridge room, sitting on a built-in stool next to the helm stand.

'What was all that about, earlier?' he asks.

'What?'

He waves to the boat. 'The whole Eros thing and the card?'

'Oh, he gave me a couple things to help save my family—'

'Right,' he says, gripping tighter to the accelerator. I'm afraid he'll get speedy like he did in the van. 'And when did that happen?'

'This morning, when you couldn't find me.'

Ben slows the boat to an idle and turns to face me. 'You're serious?'

'Yes.'

'I was that close to a god?'

I can't tell by his expression if he is mad or curious, or both. 'I was pretty surprised about it myself. All the years of learning about Eros, I never thought I'd meet him. I didn't even think the gods came to earth.'

His eyes narrow and he turns back to the wheel. 'Funny how they pick and choose when to help.'

His tone is so icy he sounds like a different person. 'Sorry?'

'It's just . . .' He glances over, returning his attention to the river and accelerating. 'Would've been nice if one of them helped my family. Seems a waste of whatever power they have to help some kid buy a boat.'

There's that word again, *kid*. Hearing him call me that stings more than I'd like to admit. But I understand he's upset so I try to ignore it. 'I'm going to explore below deck,' I tell him.

I descend the ladder into the galley, taking deep calming breaths. My stomach rumbles so I rummage through the cupboards, finding a couple of cans of beans and a six-pack of apple sauce. Not much, but it will do until we restock. I sit on the small booth-style table and eat an apple sauce. My eyes grow heavier with exhaustion. I fold my arms and rest my head, surrendering to a much-needed nap.

When I wake, I continue exploring. There's a closet-like room jutting from the wall. I open it to find a toilet, with no sink.

At the end of the galley is a bright yellow door. It stands out against the industrial grey colours the rest of the boat's decorated in. Curiosity gets the better of me, and I look inside to find a colourful array of clothing and accessories, similar to what Heinz's statues were dressed in.

I pull out a green wig and try it on, giggling at my appearance in the nearby mirror. I grab a few more items: a bright red oversized bow tie and pink furry handcuffs with the key in them. Then I head back to the deck, hoping my ridiculous look will cheer Ben up.

When he sees the green wig and red bow tie, he laughs. It's an airy throat laugh but it's a start. 'What's down there?'

'You know, typical Heinz and Frieda stuff.'

I hold out the fuzzy handcuffs and his eyes go wide. 'Aren't they too old for that?'

I laugh my way over to his side, sticking the wig on his head.

'You were out for a few hours. We're already in the Gulf,' he says, pulling the green hair off and hanging it on the corner of the helm. 'I didn't stop for food yet. I figured we could do that when we gas up.'

'What?' I exit the bridge and look over the rail to the open stretch of light blue waters. The sun is behind us, which doesn't seem right. I return to the helm and notice the compass – north is in the opposite direction to where we are going. The open ocean is to my left. If we're en route to New York shouldn't the land be on our left?

'Ben?' I say slowly. 'Where are we going?'

He lets out a long breath. 'I was hoping it would take you longer to notice.'

'What?' My hands are shaking. 'Tell me.'

He sighs. 'I can't support your stupid plan, even if the gods do. I'm not going to let you turn yourself in for Marissa and Kyle.'

'What about ma and dad? And Joyce. You have no right to decide what I choose to do!'

His head snaps to me. 'You want to talk about rights? It's not *right* that you'll pay for their actions. You're not like them, Rachel.'

My chest bounces with rapid breaths. If only Ben knew how much like them I am. I plan to turn an officer. Hell, I plan to turn as many people as needed to help me free my family. But the last thing I want is for Ben to hate me. I hate it enough for the both of us.

'Where are you taking me?' I repeat.

'Mexico. The police won't look for you there. You can start a new life.'

'I don't want a new life!' It surprises me coming out. I've spent my whole life wishing for something different. But I've come to realize that though my family isn't perfect, they're *my* family. And right now they need me. 'Ben, turn the boat around.'

His brow knits together. 'No.'

'Please. You know what it's like losing a family. How can you ask me to lose mine?'

He flinches at my words. 'No.'

I throw the furry handcuffs to the ground in frustration. They skid across the deck and land by Ben's feet, sparking an idea.

When he isn't looking, I retrieve the cuffs, leaving the bridge room with its door flapping open, and head to the back of the boat. I step on the rail and climb to the other side. I struggle to get a good foot grip, turning my back to the railing, and facing the choppy waves. All that's keeping me from the ocean is my deathlike grip.

'Ben!' I yell over my shoulder. 'If you don't turn this boat around, I'm jumping.'

'Stop playing,' he calls back, his voice sounding distant over the breeze.

The white wake bubbles bellow my sneakers. 'This isn't a game. This is my family's lives.'

Ben growls and smacks the wheel and the boat slows to an idle. He comes to me and grabs my waist, pulling me over. I don't fight him as he plops me on the safe side, thinking he's won. Instead, I walk away, and as he steps after me he's jerked back to the rail by his wrist.

'Rachel!' He holds up his handcuffed arm.

'Your hero act is predictable.' I go to the bridge, cranking the wheel to the side with my whole weight and pushing down on the throttle.

'Rachel, stop this!'

He tugs the handcuff, causing a clanking racket as he tries to break free.

'I have to help them,' I say.

The boat rocks roughly under my inexperience. I steer around waves, trying to avoid them. One large one slams into the side, spilling water over the bow, and knocking me to my butt.

'Seriously, Rachel. Unhook me now!' The clanging metal grows in desperation.

'Tell me how to drive this thing.' I scramble back to my feet and grab the wheel, trying to stabilize us.

'You don't know what you're doing. Unhook me and I'll drive it.'

'No.'

'For god's sake, then, steer into the waves. The boat handles them better front on.'

I do as he says and manage to get the feel of driving the thing.

As time passes, the clinking sound of Ben trying to escape his cuffs doesn't stop, but it does slow in vigour. Every once in a while, he begs for me to let him go. I pretend I don't hear.

'How are these things so strong?' he grunts to himself.

Soon the sun begins its descent. The wind picks up, and so do the waves. With the loss of light, it's getting hard to see and even harder to steer the boat. I can barely drive a car let alone something the size of a small bus. The reality of what I've got us into starts to freak me out.

'Ben, it's dark. I can't see.'

'Unhook me and I'll turn the lights on.'

'If I unhook you will you take me to New York?'

'If you let me go, I'll lock you to the rail and take you to Mexico.'

I can't help smiling at his honesty, or the goofy look on his face.

'Oh, you're proud of that one, aren't you?'

'A little,' he says.

A big wave rocks the boat and I screech, clinging tighter to the wheel. The clinking of metal stops. Finally, he lets out a long sigh. 'Please, Rachel, consider Mexico.'

'I can't do that to my family and friends.' *I wish I could tell you everything, Ben.*

'Listen, I know it's hard to understand, but it was their actions that led them where they are, Rach, not yours. You shouldn't have to do this.'

'How can you say that?'

'Do you even have to ask?'

For the most part he's right, but he's the one who doesn't really understand.

When I don't reply he continues. 'I lost my whole family because of one drunk bastard's decision. The court only gave him four years. Four! He took everything from me. I can't believe their lives are worth so little.' He pauses. 'Now you're the closest thing to family I have and you're asking me to hand you over. Not gonna happen.'

It takes me a while to process what he's saying. I couldn't imagine the pain. 'I'm sorry about your family. What happened wasn't right. But if you won't do it for me, will you at least do it for Kyle and Joyce and my dad? They didn't ask for what my ma and Marissa did to them.'

He stops wrestling the cuffs.

'I'm like them, Ben. As much as I hate it, I am. I can hurt you, or someone else. It's only a matter of time. I hate it, but it is what it is. If anyone should pay for that it should be me, not them.'

'Fine.' He growls and pulls one last time on the handcuffs. 'I hate these things.'

I slow the boat. 'You'll help me?'

'Rach?'

'Yes, Ben?'

'You know that I'm doing this for you, right? Not them.'

Thirty-Seven

The boat's interior light illuminates my way. It's dark and rocky, so I take my time, struggling to balance, as I head to Ben.

'Hurry,' he says.

'A little patience.' I reach him and fumble with the cuff.

'You left the boat running – we're drifting god knows where.'

The key's in the lock and it's one twist to let him go, but I pause. 'You promise you won't take me to Mexico?'

He tilts his head and narrows his eyes; the light from the bridge doesn't cut enough through the dark for me to see their blue hue, and I miss it.

'The one thing our friendship has going for it is that we're honest with each other, Rach. That's not going to change now.'

I swallow the confession creeping to my lips.

He watches my change in disposition and nudges my arm. 'I know there's something you're not telling me. You took off on me pretty quick when we started talking about Eros, how could I not? But I trust you. You'll tell me when you're ready.' He wags his arm, reminding me he's still attached to the rail.

I smile and uncuff him. He rubs his wrists, and stretches his back. I can't help noticing his skin is red from all the tugging, and I feel bad for that.

I reach out, hesitating when my gift surges, and run my gloved fingers over the raw skin. There's a faded bruise by his knuckles from the incident at the church. 'Ben, I'm sorry . . .'

'It's nothing.' He smiles and goes to the helm stand, pushing a button that causes low lights to shine out from the boat. 'It's choppier than I thought. These lights don't really do anything to cut through the darkness. I think it's better if we anchor closer to shore. We can keep going in the morning.'

I grip the rail and glance out at the waves. I am tired – fighting back my gift takes more out of me than I'd like. I could use the sleep.

'Plus,' Ben adds over his shoulder, 'with the extra time I may be able to convince you to change your mind.'

'I don't think so.' I walk up beside him, and he flicks the oversized bow tie I forgot I was wearing.

'Since you're an expert captain now, can you hold the wheel while I lower the anchor?'

I nod and shuffle in front of him. He stands behind me, the heat of his body making my skin tingle. When he leaves, it feels like a blanket is ripped away, exposing me to the cold.

He sets to work lowering the anchor. His back tightens under his thin white V-neck, and shadows define his toned arms. The bridge room is getting hot.

When he finishes, he stands on the bow, waving at me through the glass. I take in the way his shirt sticks to his chest in the wind. It makes the muscles in my stomach contract. It's going to be a struggle to fight back my feelings over these next few days alone with him.

'Should we share the bed downstairs?' he asks, pushing through the door into the small bridge room.

I inhale quickly. Share a bed with Ben? I doubt I could contain my gift if I did. The van was hard enough. But I only have a few days with him before we reach New York. Then I may never see him again, and even if I do, I won't know who he is. Maybe this trip is a stolen gift? A chance, just to be close, one final time. My stomach aches from my tightened muscles, and my gift tingles under my skin. When the taste of copper floods my mouth, I realize I'm biting my cheek.

'It's warm out,' I say. 'Why don't we pull some blankets and sleep on the deck, under the stars?'

He returns to the bridge room and closes the door. 'Warm? We're inside and you're practically shivering.'

That's not from the cold, Ben, that's from being close to you. 'The blankets will help.'

'All right.' He lowers himself down the ladder to the sleeping cabin. When he comes back, he has only one blanket and pillow. 'I'll stay up here, you get some sleep in the bed,' he says

My lips open to protest. 'But—'

'Don't worry about me, Rachel.'

We stop in Outlet Bay to refuel. I grab the groceries and head to the internet café, finding a computer at the back. I bring up a private window and search: *how to fake getting shot* and *what do police do with a body found at a crime scene?* I read everything I find about film production shooting scenes and coroners and medical examiners until a plan begins to form.

I open another window, pull up Quiver and click into my chat with Surrender2Love.

ME: *Get ready. I'm a few days away from New York. You'll need one of those stunt man bullets that make it look like I'm bleeding.*

I check again for Paisley, but she's still offline and there's no update from her mom. Marissa's offline too, and my stomach sinks just thinking about what she must be going through right now. I push the feelings aside and return to the search results – this is how I help them now. Out the corner of my eye, I see Ben enter the café. I panic and close all the windows, ending my session. He doesn't know about the staged shooting. He'd never let me go through with it. I grab the groceries and make my way over. He's smiling from ear to ear and gripping a comic book.

'What do you have there?' I nod to the comic rolled in his hand.

'Don't mock *The Punisher*. Last time someone made fun of me for reading it I got in a fight and broke my nose.' Now that he mentions it, his nose does slant a little to the left.

'I would never.' I fight back a smirk. 'It's just, I didn't take you for a comic guy.'

He chuckles. 'I'm a reader. But my love for comics I get from my mom. She was a Spanish teacher and the only way she could get me to learn was buying me Spanish translations of *The Punisher* when I was a kid.' He smiles down at the cover, absently running his fingers over it.

He clears his throat and takes the groceries from me, leading me out the store.

A heavy whacking sound fills the air.

'A helicopter,' I gasp out loud. 'There was one at the church and it sounded like when Kyle and Marissa—'

'It's probably nothing, Rach.' Ben ushers me forward. 'Let's head to the boat,' he says, reassuring me, but as we walk away, he glances back.

♥

291

The night sky presses down the sunlight, leaving a strip of fiery orange on the horizon.

'I'm going to head to shore and find somewhere to set anchor. You excited? We're a few days behind schedule, but . . . one more sleep,' Ben says, pouring the last of the tea into the thermos lid and handing it to me.

'I'm nervous, actually.' The closer we come to New York, the more worried I've become about losing him, and about making sure my plan works. Everything hinges on me using my ability. Something I've never done on purpose before.

He frowns and tosses the empty thermos on to the captain's chair. 'Changed your mind?'

I cup the tea, savouring the warmth, watching the steam rise to the wood-panelled roof, fogging the dome light. Part of me wants to follow him to Mexico. If only for another week or two alone in the boat. 'You know I haven't.'

'All right then, your turn to do dishes.'

I glare at him and he smiles a mega-watt smile back.

We find a cove to anchor in and Ben starts setting up his bed under the skylight in the bridge.

'You know what?' I say.

He pauses, folded blanket in hand. 'What?'

'You can't have all the fun. I'm sleeping up here too.' With the best pretend-mad face I can muster, I stomp the

292

short distance to him and take the blanket out of his hands. 'We need another blanket.'

He laughs his way down the ladder. A few minutes pass, then Ben grunts as he makes his way back up.

An edge of a mattress appears over the top. It falters up and down looking like it's about to fall.

'A little help, please?'

I grab the corner, pulling the heavy mattress on to the deck. It clears the opening, and I fall back, the bed crashing down on top of me.

Ben lifts the corner exposing my face. 'I brought you the mattress. I know how much of a princess you can be when your demands aren't met. Last time I was left imprisoned to the rail, Marissa, oops, I mean Rachel.'

'That's it!' I push his knees, buckling him to the deck, then I crawl out and scramble to my feet. 'Where are those darn handcuffs?'

Ben pushes on to his elbows. His eyes widen, but a smile spreads over his face. 'I threw them overboard. What else you got?'

I smack him with the pillow. 'If you weren't so cute, I'd be really mad right now.' The words escape before I realize what I'm saying. I stop mid swing, eyes wide, waiting for his response.

His smile hardens into a thin line. He pushes off the floor and steps closer to the door to the outside deck. My heartbeat races, slamming nervously against my ribcage.

He's deep in thought, too deep. The muscle on his jaw contracts, the same way it does when he's angry.

Say something, please, Ben.

He opens the bridge-room door, and walks over to the rails. A gust of salty wind pushes strands out of my ponytail. I raise a shaky hand, trying to brush them from my eyes, but they keep slipping through my gloved fingers. After a few more tries I give up, pulling the elastic from my hair so I can start over. Ben leans against the railing, arms crossed over his chest, watching me standing in the doorway to the bridge.

The tight feeling in my stomach returns. I hold my hair back, trying to get it under control. There's a twinkle in his eyes that I've never seen before. He walks to me, slow, cautious steps, stopping an arm's length away. All my nerves start firing. It's the most intense I've ever felt. I might explode at any moment.

I ache to kiss him, to test if reality is better than my dream. I put the elastic in my mouth, hoping to distract my lips, and I work to contain every stray strand of hair.

In a last act of defiance, the desire in me takes control. I look back at Ben, hoping to catch that strange look one last time. It's gone. His face is blank, void of emotion. He steps closer.

'Don't do that,' he says.

I freeze.

'Your hair.' He steps closer, so close I could lean forward and touch his lips with my own. 'You look really . . .' For the first time since we met, Ben sounds unsure, stumbling over his words. '. . . *pretty* when it's down.'

I gasp, dropping both hands to press my flipping stomach.

Between blowing strands, his eyes fixate on me – my hair, my skin, my neck, my lips. His eyes burn a trail everywhere they go.

Suddenly, I'm doubting everything. Having him, being able to touch him freely, feel his skin under my hands – it's better than never being able to look at him again. *Or looking and not remembering.* Maybe Ma was right in turning Dad. Maybe being selfish is the only way to find happiness as a Hedoness. I could make Ben mine for ever. It's what I'm made to do – it's my gift.

I push back the niggling doubt and let myself fully absorb the pleasure coursing through me. I close my eyes, concentrate on my tight muscles, on the tingle of anticipation on my lips. My gift moves me from deep within. A symphony of pleasure and power. I open my eyes, locking on Ben. I can take him.

But then he smiles.

And I feel so wrong.

More than I want to be happy, I want Ben to be happy.

I'm about to return to the bridge room when he steps so close I can feel his breath on my skin.

'I think you seriously need to reconsider Mexico,' he says. His eyes flick to my lips. 'The idea of you in jail . . . it splits me up, Rach.'

I want to, I so badly want to my entire body hurts. I take in large mouthfuls of the salty air, trying to calm the buzz inside. I have to shut off my gift, before I do something I'll regret. The only thing I need to focus on is getting to New York, and ending this curse once and for all. Then future girls can be with the boys they love.

'We're almost there,' I say, turning to grab a blanket and pillow and heading below deck.

I'll protect Ben from everything. Even myself.

Thirty-Eight

I lean against the railing, watching New York come into view.

We've only had a few hours of sleep. Ben tossed and turned and finally lifted anchor early morning. The roaring engine woke me up.

We pass Staten Island and Jersey City in the still quiet darkness. But as we near the blue-green Statue of Liberty the sun begins to rise over the buildings, waking the sleepy city. A blazing glow falls over the water, turning the buildings black in its shadow. It's a beautiful sight to see, especially the way the shadow of the statue stretches and wakes with the sun.

Something about the giant statue is comforting. After all, I'm about to do just that – sacrifice my life for a greater liberty. If everything goes as planned, I'll be freeing countless men like Dad. Men who forgot the simple joys of choosing love, caring for their children, or living life to the fullest for themselves.

I glance back at Ben. His eyes are hard in front as he guides us deeper into the bay.

There's a chopping noise overhead and I look up to see a helicopter. I head into the bridge room. Ben stiffens as I come up behind him.

'Almost there,' I say.

'Yeah. Almost.'

I glance through the skylight to see the helicopter flying lower. 'Is that the helicopter from Outlet Bay?' I ask.

'I doubt it,' Ben says, nodding to the wheel. He slows us down and switches places.

I focus on the water. There are more boats and buoys everywhere here – it's not as easy as driving in open ocean.

'I don't think so. You're just being paranoid.' He smiles and steps beside me, grabbing the wheel and bringing us back up to speed. He's probably right. I have so much I have to do before the turning. My mind's inventing problems.

We manoeuvre through the straits and slip into one of the water taxi docks.

'Help me with the dock lines,' Ben says, his muscles tighten under the heavy coils of rope. 'We have to hurry before someone asks for a permit.' He nods to the ropes by the stern.

I try to lift the pile and barely get it an inch off the deck. Ben's already secured the front of *Betsy*, and heads my way. I'm no help to him so I hop over the rails, lowering myself to the dock. 'I'll go find us a taxi.'

He stands, uncoiling the next pile. 'Maybe we should stick together.'

'I won't be long.' It's a lie, but I can't risk Ben trying to stop me.

I slip through the dock gate and head to the street. I've lived in New York City my entire life and I've never felt more pride for it as I do now. The city comes alive before me. Steam rising from grates, the honking of horns, the clanging of bike bells, the smell of people, garbage, cars, fresh coffee. It brings back a familiarity that I desperately missed.

I stand on the corner, waving at every taxi that passes. Some drivers smile and continue on, some don't even make eye contact. This part of getting a cab used to be annoying, and now it's as welcome as an old friend. Finally, one pulls over and I pop my head in the front. 'Morning.'

'Morning, miss. Where to?'

'The office of the Chief Medical Examiner, please.'

It feels good to be back in my city. I find myself smiling as we pass familiar places, almost forgetting what I've come home to do. I plunk my Olympus credit card info into the touchscreen, paying to access the Internet, and bring up Quiver. Surrender2Love is online – I open our chat thread and type.

ME: *I'm in New York. Heading to complete my plan. See you soon.*

S2L: *Roger that, I'll get in position.*

I bring up my chat history with Marissa, and even though she's offline I type a quick message.

ME: *I hope you and Kyle are OK.*

I want to say more, to tell her about meeting Eros and all that. But she wouldn't understand why I'm about to do what I'm about to do, and I don't even know if she'll see it.

The cab pulls up to the stop. 'Keep the meter running, please.' The big glass building presses down on me. This is it. This is where everything changes. I tug on my gloves and step towards it.

The doorman ushers me in with a smile and motions to the reception desk.

'Can I help you?' a lady asks.

'I'm here to see the Chief Medical Examiner.'

She directs me down the hall to a large empty waiting room. There's a man sitting behind a desk and he looks up from his file as I enter.

'Do you have an appointment?' he asks.

'I'd like to see the Chief Medical Examiner, if possible. Is he in?'

He sets the file down, an annoyed look crossing his face. 'Yes, but he's not available. What's the reason for your visit?'

He's rude – that should make this easier. But it doesn't. I'm fighting back the urge to run as he frowns at me, teetering in place before the desk.

300

I can do this, I'm a fighter.

'I just wanted to ask a few questions for a class project. But thank you for your time.' I take off my glove and offer him my hand. He does a half eye roll and reaches forward. The closer we come, the more my outstretched arm shakes. Just as we're about to touch, a tear trickles down my cheek. His eyes register something's wrong. He pulls back, but my fingertips brush his. Power pushes against my skin, and for the first time in my life, I let it free.

The man's eyes roll back and his body convulses as the strength pounds through me, cutting me up, stabbing and stinging and burning me alive. I force my lips shut and smother the urge to scream. Then it shifts, and the pain falls away, and my nerves tingle with a satisfying sensation that calms my entire body. Still, I refuse to savour this moment. I've become the person I hate. 'Take me to the Chief Medical Examiner,' I say.

The taxi pulls up to the kerb by the dock. It's been almost an hour – Ben's going to be furious. I pay for my fare and give a fifty-dollar tip. 'Can you wait for me? I have somewhere else to go. I'll just get my friend. Keep the meter running, I'll make it worth your time.'

He looks at the tip amount on the receipt, then back at me, and nods.

The cab pulls into the bus lot, and I squeeze through the sloppily chained dock gate, rushing down the short ramp, around the corner . . . I freeze.

Ben stands on the edge of the wharf a few yards away. His back to the water, his arms raised. A man and woman in black point guns at him. I cover my mouth to keep from screaming. My heart races madly. His eyes flick to me and back to them so quickly they don't notice. He shakes his head, just enough for me to know the warning.

I glance around, not sure what I should do. Do I leave Ben and try to break the curse? Or do I do for him what he's done time and time again for me. Do I save him?

I spot an oar in a nearby boat. I slink along the dock, quietly, taking careful steps. The red potion around my neck burns in reminder of what I'm risking.

'Where is she?' the woman yells, shaking her gun.

Something about her is uncomfortably familiar. I struggle to place it and when I do, ice goes down my spine – she's the same lady I saw getting out of the helicopter at the church.

'Rachel's in the boat.' Ben slowly points to *Betsy*, and when they look, he takes the chance to caution me with his eyes. He wants me to stop, to run. Instead, I reach up on my tiptoes and grab the oar, careful not to knock the empty cans of beer resting on the wooden rail. I slide it over the side and just as the tip clears the edge, I bump a

302

can and it falls. I take a heavy step forward, managing to catch it, but the oar hits the side of the boat with a smack. The gunmen stiffen, and start to turn.

I panic and throw the can to the far side of the dock. They follow the splash, and Ben motions his eyes to the guy on the left. *No time to hesitate.* I charge, oar raised high, and whack him in the back. The wood splinters over his head, and the man falls into the cold Hudson. Behind me there's a scuffle, then a gun blast. I dive for the dock, rolling to the side to see Ben wrestling the lady. I scramble to my feet, grabbing the broken oar.

From my angle, it looks like she's trying to kiss him.

The Committee.

Ben pushes her face back with one hand while the other tries to get the gun. My heart races, and I slam the oar over her wrist. She drops the pistol and Ben punches her. She tumbles back. Ben uses the opening and grabs my hand, kicks the gun in the water and drags me after him, the oar still locked in my grip.

I'm panting so hard my lungs hurt. I've never been more thankful for the gloves, because with my heart racing and Ben's hand in mine, I have no control.

The woman clambers to her feet behind us. The man pulls himself out of the river. They're on our tail, shouting at us. Ben pushes me through the gate ahead of him. I stop and turn around.

'Rachel, leave it!' he shouts.

I shove the splintered oar through the chains, bolting the door. 'Over there.' I point to the cab. And we rush for it, as they climb the gate behind us.

I dive in the back, Ben behind me. 'Drive!' I scream. The driver jolts alert, sitting up and starting the engine.

'Hurry!' I pat the seat impatiently.

They're over the gate, chasing after us.

The driver's eyes widen, and he pulls into traffic as the gunmen step into the road. They throw a rock at the cab, shattering the back window. A rain of glass falls over us.

'What the—' the driver says, ducking, and taking his foot off the accelerator.

'Drive!' says Ben. 'Turn left!'

The driver listens, cutting off a town car, and weaving between buildings at ungodly speeds. I cling to Ben as he watches out the back.

Finally, we turn on to Bowery and merge with a sea of taxis.

'We lost them,' Ben says.

We all let out a long breath.

I brush glass off my body, realizing I'm bleeding somewhere. My heart still races like crazy.

The driver spins in his seat. 'I'm calling the cops and you're paying for that window.'

'We will,' I say. 'I'll pay for a week of work while you get it repaired too.'

'Yeah?' He looks to Ben to see if I mean it.

'She's good for it,' Ben says.

'No need to call the cops,' I tell him.

'My insurance says otherwise,' the driver says.

I take a deep breath and glance at Ben. *It's time.* 'Just take us to the precinct on East 67th.'

Ben raises a questioning brow. He's still panting hard from the fight. But he smiles at me. 'Thank you for what you did back there.' He wraps an arm around my shoulder and sinks back in the seat, and I want to lean into him, to let him stay like this, to savour this last time together. But when I touch him now all I feel is the impending loss.

'One last chance,' he says, nudging my side. 'Mexico?'

I smile at his determination and stare out the window. My smile slips when the familiar thump of helicopter propellers drowns out the traffic noise.

'We're surrounded by taxis,' Ben says, noticing my sudden shift. 'We're fine.'

'As long as they don't spot the broken window,' I say. This makes his smile slip too.

I try not to worry. I'm minutes away from walking into the station, taking a police officer hostage and demanding the release and pardon of my friends. Whoever is in the helicopter, the Committee or police, they won't be able to stop me then.

Thirty-Nine

As we drive deeper into the heart of the city, the awkwardness in the cab can be cut with a knife. The cab driver keeps glancing at us, and Ben leans back, watching the helicopter circle above.

'East 67th, eh? You kids going to the protests?'

Ben sits up. 'Protests?'

'Mostly about the monsters taking our boys. But some people are protesting that the cops got some Sisters of the cloth locked up. A couple of my buddies who drive the east routes have been complaining about business. Most of the roads are blocked by crowds.'

I glance at Ben, eyes wide. This is what Paisley was talking about.

'How long have they been in custody?' Ben asks.

'A couple of weeks. I'm not sure. The cops keep breaking it up, but the protesters just come back. It got bad down there the last couple of days.'

'Maybe we should avoid that area of town,' Ben says, his words thick with hope.

'No, I'd like to see the protests.' I sit forward as the driver slows the cab and pulls over.

'Why are we stopped on Lexington?' Ben asks.

The man points down the road to a throng of people. 'This is as close as I get.'

A group of women hand out picket signs to passerbys that read *Save Our Boys*, *The Vampires are Here*, and my personal favourite, *GET THE MONSTERS OUT OF NEW YORK*.

'You kids be careful,' the driver warns as Ben opens his door.

I hand up the Olympus card. My free hand goes to the vial around my neck, feeling the cool hard glass. My heartbeat quickens again. I'll have to drink it soon.

The driver passes back the point-of-sale machine and I enter in a twenty-thousand-dollar tip. That should cover the window and his time off work, with a bit extra for any trauma. When the receipt prints, the driver's eyes widen.

'Miss, I think you made a mistake.'

'No. Please, you keep it,' I say, as I hurry from the cab.

'I won't call the cops,' he yells after us.

Ben jogs to catch up and positions himself protectively in front of me, leading the way through the crowd, deep into the heart of the mob. Every once in a while, he turns around and mouths, '*Mexico*?' Each time I force a smile and push him forward. This is my destiny. Eros said so himself. We were always going to meet, I was always going to be the next one to try and break the curse. That's how I'll be remembered – like Lady Liberty or Joan of Arc.

I feel for the protection of the vial, keeping my hand there, pinning it down for fear it will somehow get bumped off by a passing elbow or a waving sign.

People push into my back, front, sides. It's impossible to avoid them. I fight down my gift as it stirs at the contact.

The large brick building of the police headquarters comes into view over the crowd, and Ben holds up his hand, stopping me. Remnants of burning metal scatter the front stairs, and the crowd-control unit has masks, batons and shields blocking anyone from entering.

A news helicopter hovers above, filming the scene below. A blue-and-yellow one hovers there too.

'Rach, this isn't safe. We should come back when this all dies down.'

'It's never going to be safe,' I say, pushing past him for a better look.

I have to find a way into the building. How else will I be able to put on the show of a lifetime? *A show*. I don't need to be inside to do that. A new plan starts to formulate and I glance around, looking for where to take my stand. What I'm about to do is dangerous – I need Ben far away. Knowing him, he'll try to stop me, or protect me, and that won't do either of us any good.

'They'll let you in. Go check that everyone is OK. I'll look for your signal. If they're all right, we'll leave and come back tomorrow.' It's another lie, but I can't tell him that I don't want him anywhere near me when this plan goes down. I won't make him watch me get shot, even if it is just pretending and even though after I drink Eros's potion, I'll likely be a random stranger to him.

He narrows his eyes in question, and I hold my breath, hoping he doesn't see through my lie. I'm hating all the lying I've been doing.

'What makes you think they won't arrest me?'

'Because you're going to find Ammon and tell him you escaped your kidnapper. It will buy us some time.'

He runs his hands through his hair, and clenches his jaw. 'I don't like this, Rach. I don't like lying.'

'I know. I don't like to ask you to do it either.' I feel even worse about it than my lying to him. I bite my lip to keep it from quivering.

'Hopefully Ammon won't ask how I got here, and I won't have to lie.'

'Thank you,' I whisper, stealing the last moments with him, trying to memorize everything about his face – the little scar on his forehead, the bends of his lips, his nose that slants to the left from being broken over a comic, the golden highlights in his hair from time on the open ocean – our time – the strong line of his jaw, his cold, hard, calculating, endlessly blue eyes that

309

have given me more warmth and love than I could've ever hoped for.

He'll never even know the effect he has on me.

Benjamin Blake has taught me real love.

He squeezes my shoulder, one last touch, like a part of him knows this is goodbye. 'Meet me at the boat tonight?'

I nod, fighting the surge within, and the desire to hug him. But he turns before I give in, and is swallowed into the crowd. My knees buckle. I struggle to breathe. My shaky hands grasp for the vial – the pain of losing him is so great, so all-consuming, that I know unless I drink this now, I'll never find the strength to. Besides, the sooner I drink it, the sooner I'll forget and the pain will go away.

I slip it off the ribbon and uncork it.

'Keep them safe. Give me courage to do what I must, protect me, and . . . please don't let getting fake shot hurt.' I bring the glass to my lips, tipping the serum in and letting every last drop of the sticky sweet substance drain down my throat.

Forty

A part of me expected to forget Ben right away. Eros said the cost of the serum is to forget him. Maybe it takes a while for that. Even though the pain of knowing it's coming fills every part of me, I must push on.

I don't have long until Ben realizes I've tricked him. I have to work fast. On my left a man with long multi-coloured dreadlocks stands on a flipped-over car, megaphone in hand. 'Chase the monsters out of New York!' he chants into the speaker.

The crowd mimics him, their voices drowning out the helicopter's choppy threat. I elbow my way over. It takes all my focus to hold my gift back. When I make it to the car, I use the side-view mirror as a foothold to climb up.

The man stops chanting and looks at me in question.

'I'm going to end this thing,' I say.

'Oh yeah, and how's that?'

'I'm the reason it started.'

He crosses his arms, his dreadlocks hanging over them. 'You don't look like a vampire alien.'

'You ever seen one?' I ask. He doesn't answer, so I grab the megaphone.

'Be my guest,' he says, sarcastically, then climbs to the back of the car, out of my way. Now that his chanting's stopped, the crowd peters off in different directions, most shoving closer to the station.

I struggle to wrap the megaphone strap around my wrist, realizing my gloves are still on. I pull them off, toss them over the side, watching them float to the pavement. My skin suddenly feels so cold, so exposed. For a second I reconsider everything. Can I really do this? And if I don't, Ben won't realize his dream, my dad won't be free, future generations of Hedonesses will never know real love. My hands shake as I bring the speaker to my lips. My heart hammers away. Eyes turn and lock on me. Waiting to see what the little Indian girl has to say. This is scarier than I imagined it to be. I take deep calming breaths and glance around the crowd. Some people laugh and drink, others proudly display handmade signs. None of them suspect what's about to happen.

I spot a familiar form on the precinct steps.

Ben.

And now that he sees what I'm up to he's heading back through the crowd. I have to act now – *be a fighter*.

My thumb fumbles to press the button. 'Officer Ammon!' My voice squawks through the megaphone. 'Ammon? I have what you're looking for.'

312

One of the riot patrolmen returns my call through his loudspeaker. 'You there – what do you have?'

'I'll only talk to Ammon,' I say back.

The officer turns and points to someone near the door. 'Go get him.'

I teeter on the upside-down car. Trying to look as brave as I can. The crowd around watches me curiously. Soon there are shouts, and some of them point to a window above the stairs. Ammon hangs out, megaphone in hand.

'This is Ammon,' he says.

The crowd-control officer points to me. 'The girl on the car says she has what you're looking for.'

Officers exit the precinct, pushing past the line and tunnelling through the crowd towards me.

Ammon shields his eyes and scans the chaos, soon picking out the upside-down car.

It's now or never. I take a deep breath. 'Please let the serum work,' I whisper. Then I glance to where I last saw Ben, searching desperately through the crowd for him. I find him, halfway between the precinct and me, and as his eyes lock on mine I feel at peace. Forgetting me is what's best for him, for everyone. He'll get his dream back. He'll get to be an officer. I square my shoulders and lift the megaphone back to my mouth. '*I'm* what you're looking for.'

The crowd erupts in chaos, people throwing questions, some cheering.

'You arrest nuns over a girl?' someone shouts.

'That can't be a vampire,' another says.

'What are you waiting for?' Ammon yells, the speaker screeching with feedback. 'Get her!'

This is it.

The guy behind me climbs off the car. 'Come on,' he says, holding his dreads back and waving me down. 'The fuzz is coming.'

But I don't move. Instead I find sturdy footholds and brace for the oncoming officers. The angry mob turns curious, parting to let the crowd-patrol unit pass without a fight.

Soon two armed men are standing beside the car.

'Get down!' one says, holding a black gloved hand out.

I don't move, don't even look at him. I scan the officer's faces for Eros, panic rising when I don't see him. I take a deep breath. I have to trust he'll be here.

The car shakes as the other officer climbs the side.

I steady myself as he reaches for me.

'Don't touch her!' Ammon warns through the megaphone. The officer starts to pull back, but I grab his arm. He loses his footing and stumbles to his knees in front of me. In two quick movements, I stand behind him and hold his head to the side, neck exposed. I slip my hand under his sleeve and inject my power into him. He starts to convulse, and I struggle to hold on, struggle

314

not to scream. When my pain subsides, I whisper in his ear, 'Do not move, and do not say anything.' My teeth hover over the gentle flesh of his neck.

He stops convulsing but his body ticks as the power pushing into him fights his desire to obey me.

The crowd gasps, stepping back.

Police officers swarm the car.

Ammon shouts orders to men in the room.

My hands shake as I bring the megaphone back to my mouth.

This is it. I have to be convincing.

'The police are holding the Sisters, students of St Valentine's Catholic school, and some of their parents because of me. Release them or there will be bloodshed.' Hundreds of confused faces stare back. The only way to get them to believe is a demonstration. I gag, thinking about what I'm about to do – but it's necessary. I need to cause fear.

I close my eyes and open my jaw wide, sinking my teeth into the officer's neck. He cries out, but it isn't just because of the bite. It's because I inject him with my gift again, and again. I can't control my power when it comes to my lips. I wipe my mouth, wishing I'd brought water to clear the taste of his salty skin.

All around me people scream.

Some run, others manoeuvre behind the police barricade, too fixated by the gore to turn away.

'I am not from Earth!' I yell into the megaphone, the nerves vibrating my voice, making me sound extra fierce. A part of me wants to laugh when Ammon's face pales and the expression of *I knew it* crosses his features. 'My species is an advanced version of what you humans call vampire. For some time, I've taken over this human body, possessing the minds of others around me, forcing them to do my bidding, just as I have this officer. I am the only one of my kind on Earth. I have come to make a way for my people.' I pause for dramatic effect, wishing Paisley was here to see this.

All the officers' eyes and guns are trained on me. I take a deep breath and raise the megaphone. *Eros, where are you?* 'Watch what my powers can do.' I turn to the officer in my grip. 'I want you to shoot at Ammon!' I say, adding so only he can hear, 'But don't hit him.'

The officer picks himself off the car and unhooks his gun.

Forty-One

The echo of bullets silences the crowd. The riot officers form a barricade around the car. Ben's behind them, trying to squeeze through.

'Rachel!' He pushes at the line. One of them turns, slamming his baton into Ben's stomach. He gags out a breath, and continues through the pain, shoving forward. I have to stop myself from jumping off the car and rushing to him.

'Rachel, don't do this.' He reaches for me, stretching as far over the officers as he can.

I can't stop – stopping is no longer an option. Instead I order the officer to shoot at Ammon again, buying time until Eros gets here. I scan for him and a riot officer on the other side of the barricade catches my eye. He raises his gun. My heart drops. He's not Eros.

Not now. Not yet. Not before . . .

'No!' Ben shouts, seeing the same thing I do.

His eyes fix on the raised gun, on the man's finger flexing on the trigger.

My eyes fix on Ben.

An ear-shattering blast rings out.

There are screams. The officer in front of me falls off the roof of the car. Ben's shouting something and running for me, but I can't make it out with my ears still ringing from the blast. He pushes a man aside, and forces his way over. His gaze flicks to my hands instinctively clutching my stomach. It's so insignificant a look, I almost miss it. Almost. My eyes trail down.

Thick blood, *real blood*, seeps between my fingers.

My shaky hands slip under the shirt, stinging when it brushes torn open flesh.

Eros was wrong.

The serum didn't work.

I've been shot.

Ben climbs the car so fast nobody attempts to stop him. I teeter, my body weakening under the sudden pain and loss of blood. I collapse to my knees, he catches me and pulls me into his arms.

'Rachel!' He lays my head on his lap, putting pressure on my wound. 'You promised me you'd wait. You promised,' he says, frantically trying to stop the bleeding.

'Ben,' I choke over a mouthful of blood. 'Please.' My shaky hand rises to his. He grabs it and holds tightly. 'Don't forget me.'

'Never.' Ben clears his throat and brushes a stray curl from my face. 'Wait for me in Elysium.'

After all we've been through. This is how it ends. I should've known Eros would let me down again.

The crowd stands back, watching as my life seeps away. If I have to die, in his arms is how I'd want it to be. I smile, my eyes locking on his one last time, and I let out a long ghostly breath. There's a release, a freedom I've never felt before.

'No!' he cries, clinging to my limp body and rocking me in his blood-soaked arms. He lays his ear on my chest, listening as my power fades away and my heart ticks its last tick.

Forty-Two

The sun beats down on the black-clad attendees as they file into St Valentine's graveyard on a sunny afternoon. Ben keeps his eyes down, watching the grass squish under his steps. He follows the crowd of black trousers and shoes being herded to the graveside. Soon they begin to slow and peter out at the sides. But Ben continues forward until he nearly runs into the open white coffin.

Inside, instead of a body, lies a gold urn stuffed with ashes, track ribbons, a Wonder Woman T-shirt, a package of hair elastics and a slew of family pictures. He reaches in and absently trails his finger over the cold, hard, ash-filled container, before slipping the boat keys from his pocket and laying them in the casket beside the other objects. After a few silent moments, his head jerks up and he glances around the crowd of people, every friend and loved one. He wanders away, finding a place between Paisley and Kyle and stands stiff, staring at the casket.

Kyle rests a bandaged arm on Marissa's shoulder. Tears stream down her face, her body shaking, as she turns to Ben and grips his hand. 'I have no one now,' she says.

Kyle leans over. 'You have me, my love.'

Ben pulls away. 'I can't believe you'd bring him here, like *that*. Don't you have any respect for Rachel?' His tone hints that he hates himself for having once felt drawn to her.

'Don't talk to her like that,' Kyle says, wrapping his arms around Marissa's shoulders.

Marissa cries into her hands. 'I don't know how to be on my own.'

Ben's face goes through every emotion, anger, guilt, sadness, before settling on compassion. He turns to Marissa. 'You are much stronger than you give yourself credit for. Let him go, find your own strength, and don't let Rachel's sacrifice go to waste.' With fists clenched, he turns and walks to the other side of the crowd near Officer Ammon.

Ammon leans over to Ben. 'The Chief Medical Examiner cleared her autopsy and ordered the coroner to cremate her. Can you believe that? Not even getting a second opinion on what could be a first extraterrestrial discovery. He should lose his job.'

'Just leave it, OK,' says Ben. 'I knew her, she wasn't a monster or one of your alien freaks. She was just a normal girl.'

'Our family celebrated a private cremation ceremony earlier today,' Mrs Patel says, drawing the crowd's attention. 'Rachel loved New York and she'd have wanted to be buried here. This graveyard holds many important Hedonesses. It's unconventional to bury an urn in a coffin, we know . . .' She continues her speech to the crowd, standing strong, shoulder to shoulder with her mother. Their hands are clasped, chins held high, two generations of Hedonesses burying the third. Their only show of grief is their tears. Mr Patel smiles as he watches a blue-and-yellow helicopter circle above. . .

Soon the ceremony is over, the coffin closed and moved to the belt by six Sisters from St Valentine's, the wheels squeaking as it's lowered. Ben turns from watching and focuses on something in the distance. His legs twitch to run, to flee. But he stays to the end.

I stay too, watching from the headstone's shadows.

Forty-Three

I shift to get a better view. The movement catches Ben's attention. His curiosity gets the better of him and he loops through the attendees and towards me.

He's faster than I anticipated, so I run. I can't let him catch me.

He picks up his pace. 'Hey! Hey, wait.'

I push my legs as fast as they'll go, but soon he's an arm's length away. He dives, pinning me to the sharp graveyard grass. We wrestle – I'm strong, but he fights fierce. I bat away his arms as he tries to pull the cloak from over my head.

He pauses, grabbing my hands and staring at my red gloves.

'Rachel?' It's barely a whisper.

I stop struggling, laying deathly still beneath him.

'Rachel?' he asks again, pulling back the hood.

When he sees my face staring back, my freckles, my brown eyes, my curls, he nearly faints. 'I don't understand. I watched you die. Then just now I thought I saw you . . .' He mumbles as he pushes himself off and slumps against a gravestone.

'Please, let me explain,' I say, moving to my knees, curls spilling down my cheeks.

His eyes snap at me. 'Let you explain? Do you know what my life's been like for the last couple of days? Why . . . why did you do this to me? To your family, your friends? You know how hard funerals are for me.' His voice wavers as he fights back the overwhelming sadness and anger.

'Eros said he'd help break the curse,' I blurt. 'He said you wouldn't remember me. That none of this would hurt you. I thought I was doing the right thing. For them, for you, for everyone.' The desperation in me is palpable.

'Eros?' Ben whispers the name, rolling it over his tongue like it's all too much to believe.

I crawl to him, holding his hand firmly between my red gloves. 'Please. Ben. I didn't think it would happen like this. I had no other choice.'

'There's always another choice.'

'Not for me.' I drop his hand and turn my face so he can't see the single tear that falls down my cheek, but he sees.

So I stand and walk a few paces. I'd run, but his presence holds me like an anchor.

'How . . . how did you fake it?' Ben demands, pushing off the ground.

I wipe my eyes, my bottom lip quivering. 'Eros. He, uh, he gave me this potion that was supposed to keep me from getting shot and . . .' I don't want to tell him this part, I know how he feels about the Hedoness gift, but I can't lie to him any more. '. . . I turned the medical examiner so that everyone would think I was dead.'

'You turned someone?'

I face him, lifting my chin, trying to be brave like the other women in my family. But my shaky hands give me away.

'Getting shot was supposed to be staged. It wasn't supposed to actually happen. But then . . . I don't even know . . .' I look up. 'I woke in the morgue—'

'Why didn't you warn me?'

This is it – this is the moment I confess everything, and I need to be brave. I square my shoulders and lift my chin. 'Because I'm in love with you.' The words roll from my tongue, my heart lurching forward, trying to catch them and take them back for safekeeping. 'I thought I was doing what was best for you.' I wait for him to say something, anything. But I'm met with a blank stare. Somehow that's worse than him telling me he doesn't feel the same.

'Please, Ben. You have to understand.' I try to keep the desperation from my voice but it's impossible. My whole body is shaking. 'I couldn't bear the thought that my touch would change you . . .' Tears well in my eyes as the confession spills out. '. . . You're better off without me.'

The weight of my feelings is too much. I bend forward, pressing on my stomach, hoping the small act will somehow hold me together. Confessing this hurts much more, much deeper than I could've imagined. It makes me physically ill.

A strong arm wraps around my waist, another around my neck, pushing me firmly into a tree. I gasp, my lips parting. Ben's mouth smashes into mine. He holds me tight to his lips, muffling my cries under his warm breath. He consumes me. My body aches to be closer, to make up for every second we spent apart; it speaks the words I fumble through. I claw at him, pulling him nearer, our lips dancing as tiny sparks come aflame inside me. A pleasure so intense, so satisfying, it caresses my skin as I'm seized in Ben's embrace.

In a first kiss shared between lovers.

It should be heaven, perfection – I told him I love him and he showed me he feels the same. But this isn't what I wanted. I don't want to win him only to lose him. And the electricity inside me is taking him away.

I feel his will leaving, the otherness creeping in. My arms and legs refuse to work as I sob against his lips. A grief so immense crumples me in half from the inside out. I'm giving a goodbye kiss to the boy I love. All that he is, is dying in my grasp – bolt after bolt of my wicked love consumes him, fills him, takes him further from me.

I want to run away.

I want to melt deeper into him.

The gift in my acidic blood slices through, breaking our sealed lips for a second, enough for my anguished cries to ring out. With each shock he jerks back, but his grip on me doesn't falter. His lips remain stubbornly and firmly locked on mine. Then suddenly he pulls apart, my mouth ice in his absence. Those endlessly blue eyes look through me, deep into my soul.

'My love,' he whispers.

Forty-Four

'No,' I push away from him.

Tears stream down my cheeks, blurring his face. He's a distorted image on a wave-rippled surface. I've wanted him. I've wanted to hear those words. But this isn't Ben – this is a shadow of the boy, a sick trick to make me think I've been given the one thing I want more than anything. True Love.

My arms feel detached the moment the warmth of his body leaves my palms. 'Go!' The pain rips through me and I collapse forward, unable to bear the weight of the words I'm about to say. 'Leave me.' My voice breaks. 'Go. Get out of here. Forget you ever knew me. Find someone else to love.'

Ben stumbles back, his eyes flooded with alarm. Still he turns and leaves. And in that moment my heart shatters all over again. I fall to the ground, wishing I'd never believed Eros and taken his stupid serum. And that I'd never known the feel of Ben's lips on mine. Each step he takes away pulls at my seams.

Step.

Tear.

Step.

Tear.

He holds a corner of my soul and unravels me from the inside out.

This loss is too much. I won't survive it. I turn my head from him. I can't bear to look, to see him this way. This isn't Ben – the Ben I love is gone.

With my last ounce of strength, I push off the ground. Even though it pains me, literally pains me to watch, I know I must. Seeing the body of Ben, the shadow of him, stumbling through the graveyard, will give me the courage to go on, to find Eros and make him reverse this curse like he promised.

I will my legs to walk to a different tree, each step feeling foreign. I collapse against the rough bark, tears staining my face. In the distance Ben staggers, pauses, mumbles to himself, then continues on. This pattern repeats – he's confused, he's trying to reconcile the pull to me and his desire to obey my command.

He stops again, looks down at his feet. His shoulders tense, and his head droops. He lifts his hands, runs his fingers through his hair and turns around. His dark blue eyes search until they find mine, and when they do, he takes long, determined steps to get to me.

I suck in a breath.

'Rachel, I—'

'I don't understand – how are you disobeying? I took your will . . . you should be . . .' My legs collapse. I grip the tree for support.

He smiles, looking down at my hands, fingers clinging to the bark. He pries my grip free, slowly pulls off my glove and trails the tip of his finger over my exposed skin.

I feel the shiver deep in my soul.

With one hand he undoes his tie, unbuttons his shirt, while the other slips my bare palm over his heart, trapping it there. 'I don't know why.' He pauses, those eyes holding mine. 'Maybe it's because I've spent every day since my family died looking for something more in this world. Or maybe,' he pauses, 'it's that I gave you my heart before you ever took it.'

'We come to love not by finding a perfect person, but by learning to see an imperfect person perfectly' – Sam Keen

Epilogue

I watch my family bury me – one shovelful after another – dirt raining down on a small white casket. I imagine I'm inside the box, staring up at the tufted satin, listening as each rhythmic smack of dirt entombs it. If it weren't for Ben's hand in mine, holding me together, I'd have run over there already. Across St Valentine's cemetery, and right to my mother. To my family and friends surrounding the open grave as they watch the coffin disappear underground. *My* coffin. They deserve to know that the girl they're mourning isn't me. I'm alive.

An agonizing scream echoes through the graveyard. My father falls to his knees, clawing at the ground where he thinks my body is.

'I never knew her,' he cries.

Kyle drops next. The crowd stirring at the change.

'The gift,' Ben says. 'It's leaving them.'

I take a hurried step towards my dad. Ben's grip tightens on my hand and he pulls me back to him. 'We'll see him soon,' he whispers. 'As soon as it's safe.' He points to Officer Ammon. My spine curves into his body and his arms secure around my waist. I've never been touched this way and my entire body shakes.

'But—'

'No buts,' Ben says, giving my hand a quick squeeze. 'It'll be best if we tell your family in private, back at your home. Tonight.'

If my parents would only look this way they'd see us watching from behind the headstones, hidden in the shadows of the old oak tree. But the men are too dazed and confused to notice anything, and the women whisper among themselves, probably about the recent changes in their bodies. I feel it too, the lack of buzz, the numbness. I've been so used to being a Hedoness, I didn't realize what it would feel like to not be. Somehow, someway the curse is gone.

I lean further into Ben. Like it or not, he's right. If I walked over there now, Ammon would be the least of my worries. My family would lose it. I can just imagine Nani pointing and screaming, *'Ghost!'*, and Ma ordering them to dig up the coffin to see if Nani's right.

For now, I'll have to stay dead.

Ben runs his thumb across my arm and electricity resurges under my skin. I pull away, my heart speeding into a familiar panic. Then I realize it's different from Hedoness power – this is my body's uninfluenced response to his touch. It's everything I've ever wanted, and it feels amazing. I push past the urge to put distance between us and I nuzzle in tighter, treasuring this new sensation of skin on skin.

Our moment is interrupted by the rumble of a helicopter fading in and out above. It's likely the Committee checking to make sure I'm no longer their problem. It brings me a twisted satisfaction knowing that we ended their ability to exploit Hedonesses. Some of the funeral attendees look up at the sky. My heart hammers faster, hoping my family will turn and see me, but they never do.

'After the scene at the precinct it's probably a news chopper,' Ben says, glancing up. 'The whole world is watching – what the—?'

I follow his gaze, expecting the blue-and-yellow Committee chopper. Instead my eyes land on a cloaked figure sitting in the top branches of the oak tree.

Ben's body stiffens and his grip on me tightens. 'Who are you?' he asks, his voice filled with unspoken warnings.

I don't have to see the stranger's face or hear his answer to know – the golden bow and arrow slung over his shoulder is all the evidence I need. I recognize the engraved celestial battle scene, and the white-gold-framed amethyst handle. It's the same one from the St Valentine's library painting. Though I didn't see the arrow when we last met, and it wasn't glowing in the painting, it is glowing now.

'*Eros.*'

'Hello, love.' He pulls back his purple hood and lets his blonde curls loose. 'Ben.' He nods.

Ben glances between the two of us, his gaze cementing on Eros. 'You.' He sucks in a sharp breath, and his hands tighten into fists. 'You're the one that talked Rachel into getting shot.'

'A small price to pay for a greater good, no?'

Ben eyes widen and he turns to me. 'Is he serious?' I open my mouth to answer, but Ben cuts me off. 'If something had gone wrong she could've died.' He points at Eros as if willing his fingers to shoot daggers.

Eros doesn't seem concerned. 'You're welcome,' he says, adjusting his bow and grinning down at us. 'Let's just say I knew the ambrosia would eradicate any chance of that.'

'Ambrosia?' I ask.

'The vial,' he says.

Ben surges forward and I grab his arm, afraid he'll yell and draw attention. He relaxes into my grip, though the frustration doesn't leave his face.

'What are you doing here,' I ask, 'and why are you in the tree?'

Eros smiles. 'I wanted to make sure my plan worked. But I didn't want to interrupt your moment.'

'Your plan?'

'The only way to break the Hedoness curse is for a man to knowingly give his heart to one. Ben needed an extra nudge.' He smiles at Ben. 'Your family's death had shut you off to letting people get close to you – it demanded another tragedy to teach you to not waste a second you could be spending loving someone. Rachel's death did its job.' He waves the glowing arrow. 'See, it's as good as new. Now I'll be the only one dictating love, not teenage girls.'

Ben drops my hand and crosses his arms. So that's what Eros meant when he said I had what was needed. What was needed was Ben.

'Precisely,' Eros nodded having heard my thoughts.

'And why the tree?' I repeat.

'This made an inconspicuous perch.'

Ben lets out a scornful laugh. 'If you wanted to be inconspicuous, you should've rethought the purple cape.'

'It's a cloak,' Eros says, in a monotone.

'The glowing arrow isn't helping either.'

Eros ignores him and looks at me. 'Good job on the funeral arrangements.' He motions towards the distant crowd.

Ben grumbles, 'She wouldn't have needed a funeral if it wasn't for you.'

'I suppose you could look at it like that,' says Eros, 'or you could look at it as your chance to be with Rachel. But listen, I'm not here to argue with you, Ben. I'm here because . . .' Eros's attention trails off as he watches the helicopter circle around.

'Because what?' I say, but he doesn't even bother looking down. 'What?' I fight the urge to yell, conscious of my funeral happening a short distance away. The last thing I need is to draw attention to the three of us. Eros's arrow is practically a beacon as it is.

'Is he always like this?' Ben asks.

I shrug.

'Eros,' I sigh, 'because what?'

His head drops and he leans forward like he's about to tell us a secret. Ben and I step closer, careful not to stand on the grave in front of us. Eros leans in further still.

'Dramatic,' Ben whispers as Eros leans in a little too far. He slips from the branch in a flurry of purple robe and golden bow and falls hard into a heap on the unmarked grave at our feet.

I gasp, drop to my knees, toss the bow aside and dig through the layers of cloth, looking for his head. When I finally unbury his face, there's no bruises or bleeding, but he isn't awake either. My hands rush to the side of his neck, fingertips searching frantically for a pulse. When I feel the gentle beat, I exhale in relief.

'Eros?' I pat his cheek.

Ben crouches beside us and tries to pull me back. 'Rachel, stop.'

'He could be hurt.' I pull away from Ben and nudge Eros.

'Rachel,' Ben says more firmly, but I continue, shaking the god until his curls bob and his teeth clack.

338

'Rachel. *Stop!*'

I freeze, dropping my grip and watching Eros's head fall back. Ben's never spoken to me like that. 'But—'

He grabs me, pulling me away like he thinks the god's about to explode, and settles us behind a headstone, sheltering me with his body. 'Rach, he won't wake up.'

'Don't say that.' I push away, twisting to face him, but Ben isn't looking at me. I follow his panicked gaze to a small blue-and-yellow dart sticking out of Eros's shoulder, partially covered by his purple hood. My heart quickens, and a new sense of dread washes over me.

'Stay here,' Ben orders. He crawls on his stomach, across graves and rusted patches of grass, dirtying the nice black suit he's wearing. *A suit he wore to honour me.* When he's within arm's reach of Eros, he dislodges the dart and turns it in his fingers, looking it over.

Ben waves me back, but I ignore him and rush to his side. I kneel there, clinging to Eros's hand, remembering the relief his touch once gave me, and wishing he'd just wake up. 'What is it?' I ask.

His blue eyes knit together, focused on inspection. 'I'm not sure. My guess is it's a tranquilizer dart. It looks like one my dad had in his fishing kit. Whatever it is, we need to get out of here. Now.'

'We can't just leave him,' I say, taking in the peaceful way he seems to sleep. I can only imagine who'd want to get their hands on a god.

Ben grabs my arm and ushers me lower to the ground. His jaw tightens. 'We don't know who shot him. They're probably close.'

My stomach twists at the thought. 'Close is even more reason to get him out of here.'

His grip on me falters. He leans in. 'At least stay low until we come up with a plan.'

The concern in his eyes is enough to make me listen. I crouch by Eros's feet, ignoring the sting of gravel pressing into my knees and busying myself with wrapping the cloak around his legs. It's not a completely idle task – I don't want to trip on it later. It's already going to be hard carrying a body out of a graveyard unnoticed, I don't need to delay our getaway.

'We shouldn't leave that,' I say, nodding to the glowing bow and arrow half buried in leaves.

Ben takes in our surroundings, before finding it safe, and darting for the bow. He grabs them both and returns, kneeling beside me, helping wrap it into the cloak.

'You take his arms, I'll get his legs,' I say, but the only part of Ben that moves are his eyes. They flick to mine, and he gives me *that* look. The same one he gave in the crowded streets in front of the precinct before I was shot.

It's his goodbye.

His eyes roll back and, he struggles to speak. Still, I'm certain the word that he's mouthing is '*Run.*'

'No!' I gasp, dropping Eros's legs and reaching for Ben. I'm too late.

He falls through my fingers, landing twisted over Eros – a blue-and-yellow dart sticking at a strange angle out of his neck.

I rip it out and clutch his body, trying to crawl us back towards the safety of the tree. Eros lays exposed. I can't protect them both, and if I have to choose, it's Ben.

Always Ben.

I choke back tears and clear my throat. 'Benjamin Blake, don't even think this means you're getting out of meeting my Nani.' I say it as though he can hear me. The truth is I don't know if he can, but I can't think like that. 'Stay with me,' I exhale. 'Please.'

His body is folded, limp. It makes it impossible to move without standing. In my current position, I'm an easy target. The blue-and-yellow helicopter begins to descend a short way away in a clearing of trees. Ben's voice fills my head, telling me I'm being unsafe. It takes everything in me to drop him and dive for my own cover.

I lean against the oak's trunk, trying to catch my breath and think about what to do. Eros and Ben lie in a heap of twisted black and purple limbs. I'm not sure how to help them. I choke back the sob filling my throat and slink up the trunk, trying to get a good enough visual to see if the shooter is in the helicopter.

A sharp sting sears into my skin, spreading its wildfire down my spine. I suck in a breath and reach over my shoulder. My shaky fingers find the plumes of a dart lodged between my blades, shaft pointing up.

Sleep sinks quickly into my body, its blackness infringing my sight. The old oak's branches become dark twisted arms reaching down. My eyes strain for Ben, to hold on to one last memory of him, to add something more to our short time together.

Every angry slap of the helicopter propeller sends a shiver down my back. My legs wobble. Shadowy figures approach from the side. I blink, trying to clear my head, to steady my shaking fingers as they claw for the dart, wishing it was Ben's hand they were reaching for instead.

Still, gravity pulls me hard to my knees, and I fall . . .

. . . landing on Ben, and Eros.

And the unmarked grave.

[*To be continued* . . .]

Acknowledgements

We've come to the portion of the novel where I, the author, am to find a witty way to express my gratitude for all those who've helped me reach this wild dream of publishing Arrowheart. Having tried many, rather unsuccessful attempts at such appreciative wit, I'm retiring to the tried and true thank you list. I have three thank yous to make:

1. First, I must thank my parents, without whom I would literally not be here. Mom, it was your love, support and unwavering belief in me that brought me through my hardest trials, including chronic illness, to achieve my dream of being a writer. Knowing you thought so highly of me, helped me find value in myself. You are the fiercest woman I know. And Dad, though we don't always see eye to eye (I had a short joke here, but Dave made me take it out) it is your stubbornness that I inherited. A stubbornness that's kicked my butt every step of the way and

made me want to be the best writer I can be. For that I'm thankful.

2. The second most important thank you goes to David. While my mother taught me I could do anything, and my father taught me to pursue excellence in all I do, you taught me I can be anything. And your example in my life has taught me that I want to be the best person I can be. You once told me that you wake up every day with the goal to leave the world a better place than you found it, but you didn't need to tell me that. I'd already seen it in the way you loved the world and everyone in it, and the integrity and kindness that is foundational in your soul. I never thought I'd meet someone like you. Getting to do life together makes me the luckiest girl in the world.

3. Those of you who know me well know that three is my favorite number. Therefore, it's safe to assume this thank you means a whole lot to me too. And since I still have so many people to thank I'm cheating on my three thank yous . . . slightly:

a. My grandfathers, who aren't here to see this, still I'm hoping this reaches you, wherever you are: Papa, it was your love for the written word that introduced me to the beauty of prose, and Opa it was your ability to spin a 'Flax-Golden Tale' that made me want to get lost in the wonder of stories. I miss you both dearly.

b. My grandmothers: I never questioned my value as a woman thanks to having you two inspirational role models. Nana, thank you for teaching me that kindness and generosity is a most powerful magic, and Oma thank you for teaching me that hard work and a bit of housework is a form of magic too.

c. My brother, Little Buddy: It's arguable I wouldn't be a writer without you. It was our mutual love of books, actually any form of imagining, that opened this door for me, and your strong encouragement pushed me through it. Thank you for helping me follow my heart. I'll be forever grateful.

d. My sisters – Megan, Emma, Hannah, Rhea: You all mean so much to me. Life is never lonely with you. I know that no matter what I do, if I needed you, you'd all be there. It's like having four personal assassins. *insert appropriate gif*

e. Victoria and Isaac: I'm so proud to be your aunty. You never cease to remind me that wonder is magic. I can't wait to see which wild dream settles in your heart. I'll be the one yelling, 'You can do it!' and stuffing you full of candy before sending you back to your mother.

f. My foster siblings: My life was enriched by growing and learning and doing life alongside you all. I love you like you're my blood.

g. Pat (and Steve): You gave me the best gift ever with raising such a stand-up son. You also embraced me as a daughter and have supported and encouraged me in this journey. You taught me that anything is possible with a well-thought plan. Thank you!

h. My Step Dad: Thank you for loving my mom and my family. We're so lucky to have you in our lives! You really are Superman.

i. Erin, Monica, Leah, Lindsey and Fallon: You complete me. You're my writing soul sisters. Love you forever.

j. To my agent Sarah Manning, who is as brilliant as she is hardworking: I'm convinced Shakespeare was picturing you when he wrote his iconic line, 'Though she be but little, she is fierce.' Thank you for taking on whatever unusual thing I throw at you, you're the best.

k. To my editors Sarah Lambert and Naomi Greenwood, and to Kate Agar, Sarah Jeffcoate, Natasha Whearity, Samuel Perrett and the rest of the team at Hodder: You made this dream come true, and you've taught me so much already. It's been a treat working with you and watching you do your bookish magic.

l. To Durriya, Natasha and Alka: Thank you for sharing your heart, life and experiences with me, and helping me make Rachel's story the most authentic I could.

m. To my Wattpad family: I found myself when I started writing, and I started writing on Wattpad. HQ (the CIA), my writer friends, and of course my readers, your support and encouragement has made me excited to get up each day and keep pouring everything I have into my stories. You will forever be treasured by me.

n. The writing community, specifically #1linewed, Electrics, and the Pitch Wars crew: I am so lucky to do what I love, and I'm even more lucky to be a part of such a kick ass community. Writers/Readers truly are some of the best people in this world.

o. To Vinoo and Juli: Thank you for making my world a bigger place.

p. To my friends and family not mentioned (Aunty JoJo, Funky, my cousins, Aunty Lynda, Uncle Ernie, Genny Penny, K$, Nicole, Tiff, Debbie, Ali and more): I'm sorry I'm an author-hermit and don't see you as often as I'd like. I promise, you're all important to me.

q. And finally, to my readers, the ones who've been there from the beginning, and the ones who just found me: I can't wait to get to know you all better and hear your thoughts on *Arrowheart*. Thank you for supporting me, it means more than words can express.

Never forget to follow your own arrow!

All my love, Rebecca

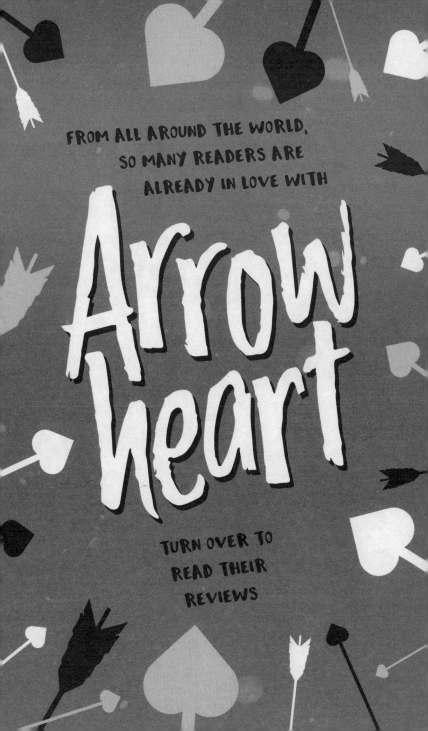

FROM ALL AROUND THE WORLD,
SO MANY READERS ARE
ALREADY IN LOVE WITH

Arrow
heart

TURN OVER TO
READ THEIR
REVIEWS

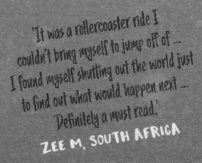

mythology mixed
hint of love.'

'It was a rollercoaster ride I
couldn't bring myself to jump off of ...
I found myself shutting out the world just
to find out what would happen next ...
Definitely a must read.'
ZEE M, SOUTH AFRICA

'Hooked from the start.'
SARAH D, UNITED STATES

'A fantastic read from beginning to end!'
KENNEDY M, UNITED STATES

'I love everything except for Marissa. I want to punch her. Best Book Ever!'
JESSE K, USA

'Romantic, funny, Makes me want
DEBRA

'This is a truly phenomenal book! I enjoyed every second of reading it. It has such a uniqueness and originality that I never knew what to expect in the next chapter. I couldn't put it down!'
TEE B, USA

'I fell in love with Rebecca Sky's writing from the first sentence.'
MIKAYLA B, UNITED STATES

'Brings Greek myths into the modern world in a fabulously original way.'
BELLA H, ENGLAND

heart-breaking.
to fling an arrow at Eros.'
USA

'Love always
wins in the end.'
KATE B

'An intriguing plot with an endearing character!'
A J K, PAKISTAN

'... made me scream so much in excitement and frustration.
It also made me cry. BUT THE STORY IS AMAZING!!
I FELL IN LOVE WITH IT!!'
FRANCESCA T, PHILIPPINES

'I could not stop reading it and I fell
in love with the characters!'
EMILY E, USA

'Incredibly written characters! I felt very strong feelings toward each and every one (especially a certain few). Definitely a must-read!'
JENNA B, CANADA

'I stayed up all night reading. The ending had me in tears.'
HANNAH H, CANADA

'Thrilling, heart-warming and just all round lovely. I can't wait to get a copy.'
JESSE B, NIGERIA

'Love is a curse but true love is a blessing ... [a] masterpiece.'
ANJALI J

'Addictive, charming and beautiful!'
KEVINA O, USA

'Captivating. Beautiful. Stunning.
This book puts a challenging flip on love,
that you've never seen before.'
ESHAL K, AUSTRALIA

'A fantasy-filled read that'll
leave you wishing for more.'
CARA S, CANADA

'A dash of romance, a sprinkle of magic,
a pinch of mystery, and you have the
recipe for an amazing book!'
BRYAN B, CANADA

'Arrowheart is one of the most intriguing books
I've ever read. Ever.'
TOPHIE J.S, NIGERIA

'I have never felt this many emotions in one go before ...
An AMAZING author.'
SYEDA B, UNITED ARAB EMIRATES

'Heart-warming
and heart-breaking
at the same time!'
LARA Y, USA

'Simply amazing.
A must read.'
SYDNEY K, USA

BKMRK

Find your place

Want to be the first to hear
about the best new teen and YA reads?

Want exclusive content, offers
and competitions?

Want to chat about books with people
who love them as much as you do?

Look no further...

 @TeamBkmrk

 @TeamBkmrk

 /TeamBkmrk

 TeamBkmrk

See you there!